SO-ABA-735

"This book is very well written. It brought back a lot of memories."
—*Martin J. Payton, Blue Bell, PA.*

"After reading the first few pages of this book I really wanted to read more."
—*Raymond Tulisalo, North Bay, Ontario Canada*

"These tales are hilarious. I laughed a lot. The story about the 'fum' broke me up."
—*James Plaziak, Narragansett, R.I.*

"We've been to Martha's Vineyard quite a few times. I thought your descriptions were perfect. I felt like I was there again."
—*Sharyn Patriarca, Cranston, R.I.*

"I burst out laughing when I read about the prank Ralph pulled when he changed the sign in the restaurant from, 'Hello, Please wait to be seated' to read, 'O Hell, Please wait to be seated'."
—*Marie Peyton, Swinford, Ireland*

"I could relate to the time when I was a teenager. Boy, the root beer stand brought back memories."
—*Leonard Berliner, Quechee, VT.*

"@ & Q #. A 1948 Studebaker. The cellmates looked forward to all the readings in the cell block as you finished each chapter."
—*Walter, Hollywood, FL.*

"Sex—No sex—Sex sells! Seriously, I really enjoyed the readings."
—*Stan Fabiano, Pennsylvania*

"It would be a good idea to publish excerpts of this book in the newspaper."
—*Ewa Kozyra, Krakow, Poland*

"Thank you for sharing your work with me. I had many good chuckles over the different experiences–all of them unique. Certainly your delightful humor comes through in each chapter."

–Bridget McTavish, Ontario Canada

"Nice job! Enjoyable read. Chapter 17 ends on such a fitting note."

–Dennis Flaherty, Vernon, CT.

Friends Are Thicker Than Water

Tales of a Misspent Youth

Donald C. Payton
With Patrick J. Payton

Friends Are Thicker Than Water

Tales of a Misspent Youth

By Donald C. Payton

With Patrick J. Payton

Original Poetry by Patrick J. Payton

****

Anonymous Poems

iUniverse, Inc.

New York Bloomington

Friends Are Thicker Than Water
Tales of a Misspent Youth

Copyright © 2009 by Donald C. Payton with Patrick J. Payton

iUniverse books may be ordered through booksellers or by contacting:

iUniverse
1663 Liberty Drive
Bloomington, IN 47403
www.iuniverse.com
1-800-Authors (1-800-288-4677)

Because of the dynamic nature of the Internet, any Web addresses or links contained in this book may have changed since publication and may no longer be valid. The views expressed in this work are solely those of the author and do not necessarily reflect the views of the publisher, and the publisher hereby disclaims any responsibility for them.

ISBN: 978-1-4401-3214-8 (sc)
ISBN: 978-1-4401-3216-2 (dj)
ISBN: 978-1-4401-3215-5 (ebook)

Printed in the United States of America

iUniverse rev. date: 4/9/2009

Friends Are Thicker Than Water

Tales of a Misspent Youth

By Donald C. Payton

With Patrick J. Payton

Edited by Patricia J. Payton

Creative Writing Advisor
Patrick J. Payton

Technical Editing Advisors
Dennis Flaherty,
Marianne Douglas–Horizon Enterprises

Advisors
Ina Yalof, Bridgitte McTavish, Dr. Michael S. Payton

Proof Readers
Donald C. Payton, Jr., Leonard Berliner

Computer Consultant
Stanley Steliga III

Web Designer for www.DonPayton.com
Marianne Douglas–www.HorizonInternet-Marketing.com

A special thank you to the people who made this book possible:

My heartfelt gratitude to my son, Patrick, for his creative input, enhancement and poems, my wife, Patti, for her devotion to this work and my brother, David, for his creative adaptation of this book into a musical. Thanks to Cathy St. Jean for her initial typing of the chapters and to Angel Zaninni for her encouragement and promotion of this book.

Friends Are Thicker Than Water

Tales of a Misspent Youth

DEDICATED

TO

GEORGE MCGONAGLE

ROUND TREE
By Patrick J. Payton

Once there was round tree.
So perfectly round was he.
At dusk he cast a round shadow
And in afternoon round shade.
His trunk was strong and branches
Made up a beautiful round ball
For his canapé to rest.
He was round like the world,
Round like the sun and moon
And dotted stars at night.
One day it rained.
It rained and rained.
A rain drop landed on his round shoulder
And whispered
I am round too.
Then the drop changed, as she slid away.
She was not round for long thought the tree.
She disappeared.
That was the best day the tree could remember
Out all of his days.
And he slowly began to change.

Friends Are Thicker Than Water
Tales of a Misspent Youth

Prologue

I pointed to an area on the far right of the cemetery now covered with headstones.

"Zeke, that's where we played sandlot football when I was a kid. I can still hear the crack when I broke my nose playing right there. You never forget that sound. I was playing against a gang of scrappers from Central Falls. Ray Oney threw a block on one of our opponents. The wily kid spun off him and his head slammed right into my nose."

Zeke looked bewildered, "Hey wait a minute. Hey…wait a minute. It was you who broke his nose. I remember that day. It was 1948, my first summer working at this graveyard. It was you I helped carry across the street to the home of the Darlington Braves Baseball Coach, Roy Norman."

"I don't remember *who* carried me to Mr. Norman's house, but it was Ralph McGreavey's head that broke my nose. I remember that!"

Zeke looked at Ralph's tombstone, "I remember that boy. I remember that look. I remember how he looked up from the ground, with blood streaming from a gash on his forehead. He asked me, 'Is he going to be all right? I mean, is he *really* going to be all right?'"

I mused, "Yeah, Zeke, I was all right, but I didn't see Ralph again until our sophomore year at Saint Raphael Academy."

Zeke shook his head, "Well wadda ya know, wadda you know!"

"Little did I know that this first encounter would lead to a friendship full of unexpected escapades prompting my father to say that Ralph was having a misspent youth and I was going along for the ride."

Chapter 1
Echoes from the Past

Stepping out into the clear, refreshing Vermont air long before daybreak, I took a deep breath. I thought, *"This is going to be another long day in the life of this salesman."* But I was looking forward to my first long ride in my new STS gold Cadillac. This car has more electronic features than I'll ever know how to use. I headed up the long gravel driveway and could hear the crushed stones crackle under the solid tire treads. It felt like I was riding on polished glass gliding down the interstate. Familiar 50's music enhanced by new technology brought me back to another era. New Hampshire's White Mountains were totally obscured, covered with thick fog that probably wouldn't burn off for a few more hours. It was still the middle of the night for most people.

A little over three hours later, I spotted the Pawtucket exit off Route 95. Pawtucket, Rhode Island was bathed in a golden hue. The Caddy headed down the ramp almost sensing where I wanted to go without even touching the leather-wrapped steering wheel.

1

I stopped on Walcott Street in front of Saint Raphael Academy. Everything had changed. Nothing had changed. There, still standing high on a pedestal, was the pristine statue of St. Raphael with outstretched arms. My mind flashed back to 1955 with a feeling of nostalgia. It sure has been a long time since my buddy Ralph McGreavey and I graced those halls.

I drove downtown past the pawnshop on deserted Park Street. I chuckled remembering the time Ralph and I hocked a mandolin. I decided to have a look. Early sunlight bounced off the pawnshop window. The fuzzy image of a mandolin revealed itself through dewdrops and squinted eyes. I peered deeper into the store window sizing it up. There on the back wall hung the instrument with a maroon and green body and long tan guitar neck. I knew it was not a genuine mandolin because Ralph and I had hocked it over fifty years ago. I couldn't believe it was still there.

As the door cracked open, a rusty buzzer announced my arrival. The smell of stale cigars permeated the air. I looked up and the pawnbroker looked down. I looked at the mandolin and he looked at me. His bulging eyes, enlarged by thick glasses, shifted from side to side. He was the spittin' image of his father.

He looked up through his green visor and said, "Some mandolin, huh?"

I took it off the wall and said, "I bet it's only five dollars."

He jolted. "Are you kiddin'?" He took a breath and talked from the side of his mouth. "That's worth two hundred bucks. My father got it in the shop in the nineteen fifties. It couldn't be tuned. Everyone tried. No one bought it and now it's a relic."

"I'll give you a hundred for it," I said, twanging the lowest note. I thought, "*We only got five dollars when we hocked it in 1955.*"

2

Adamant, he said, "No way! Two hundred or it goes back on the wall!"

I put the mandolin in my car. Gee, Ralph was right. Someone *would* pay two hundred dollars for it. If he were alive today, he'd get a kick out of this one. If laughter had been a cure for cancer, Ralph McGreavey would have lived forever. I decided to show Ralph good memories never die. Sometimes special things just have a way of returning to you. On the way to the cemetery, I stopped along the side of the road and looked at the mandolin, then tried to tune it. I cupped the base in my right hand holding it as if it were a football that I was about to pass. I tightened each string with my left hand but my efforts were in vain. PLUNK, PLUNK, PLUNK. I lifted the mandolin up at an angle. I could see something inside. I squeezed my fingers through the strings and pulled out a crumpled discolored price tag that had *Composant defectucux 700 FF* written on it.

I thought, *"Defectucux, defectucux. Oh, defectucux – defective. We never noticed the sticker years ago."*

My eyes gazed over the tombstones revealing many familiar names as I drove through the gates of St. Mary's Cemetery. There, on a corner lot, stood a large oak tree with three huge trunks extending from the base, its wild branches shading Ralph's gravestone with the inscription deeply etched into the shiny granite slab.

1938-1985 *57yr old*

RALPH MCGREAVEY

MISSPENT YOUTH

May He Rest in Peace

The air above the grave was motionless. Memories rolled with a tear from the corner of my eye. Reflections of Ralph unfolded. My face flushed as a deep insight inflamed my thoughts. My lips started to move, repeating words uttered long ago when I noticed Ralph smoking a long cigar.

"Do you think you live in Countryside, Ralph?"

Smoke stung his creased face when he said, "Heh, heh. My father was a doctor and if he hadn't died, I'd be one of those rich kids living in Countryside."

Suddenly an old man who looked to be in his eighties quietly came up to me. He wore a weather-beaten Red Sox baseball cap high on his head that revealed a receding hairline. His baggy, green pants were held up with faded red suspenders. He was stocky, and his sweaty T-shirt gave proof of his dedicated work.

He said, "Hey, you know this guy?"

"Yeah. He was a buddy of mine."

He continued, "I've been cutting grass here for more than fifty years. This headstone's been here about twenty years. I always wondered why '**Misspent Youth**' was engraved on it."

I said, "I know, but it's a long story."

He said, "That's okay. I've got nothin' but time." He extended his hand and said, "I'm Zeke Walters. I'm the caretaker here."

I replied, "I'm Mike Ryan."

He pulled his mower up by the big tree and sat down on an old stump. I settled on a knoll near the tree and gazed out over the tombstones into a radiant blue sky. A light breeze carried the sweet smell of fresh cut grass and the strong scent of lilacs in bloom to our perch. My mind focused clearly on visions from a time past.

"Zeke, you remember what it was like in 1955. It was a time of innocence. Those were happy, carefree times after the Second

4

World War and the Korean War, the calm before the 60's. Elvis signed on with RCA Records and Rosa Parks wouldn't give up her seat on the bus in Montgomery, Alabama. Einstein died, and imagine – Bill Gates was born."

Zeke said, "It was a different world back then."

"Yes. A good time to be young. I started to hang around with Ralph McGreavey in April of my junior year at St. Raphael Academy, Pawtucket's parochial high school for boys. We were like two peas in a pod."

Ralph had straight jet black hair. His handsome face featured prominent puffy cheeks and a square nose. He had slightly rounded shoulders accented by his lanky frame. His unique way of holding a cigarette with his index finger and thumb close to his lips gave the impression he was contemplating his next move. He was the unpredictable action man. That's where I liked to be.

Ralph had just been thrown off the baseball team. He hit a ball over the outfielder's head. It rolled into the deep grass in center field. The ball was thrown from the centerfielder to the leftfielder, then to the shortstop, and finally, too late, to the catcher. Ralph danced around the bases in reverse, going to third, to second, to first, then home, stomping on each base. You should have seen Coach Bernard's face. He was furious! He raised his fungo bat, pointed it at Ralph in disgust and hollered, "Nice show, McGreavey! You're off the team!"

Ralph took out his last bent Lucky Strike, straightened it out, lit it, and took a long drag as if it was his last breath. Next move...spring football!

Saint Raphael students had tremendous spirit. The football team elected me captain. I vividly remember that mild Saturday morning when the coaches called me off the field to tell me we were getting a new player on Monday. *McGreavey*!

Ralph was the first one in uniform for Monday's practice.

I said, "Looks pretty good, Ralph. Did you get all your gear?"

He quipped, "Everything except my oranges."

The team hustled down to the old Walcott Street practice field with our new leather Notre Dame-style helmets in hand. Our new equipment was a sharp contrast to my first sandlot football helmet, a World War II tank helmet bought ten years earlier by my father.

Coach Farley asked, "Is everyone here, Mike?"

"I think so."

"Where's McGreavey?"

"I dunno. He said something about oranges."

The long, shrill blast of Coach Farley's whistle cleared the afternoon air.

"Jumping Jacks – Ready! Begin! One, two…one, two."

From the far corner of the field a car screeched to a stop.

"Thanks for the ride, Buddy." The door slammed shut. A football helmet soared over the silver chain link fence and landed on the turf with a thud. Out sprang oranges, rolling in all directions. Coach Farley's whistle fell from his jaw as Ralph struggled over the top of the fence. The last barb hooked the seat of his pants leaving him dangling. R R R R I P!

"OOHFF!" Ralph had arrived.

Coach Farley cupped his hands to his mouth and wailed at the top of his voice, "Nice goin', McGreavey. Now start running laps!"

Ralph put his right hand on his lip and held his pants together with his left hand.

"How many, Coach?"

"We'll tell you when to stop!"

Ralph kicked his oranges into the high grass and circled the field like a superstar. The crack of shoulder pads could be heard as the contact drills began. Ralph dove into the tall grass and peeked through the cover. The coast was clear! He took off his helmet and high-cut spikes, rubbed his toes, and ate the oranges. He looked like he was in his own little world. The whistle blew to signal the end of practice.

"Everyone up!"

Ralph ran by the coaches, panting. Orange peels could be seen through the ear holes in his helmet.

"Does that mean me, Coach?"

"Oh, McGreavey! I forgot about you. You better get some water."

"Yeah! Thanks coach."

We trotted to the water bucket together, "Ralph, quit with the damn oranges and start walking to practice with the rest of the team. Try to help the team."

He mused, "I promised my mother I'd earn a letter playing sports. I'm done with baseball. Football's my last chance!"

He sounded serious, but then mumbled, "I suppose you want me to stop smoking, too."

I did—and he wouldn't. Shortly afterwards he was caught smoking in the men's room when smoke rings floated to the ceiling from his stall. He was punished by being placed in a two-on-one drill. Two offensive linemen blocked him high and low as he tried to split them. I really gained respect for him that day, because even though he took a terrible pounding, he never gave up.

One guy watching the drill jeered at him. "Shape up, McGreavey! I hope you learned your lesson, Jackass!"

It was LaFrance, a huge tackle. Ralph glared at him.

"Mike, he insulted me. I'm gonna get that bastard before the end of spring practice."

Saints scheduled a practice scrimmage against Pawtucket West. Our team was cheering as we formed a circle and passed the football to the left. Ralph ran around the group and slipped into the spot to the right of LaFrance.

When the ball came to him, he turned to his left, "Take that!" **W H A M**! The ball slammed into LaFrance's nuts. He crumbled to the ground.

Coach Farley's shadow cast over his pained eyes and gasping mouth. "What happened, LaFrance?"

"I ah, I ah, I ah, I ah…"

Ralph moved closer. "Gee, Coach, how could anyone get the wind knocked out of him in a warm up drill?" He then faded into the circle.

When Ralph didn't show up for the last few practices, LaFrance barked, "Hey Ryan, where's your pal, McGravy?"

I slanted toward him, stabbing him with my finger in the shoulder pads. I spoke sternly, "Get back in line LaFrance, before I make *g r a v y* out of you." LaFrance was lazy, a real dogger. I knew he wouldn't have lasted in a two-on-one drill.

* * * * *

After my two week spring football session ended, my brother Joe, a freshman at the University of Rhode Island, taught me to pole-vault. We used a steel clothes pole to vault over the clothesline in our back yard. It was a far cry from a regulation pit that has a box to plant the pole and soft sand to land in. Joe was a good athlete and after completing timed events in his gym class, the instructor asked him to go out for track. The team needed more vaulters, so Joe was a welcome asset.

On his initial demonstration in the backyard, the pole held tight in the ground until he got up about five feet with his body parallel to the ground. The pole slipped forward and he came crashing down on his back. His head snapped and hit the ground with a hard thump. Ralph thought that was a riot and laughed until he was in hysterics. My brother got up, leered at him, then chased him around the yard holding the clothes pole like a spear.

I chuckled, "Run for the roundhouse, Ralph. He can't corner you there!"

Joe yelled, "KNOCK IT OFF! This is nothin' to laugh at."

They finally calmed down and I tried my first vault. It took intestinal fortitude. I dug the pole into the soft, late spring grass, threw my feet up, and went over the four foot clothesline. It felt great!

I went out late for spring track. I told the coach, Father

Vincent, that I would like to try pole-vaulting. He said, "There are two old poles under the stage in the gym."

I crawled under the stage to find an old bamboo pole that must have dated back to the 20's or 30's, and a longer metal pole. It was obvious by the dust on them that they had not been used for years. I rubbed my hand across the bamboo pole. It had intervals of old, faded, white tape wrapped around it. I decided to use it because it was shorter than the steel pole and easier to handle for a beginner like me. Saints didn't have a pit. I still practiced vaulting over the clothesline before my first meet against Moses Brown in Providence.

Wally Cook was their only vaulter. He took first place, going over nine feet. I was the only other contestant and took second place, picking up three points for our team by vaulting six feet.

My teammate, Ernie Laverdeau, called over, "Hey Mike, I just high-jumped that high."

I laughed and said, "Yeah, but it beats my best vault over the clothesline."

Wally and I worked together on my technique after the meet. In a meet against Mount Pleasant at City Stadium in Providence, I broke the bamboo pole. At the height of my vault, just as I pushed down on the pole to extend my arms and twist my body over the bar, the pole bowed out like an accordion. I plunged head first, **BLAM!** into the pit below. I just missed the wooden box with my face. The smell of trampled dust flew up my nose. Dirt caked my lips. I rolled over and looked up into the bright sun, which seemed to have stars dancing around its perimeter. Johnny Miranda, a star athlete and vaulter at Mount Pleasant, came over to help me get back on my feet.

He gave me his pole and said, "Try another vault right away."

I took his advice as I didn't want to have a lot of time to think about my last vaulting disaster. The stretched fibers of the bamboo pole were like wet noodles. When I got back to Saints, I retrieved the metal pole. I used it for the remainder of the season, regularly clearing a height of nine feet.

The State meet was held at the University of Rhode Island on a Saturday at the end of the season. I stayed in my brother's dorm the night before the meet. Joe is only a year and a half older than me, but was two grades ahead of me. He was considered intelligent and gifted and was pushed ahead in school, skipping the sixth grade. He was a good influence on me. I looked up to him because he was smart and tough. He wasn't big, only five-eight and a hundred forty pounds, but he could fight like hell and never backed down from anyone. He worked at several jobs at the same time. He always knew how to make a buck.

Early the next morning we were at the field. We practiced getting my steps down on the run to the pit for two hours straight. I was always proud to wear my Saints track shirt with purple letters that stood out on the gold background. My lightweight new white silk shorts had the sides cut up three inches so there would be no restriction on my stride. I was ready! But when the competition began, I missed my first two vaults at eight feet. One more miss and I was out!

Joe said, "You're too close to the bar. You need to step back about half a foot."

I was running a little faster than I did when I practiced before the meet. It caused me to be off the mark and I threw my body up into the bar, rather than up and over it. On my next try I went back further from the start position. The timing was perfect. I vaulted over the bar, then went on a roll. I vaulted eight-six, nine, nine-six, and finally ten feet. My heart pounded with exhilaration. It was the highest I had ever vaulted! I missed at ten-six, but ten feet was high enough to tie Koko Garabedian of Classical High School for third place in Class B. There was only one medal so we flipped to see who got it. Last year Koko lost the medal on the flip of the coin; this year it was his.

I didn't have a good build for vaulting. Most vaulters have slender whippy bodies. At five-eight, weighing a hundred fifty pounds, I was built more like a fire hydrant. I used my upper body strength to pull myself up and over the bar. Thanks to Joe, in two months I progressed from vaulting four feet over the clothesline to ten feet in the state meet. Later that summer, I put on an extra twenty-five pounds to bulk up for football, my favorite sport.

Joe was not scoring many points vaulting at URI in their dual track meets. In a meet against U Conn, however, he came in second overall. The Connecticut ground crew was in the process of repairing the landing area at the vaulting pit. They had backed up a low bed pickup truck just under the bar and filled it with rubber foam. If a vaulter missed the box when he planted the pole, he would run right into the back of the truck. It was a dangerous situation and most of the vaulters were bailing out. Joe knew this was his chance to score points. He ran as hard as he could, planted the pole and vaulted right over the bar. His second vault was the second highest for the meet. Somehow Joe always turned a disadvantage into an advantage. He had a lot of guts.

* * * * *

St. Raphael held its annual minstrel show in the spring. I suggested, "Ralph, we otta' get an act together."

"Yeah. How about a quartet?"

"Great idea! Ted Molloy and Bobby Patterson are the best

singers in the Glee Club. There's our tenor and alto; I'm a baritone."

Ralph's eyes widened. He took out a Lucky, lit it, and took a long drag. "I'm your bass!"

We sounded terrible at our first rehearsal. I asked my friend, Art Maloney, if his sister, Ann, would consider coaching us. She was a music teacher at Goff Junior High School. She agreed to help us and we decided to call the group 'The Four Harps.' Ann was absolutely terrific. She picked out two songs that were corkers and had us singing *Ramona* and *Lullaby of Broadway* in beautiful harmony. I played the ukulele using chords my father taught me. Ralph created his own unique bass instrument made with a metal bucket and a broom handle and tied it all together with rope. When he plucked it, a deep bass tone vibration emerged….**FUMM.**

A week before the performance, Danny Donavan asked if he could join our group.

He said, "Mike, I'm having trouble with two of Brother Melvin's classes. It'll probably help me if I can be in his show."

We all liked Danny, so I said, "Sure."

Now we were 'The Five Harps.' This created a problem, however, because Danny had no clue how to harmonize and always sang off key. Ann was frustrated with him and finally told him to just mouth the words and not to sing at all. She put him in the middle of the group, next to me.

Show time!

Shawn O'Neill sang *Danny Boy.* His parents talked with an Irish brogue and gave him the gift of a beautiful Irish tenor voice that echoed throughout the auditorium. Jim Hennessy brought the house down with a medley of tap dancing routines. Dressed in our matching vests and straw hats, we went on stage –'The Five Harps'–four singing harps and one mouthing harp. We got a standing ovation as the crowd roared, "MORE, MORE!"

When we left the stage, Brother Melvin, a Mr. Peepers look-alike in horned-rimmed glasses, thin pale face, and meek demeanor said sarcastically, "And what the blazes do you call that contraption, McGreavey?" His eyes remained fixed on the home-made instrument Ralph was holding.

Ralph smirked as the grinning glow of a Cheshire cat came over him. "It's a Fum–everyone knows what a Fum is, Brother Melvin."

"Well, what is it?"

"All the new groups have a Fum player."

"OK, OK–What is it, BUCK–O?"

"It's three strings across a pig's ass. You pluck it with your teeth. FUMMMM!"

Brother Melvin's pale face turned bright red and his blood pressure shot through the roof! Ralph flew out the door with Brother Melvin in hot pursuit! He chased him all the way down Walcott Street.

* * * * *

The next day Ralph was in pursuit of his driver's license when he parked his mother's car at the Registry of Motor Vehicles in Providence. He passed the written portion with no mistakes.

I kidded him, "Ralph, you're smarter than the average bear!"

When the examiner came to the car for the road test, he looked at Ralph and asked, "Who drove you here?"

"My mother."

"Where is she now?"

"Shoppin'."

He looked at me. I looked away. Ralph passed the driving test, but we had to wait until the officer went inside the building before we could leave.

When we drove off, I said, "Look Ralph, there's Buckley and O'Neill at the red light."

Ralph yelled out his window, "Hey you guys, last one to the Darlington Spa buys the shakes!"

Buckley hollered back, "You're on!"

Ralph didn't have time to light the cigarette in his mouth. He yanked the steering wheel to the right as the traffic light turned green. The race to the Spa started. Our wheels screamed on the pavement sending smoke from scorched tires. Ralph roared onto the grounds of a large bus company.

"Wadda ya doin', Ralph?"

With a sly look and the unlit cigarette still hanging from the crack of his smile, Ralph hollered, "Hold on!" He drove into the right side of a long tunnel at the end of the property.

BEEP! BEEP! BEEP! BEEP! BEEP! BEEP!

Two busses passed us going in the opposite direction. We could hear the drivers screaming, "NO! NO! NO!!"

I rolled up my window and rubbed my eyes, "The diesel smoke is killing me, Ralph! Let's get outta here!"

At the end of the tunnel was light, fresh air and the law. The silhouette of a policeman with hands on hips blocked the exit.

He pulled us over with his index finger. "License and registration." Ralph handed him his spotless license.

"This smells new; did you just get it?"

"Yes, sir."

"Did Driver's Ed teach you to drive in a bus tunnel?"

"No, sir; can I, ugh, get to Pawtucket from here?"

"I'm going to give you a warning this time, Mr. McGreavey. If I see this car in a bus tunnel again, it's gonna cost ya."

"Thank you, sir."

We cruised past Brown University. Ralph looked at the entrance gates, "This is where my father went to medical school."

"Boy. He must'a been smart."

Tapping an unlit cigarette against the steering wheel, Ralph reflected for a moment. Then, looking up he said, "He was brilliant. A graduate of Brown Medical School has to be brilliant. What a future he had. What a future I had."

I said, "Do you remember when he died?"

"No, not really. I was only three but I could feel the pain. When I got older, reality set in and I understood the whole tragic picture. I was a doctor's son, Mike."

I was at a loss for words and the car became silent. We arrived at the Spa five minutes before our friends. As they walked through the door, we were already seated in our favorite booth sipping our large coffee shakes. SLURP! SLURP! SLURP!

Buckley seemed exasperated. "How'd you get here so fast?"

Ralph quipped, rolling his eyes, "We tunneled our way!"

* * * * *

Ralph took his mother's car, a 1949 Packard, to take John Manning and me for a ride. It started to rain and Ralph turned the windshield wipers on. He was dumbfounded; each time he pressed on the accelerator, the wipers stopped. When he took his foot off the pedal, they moved back and forth in rapid succession. He didn't have time to figure out what the problem was because we went around a corner and he couldn't see a thing in the torrential rain. Ralph took his foot off the accelerator to allow the windshield to clear, but we were too close to a truck that was stopped in the road ahead of us. We slammed into the truck with a loud bang! Manning hit his head on the windshield and had a large lump on his forehead. I was in the middle of the front seat and my nose hit into the rearview mirror. I ended up with three stitches on my nose. Ralph was protected by the steering wheel. He jumped out of the car to inspect it and found the front wheel caved in. He kicked the left fender in disgust. Ralph had only driven the '49 Packard once before – on the day he got his license – and now it was out of commission!

I was elated when I got to drive my mother's 1950 Ford to school in my senior year after I got my license, but joy quickly turned into a hassle when the car was towed because I illegally parked in front of the school. Ralph gave me a ride to the police station to pay the eight dollar fine to get the car out of the impound area.

There were always plenty of parking spots for the students' use, but if I arrived late they were all taken. Faculty members parked in a small lot in the back of the school and it was never full. With my habit of being late, I knew I would have trouble all the time.

I told Ralph, "An attendant guards the entrance to the faculty parking lot like a hawk, but I *have* to get into that lot."

Removing a cigarette from the top of his ear, Ralph suggested, "How 'bout wearing one of your father's old soft hats?"

"Yeah, I guess that'd make me look older all right."

Ralph added, as he tapped the end of his unlit cigarette onto the back of his hand, "You could smoke a pipe, too."

"Oh, yeah."

I took Ralph's advice. Arriving at the faculty parking lot the next day, I gave the attendant a big wave. I casually breezed right past the guard and drove straight to the back of the lot. Leaving the hat and pipe in the car, I grabbed my books off the front seat and ducked into the school through the back door.

I thought, "*No problem; so far, so good.*"

It worked like a charm, but the next day the attendant followed behind me as I drove past him. He signaled me to stop, and asked, "Are you a teacher?"

I gave a nervous laugh, but came up with a quick response, "Heh, heh. I work in the speech lab on a teaching fellowship. I'll be working with Brother James for the rest of the year."

The guard said, "Okay," and waved me on.

From then on, I was the only student allowed in the faculty parking lot for the entire school year, and I always had a place to park, whether I was late or not!

* * * * *

One day, Ralph was standing next to Hennessy on the fringe

of the gym stage watching the rehearsal of *Harvey*, the school play.

Brother Raymond walked over to them and asked, "Would you guys go over to LaSalle Academy in Providence and pick up our costumes from the principal? You can take the school station wagon. Here are the keys."

They left the school with every intention of coming right back to school when they finished the errand, but somewhere along the way, Ralph looked at Jim and said, "We've got the car and we've got the time. Got any ideas?"

Hennessy looked at his watch as he pondered, "Ya know, Ralph, the matinee's about to start at the Silver Dollar in Johnston. I tap danced there last summer for some of the shows. *It's a very interesting place.*"

"Sounds good to me," Ralph countered flicking his lit cigarette butt out the window with his thumb and index finger.

The black 1950 Nash Rambler station wagon, with the Saint Raphael school emblem and Christian Brother's decal pasted inside the rear window, headed into Johnston. When they reached the parking lot, Hennessy circled around a couple of times, then found an empty spot, right in front of the door. Ralph checked the box of costumes sitting on the back seat, smoothed Brother Raymond's folded robe, and tossed the Brother's stiff white collar up on the dash. Ralph and Hennessy strolled into the Silver Dollar Saloon just as Busty Rusty was beginning her act. When they finally got back to St. Ray's and were questioned by Brother Raymond, Ralph was targeted as someone to watch.

Chapter 2
A Few Girls–A Few Dates–A Little Trouble

Slater Park blazed with yellow daffodils. On the pond, in the center of the park, two white swans glided without a ripple, as if skating on a mirror. Flowering lily pads floated like white teacups. Azaleas and rhododendrons were in full bloom. Music from the pipes on the carousel nickelodeon drifted on the warm spring breeze throughout the park, drawing young and old near. The May air was pungent with garden aromas.

This was prom season. Maria Costa, a senior at Pawtucket East High School, had attended many of Saint's Friday night dances held in our gym. She was a petite seventeen-year -old with black raven ringlets. Radiant and bubbling with excitement, she twirled across the polished dance floor like a butterfly. Many of my classmates eyed her walking over to me as I pretended to be nonchalant.

"Mike, she said, "We have our prom coming up at the Admiral Inn. Would you like to go?"

21

"Sure."

"Do you have a friend that might wanna' take 'Toots' McGraw?"

"Yeah, I've got just the guy."

Ralph, 'Toots', Maria, and I double-dated when we went to the prom a month later.

It didn't take long to discover that 'Toots' had bad breath. "Ralph, what do you think of 'Toots'?"

"It's bad, Mike, real bad."

"Her breath?"

"Uh, huh. My carnation is already droopin'."

I looked Ralph square in the eye, "Do you have any mints?"

"I've got gum, mints, and red hot fireballs."

"Give 'em to me! Something's gotta work!"

I offered 'Toots' a piece of gum.

"No thank you."

"Mint?"

"No."

"Red hot fireball?"

"Naw." She breathed straight into my face.

I sighed, "Yoh boy!"

We danced to some of our favorite songs: *Sincerely*, by the McGuire Sisters, with their harmonious blend of perky voices, and *Cherry Pink and Apple Blossom White*, which featured the great sound of the trumpet. Les Baxter's *Unchained Melody* played as we glided on the dance floor.

The music was great, but Ralph was turning green. "Mike, I can't stand her breath. After that last dance, I'm ready to pass out!"

I leaned toward my pal, a weeping willow, and lilted, "I've smelled bad breath before, but this is the pits!"

He turned slowly, and with a coy smile, whispered, "Yeah, I know, but they don't call her 'Tits', I mean 'Toots', for nuthin'!"

She never knew why Ralph wasn't having a good time but she did know she didn't want to go to the after-prom party at Freddy Fernold's house in Countryside. We rushed her home when she complained about a toothache.

Maria said, "Sorry, Ralph. I understand."

I called my younger sister, Nancy. "Nance, how'd you like to go to a party?"

"Now?"

"Yeah, with Ralph."

"Oh, Mike. What happened?"

"I'll tell you when I see you. Just make sure you brush your teeth!"

Driving down Fernold Drive in the elite neighborhood, we immediately felt the presence of affluence as we gazed at the gracious homes in this prestigious new area. The entrance to the development of custom-designed ranch houses and spacious New England colonials was across from the country club and home to the city's prominent citizens–doctors, lawyers and successful businessmen. Short, curving roads wound past perfectly landscaped, picturesque homes. As we entered the Fernold home through double French doors, I noticed how pretty my sister looked standing under the huge chandelier in the foyer. Her golden hair rode on her shoulders as she turned her head and smiled at Ralph. They strolled into the party looking like Fred Astaire and Ginger Rogers. No one noticed that Ralph had switched dates after the prom.

I nudged Ralph and said, "Nice play, Shakespeare!"

* * * * *

I wasn't interested in getting tied down with one girl and didn't go out on many dates. I liked hanging around with Ralph. My brother had a steady girlfriend from Attleboro, Massachusetts. Her friend, Angela Bertinelli, lived in Cranston and Joe fixed me up with her so we could go on a double date. We spent most of the day swimming in the clean, cool waters of Herring Pond on Cape Cod. Then we spread a red and white checkered blanket over the bright green grass and had a picnic. That evening Angela invited me to her junior prom.

I was at the Spa with Ralph on the night of Angela's prom. "I gotta get going; the prom starts at eight."

"Augh, you've got plenty of time."

"I've gotta go all the way to Cranston."

"Okay, one last game of High Low Jack."

I arrived at Angela's house an hour late. She was dressed in a green gown of taffeta and lace. I apologized as I slipped a wrist corsage of white carnations tied with matching green ribbon streamers over her hand.

Angela asked, "Where have you been, Mike? My friends

wanted to double with us, but they couldn't wait any longer." She let out a loud sigh of exasperation. "My parents wanted to meet you."

I just shrugged and thought, *"They must have been the couple that gave me a dirty look when I passed them at the corner. I'm sure they told Angela to get rid of me."*

"Sorry, Angela."

She gave me the cold shoulder all night. I knew I was inconsiderate. I never heard from her again. The only good thing about that night was the singing group called The Eldorado's, led by Cranston football great, Mike DiNitto. Time didn't mean much to Ralph and me and this time, it cost me dearly.

* * * * *

I worked as a soda jerk at the Rumford Rexall Drug Store on weekends for Mr. & Mrs. Saltzman. Mr. Saltzman would pass me many times throughout the day without saying a word. Occasionally he would throw up his right hand and say, "Hi." I could never figure out when he was going to acknowledge me.

Mrs. Saltzman kept showing me how much ice cream I should put in the ice cream cones and shakes. She didn't realize that girls from East Providence High School qualified for an extra scoop! Billy Cavanaugh, one of my best friends at Saints, helped me get this part time job after he had worked there for two years. Billy looked like a teen idol talking and flirting with all the girls at the soda fountain. Only I knew that his favorite pastime was scanning the nude magazines whenever he could, and those that he didn't get to, went home with him under cover of a newspaper. The next day, the magazines were back on the rack, ready for sale.

We alternated taking Mr. Saltzman's dreamboat of a car into

Providence to pick up pharmaceutical items. It was a good break from our regular routine and we liked driving the big, dark blue 1955 Oldsmobile. On one of my trips, I decided to swing by Shawn O'Neill's house in the Fox Point section of Providence near Brown University. The route back to the pharmacy took me down Hope Street. I ran out of gas but I was lucky. I was able to roll right into a gas station. Just ahead, there was road construction and several heavy vehicles were moving along the side of the road. I stopped for a steam shovel putting boulders in a dump truck.

A worker in a yellow hard hat yelled, "Let's move it!"

When I got opposite the truck, I didn't step on the accelerator hard enough and the car stalled. A huge boulder rolled off the side of the big dump truck, shattering the windshield. It bounced off the shiny hood, leaving a gaping dent. Boy was Saltzy livid when the construction company wouldn't take responsibility. His insurance company paid for the repairs, but then raised his premium.

He never uttered a harsh word to me or talked about the incident and I really appreciated that. The next time he walked by me he said, "Hi."

The young pharmacist, Dick Pagleri, was fastidious and aloof. He had a hooked nose and looked like a hawk. His brown curly hair was always combed back with every strand in place. The white laboratory jacket he wore was spotless and pressed. A wall at the back of the store had a cutout open window so he could talk to customers from his small work area. Filled prescriptions were neatly stacked on the counter behind him. The constant aroma of antiseptic lingered in the air. No one was allowed in this area, and no one ever went into his space. One day I noticed a long line of customers at the prescription counter, so I went into the back area unannounced. I found Dick with his pants down!

Shocked, I hollered, "Dick! What are you doing?"

He was annoyed as he turned and looked at me with glaring eyes, "Whata' YOU doing here?"

Repeating in a calmer manner, I said, "Dick, whata' you doin'?"

His face flushed and he looked embarrassed as he pointed to a jar of ointment and meekly said, "Hemorrhoids–I'm just applying salve."

I said, "Geez Dick, people are waiting for their prescriptions!" But I thought, *"For cryin' out loud, Dick, get your finger outta your ass."*

One of my favorite customers was a pretty redhead named Janet Moran. She invited me to her senior prom at East Providence High School. I was happy to oblige because I always enjoyed seeing her.

I was all decked out for the prom and had a fresh pink carnation pinned to the lapel of my white sports coat. My black pants were pressed, the bow tie was on straight, and my white bucks were sparkling. I was raring to go when she picked me up at seven o'clock sharp in her 1953 bright red Buick Skylark convertible with long, ornate fins and loaded with shiny chrome trim. The prom was great, the band sensational, and my date, beautiful.

Janet drove me home periodically after work at the pharmacy. I sat in the passenger seat, proud as a peacock, when we rode down my street, her flaming red hair blowing in the wind. I thought I had died and gone to heaven. One day we had the radio blaring to Bill Haley's *Rock Around The Clock.* When I sprang out of the car, Bill, my slightly gray-haired next door neighbor called over to me.

As the redhead in the convertible waved and drove off, he shook his head and sighed, "Mike Ryan, I'd like to be you one week of my life!"

I laughed. I felt like a million bucks, and he knew it!

But I didn't go out with one girl for any length of time. A few weeks later I made a date for Friday night with Meridith Slocum. She attended Bay View Academy, a highly accredited school in East Providence. Meridith always looked stunning when she came into the pharmacy. I wanted this date to be special and tried to come up with a novel place to go. I made arrangements to use my dad's car. Much to my dismay, when Dad returned from his week long business trip, the car was tilting to the left.

"Gee, Dad, what's wrong with the car? I've got a BIG date tonight!"

"Oh, the car drives okay, Mike. A spring broke when I was on the Mohawk Trail."

After parking the lopsided car across from the Wannamoisett Country Club, I slowly made my way up the rambling walkway to Meridith's house. It was a big red brick house with white pillars on the portico. Above the huge entrance doors was a large, ornate light fixture hanging from a five foot gold chain. The musical chimes brought a smile to my face when I rang the doorbell. I was in awe of her family's prestige.

"Come in, Mike."

Meridith was dressed in a dark blue pleated skirt, matching vest and neatly pressed white silk blouse with eyelet trim and a stand-up collar. Her shiny, jet black hair was braided down to her shoulders.

"Boy, you look nice, Meridith!"

She put her hand over her mouth, "COUGH–COUGH–COUGH. Sorry, Mike, I've got a terrible cold but I didn't want to break our date."

The house was elegantly furnished and tastefully decorated with expensive antiques. Everything was perfectly arranged throughout the room. Her father appeared in the doorway to the living room dressed in a beige tweed jacket, blue casual shirt and tan slacks. A loosened woven necktie completed his ensemble. His mustache was neatly trimmed as was his perfectly styled salt and pepper hair.

I could feel his eyes sizing me up as Meridith said, "This is Mike Ryan, Dad."

Shaking hands, I greeted him, "Nice to meet you, Doctor Slocum."

He smiled, "Meridith tells me you're going to Boston."

"Yes, sir, to see Cinerama."

"I understand it's a spectacular advance in the motion picture industry."

I nodded in agreement. When he was talking to me, I had the feeling he was looking right through me as he slowly took his thin-bowled mahogany pipe from his pocket, raising it into his mouth. Meridith rubbed her nose with a handkerchief and walked over to kiss her dad on the cheek. I waited by the open door.

As we approached my car, she started to laugh, "Oh Mike, look at this lopsided car! COUGH...COUGH"

"Yeah, I know. It's mine!"

29

Every time I took a left turn Meridith slid across the seat until she was very close to me. The problem with the car gave me an unexpected opportunity to turn a disadvantage into an advantage! Finally she just stayed next to me and I nonchalantly put my arm around her!

"SNEEZE, WHEEZE, COUGH, SNIFF, SNIFF." Her cough became more frequent. The stuffy, hot theater made it difficult for her to breathe. "COUGH...COUGH." Turning her head away from me, she put her thumb to her nose to block one nostril as she slowly forced air through the other side.

I thought, *"She needs a doctor."*

All heads turned in our direction when she opened her small jar of Vicks Vapo Rub and the strong medicinal odor punctured the air. "COUGH, COUGH, WHEEZE, WHEEZE, SNIFF, SNIFF."

On the drive back to Rhode Island, Meridith ran out of Kleenex, and I ran out of gas. She proved to be a strong girl when she helped me push the car a quarter of a mile to a gas station. I still wanted to go parking and took her to Slater Park near the monkey island. The animals did acrobatic antics on swings, ropes, and wooden platforms as we watched them in the moonlight.

Meridith shied away from me and sweetly said, "No kisses, Mike. I can't breathe."

I didn't want the poor girl to die in my arms, so I kissed her gently on the cheek and drove her home. I thought maybe there'd be a chance of a kiss or two when we reached the portico. But I was foiled again when the light snapped on and I saw the silhouette of her father's mustache in the corner of the window. **"AH, AH, AH, CHEW...."**

I met Sue Alves at Crescent Park, an amusement park in

Riverside. I spotted her walking toward me because she was dressed in a brilliant red poodle skirt, white sleeveless blouse and had a wide, black cinch belt around her waist. Her bobby socks were glistening white and her black and white saddle shoes looked like they just came out of the box. She stopped at the cotton candy booth and so did I. I struck up a conversation with her and before we left the booth, I had her telephone number. Later that week, I gave her a call and she invited me over to her house. We never went out on a real date, but I went to her house once in a while. Her parents liked to provide pizza and soda. I enjoyed her record collection that included my favorites: *Only You* by The Platters, *Love Is a Many Splendored Thing* by the Four Aces, and *Ain't That a Shame* by Fats Domino. This was a treat for me because I didn't have a record player, never mind a record collection. We usually danced to the music in the living room. I tried to kiss her the last time I was there, but she turned her head as if to say no. I was crushed because I really liked this girl with the sweet smile and smooth clear olive skin.

I turned my head and raised my eyebrows, "Okay, we'll just be friends."

She grabbed my jacket, pulling me closer to her. I attempted a kiss.

She sighed, "Just friends? Just friends?"

Surprised, I blurted, "A-yeah...a-yeah...yeah...just friends."

As I turned to leave, I said to myself, *"I can't believe I said that! Am I out of my mind? I blew my chance."* Then reality set in. I knew Ralph and I would operate better without anybody tying us down over the summer.

We went to Warner's Dance Hall in Central Falls for the last dance of the school year. Teenagers from all over Rhode Island and Southeastern Massachusetts went to those dances. The second floor featured a local disc jockey, Ray Mahill, spinning the latest hit records. The dancers displayed a unique slow step, fondly referred to as 'Warner's Style.' The guys held the girls cheek to cheek with their left arm out straight. The extended left foot glided on the floor and the right foot slowly slid up until they were even. There would be a pause as the couple shifted their shoulders and arms back and forth. Then the same sequence started again. Ralph was a master at this dance technique and also jitterbugged with the best of them.

He danced with Marge Silva the whole time we were there. She was a rugged girl and a little taller and heavier than Ralph. She was also an outstanding athlete at Pawtucket East High School. She could throw the shotput and hammer at near record distances.

As they danced to *Goodnight, Sweetheart, Goodnight*, Ralph asked, "Marge, how 'bout letting me take you home?"

"I'm here with my girlfriends, Ralph."

"See if it's all right with them."

"Well, what about Mike?"

"Augh, he's goin' with his football buddies."

Ralph and Marge walked to Ralph's car hand in hand. He had recently bought his first car for forty-seven dollars. It was a 1938 light gray Studebaker. Black smoke fumes escaped from the straight exhaust pipe every time he changed gears with the pearl handle floor shift. We shelled out more money on oil than we spent on gas. It was his pride and joy, but anytime we wanted to go anywhere, it wasn't running. On the way to the dance, the foot pedal came off the accelerator. Ralph couldn't get it back on the pin because the pin coupling was worn out. When he tried to drive, the pedal kept slipping off. Ralph knew he had a problem and explained his predicament to Marge.

She frowned, "How am I going to get home?"

Ralph took out a Lucky Strike as he contemplated his situation. "Marge, get down on your knees under the dash and hold the pin down."

"What? Are you crazy?"

"I'll tell you when to let the pin up. Trust me."

According to Ralph, he was able to drive the car, with him shifting and steering, while Marge controlled the accelerator on command. She couldn't see where the car was going so he proceeded to drive into a secluded parking area near McCoy Stadium. When the car stopped, Marge thought she was home.

She popped up, spinning her head from side to side and hollered, "Where the hell are we?"

He whispered, "How 'bout a little kiss?"

"KISS…KISS…Kiss my ass!" She lifted Ralph right up off of the seat and threw him bodily into the back seat.

Ralph was shaking and said, "I'll take you home, Marge, but I still need help with the pedal."

In a rage she commanded, "If you don't take me right home, I'll shot put you right out the window!"

Ralph immediately left the lovers' lane and drove straight to her house. He walked home and had to leave his car parked in her driveway overnight.

* * * * *

Saint Raphael Academy held a retreat for students at Our Lady of Peace Spiritual Life Center. The center was started in

1952 by the Roman Catholic Diocese of Providence as a men's retreat house dedicated to helping people enrich their lives through the renewal of their Christian faith. Ralph and I were in a mischievous mood when we bounded off the old purple and gold Saints bus onto the sprawling grounds at the big estate in Narragansett. There were ponds, bridges, gardens, stonewalls, meadows and wooded pathways throughout the manicured grounds. The complex consisted of a large mansion and several smaller houses with underground tunnels running from the main house to the other buildings. A track ran through the tunnels and carried large wooden conveyers along the track to transport food and supplies back and forth.

Jim Buckley and Shawn O'Neill disappeared from our group soon after we arrived. This was no surprise, for Jim's freckled baby face and innocent demeanor masked an adventuresome spirit. Shawn, the shy singer, with the map of Ireland written all over his face, always had a twinkle in his eye. The bond between the four of us was tested many times. It was never broken. Whenever we met, we would smile and slightly shake our heads. The fun and good times always prevailed.

Father O'Hare, a young priest, had a nervous manner and constantly seemed to be in a hurry. He wore his robes with dignity and was proud that he was doing God's work. All of the students liked him. He approached Ralph and me. He took us to a tunnel entrance with a thick door that was ajar and popped his head inside. Father O'Hare finally said, "I think Buckley and O'Neill are in this tunnel. Please try to find them and get them back here."

Ralph and I marched up the tunnel. "Jim, Jim, Shawn, Shawn," we called up the dark shaft.

We heard an echo from the distance, "Up here. Up here.

34

We're here." Jim ran to me, "Hey Mike, look at this cool tunnel system."

Ralph took out a Lucky. "Anybody got a match?"

Mortified, Buckley hollered, "Don't light that in here, we'll all go up in smoke!"

Ralph put the cigarette behind his right ear, and said, "I've got a great idea! Let's put one of the trolleys on the track leading back to Father O'Hare."

Shawn brightened, "Yeah, we can all ride on the trolley together."

Buckley was first. He pushed the conveyor down the slanted track and belly flopped onto the descending trolley. O'Neill was next, then me. Sprinting, Ralph had just enough time to jump on top of the pile as it careened down the steep track. There was no stopping this flying four man missile at the bottom of the tunnel! **S l a m B a m**! The door split wide open, tearing apart at the hinges, as we blasted out of the tunnel. Father O'Hare was knocked ass over teakettle and the four of us were sprawled all over the lawn. We thought we'd pay with our lives for this one, but fortunately, Father O'Hare took cash.

The next day Ralph and I walked into the chapel and the pungent aroma of incense filled our nostrils. Our instruction handbook listed confession as a requirement while we were at the retreat. It indicated that the light would be on over the confessional booth if a priest was inside.

Ralph observed, "Look Mike, there's no priest in here now. Go get Buckley and O'Neill and we'll have a little fun with them. I'll be sitting in the priest's seat behind the curtain when you get back."

I thought, *"This otta' be good."*

I found Jim and Shawn walking together on the grounds.

"Hey you guys, the priest is in the confessional now. Let's get it out of the way."

Buckley resisted, "Now? But I just went to confession a few days ago!"

O'Neill meekly said, "Oh, all right. Brother Peter said we have to go to confession while we're here. We might as well do it now and get it over with."

We tip-toed down the side aisle and I entered the confessional on the right. Buckley went behind the left curtain. Ralph was pressed back against the seat and opened the sliding door halfway.

Ralph cleared his throat and Buckley started his confession. "Bless me Father, I have sinned. It's only been a few days since my last confession, so I haven't had much time to do anything yet. I overslept this morning and missed breakfast…and I–I, I *guess* I've had a *few* impure thoughts."

Ralph abruptly slid the door wide open, pushed his nose tightly against the screen and whispered, "Did you get any nookie?"

"McGreavey!" Buckley was mortified and yelled, "Jesus, Mary and Joseph! That's a sacrilege, McGreavey!"

* * * * *

Tommy Shapiro's father owned the Pocasset golf course in Tiverton. Tommy invited us to play, free of charge, on the last Saturday before school ended. We welcomed this opportunity because it was a great chance to play another course and, as always, we were short of funds. Ralph's car was kaput. We had to thumb to Tiverton. We hid our golf clubs behind trees on the side of the road. When a car stopped, we made a bee-line for the clubs. It took us a long time to get to Tiverton.

Ralph didn't tell me that he planned to meet a former girlfriend, Molly McGuinnis, in Tiverton. She lived next door to Ralph's cousin Paul. She was waiting for him at the corner of River Road because Ralph wasn't allowed to go back into her house. I sat on a stone wall while they talked and could hear parts of the conversation.

"You shouldn't have said all those terrible things to my parents, Ralph. You know my father's a staunch Irish Catholic."

"Will they ever forgive me, Molly?"

"I don't know. The Irish are not all pig farmers. You're not Scottish; everyone knows you're Irish."

"I was just mad 'cause they were giving me a hard time. How'd I know they'd come home early? We were only kissing on the couch."

"If you can't control your emotions, I guess there's no future for us. Goodbye, Ralph."

It started to rain so we headed home. I thought, *"So much for our free round of golf."* The heavy downpour soaked our clothes right down to our skin. We shivered as our stomachs growled from not eating all day. We stopped under an awning in Fall River while Ralph tried to light up a Lucky, but the matches were too wet to ignite.

"We're goin' in this grocery store, Mike. Keep the owner busy. I'll put some blueberry pies under my shirt."

"No way, Jose. Your shirt will bulge. Besides, I don't want to steal anything."

Ralph ignored me and entered the store by himself. With hands cupped around my eyes, I looked in the window and saw him stuff pies under his shirt. He headed toward the door. I was stunned when the store clerk walked up to him. I thought, "*Oh no! He's caught in the act.*"

Ralph quickly turned and dropped four small pies and a carton of Apple Cherry Berry Juice on the counter. Then he whipped money out his wallet and paid for them.

As soon as he stepped out of the door, I grabbed him on his wet shoulders. "Hey, where'd you get that money, Ralph? I thought we were broke!"

With a sly look on his face he answered, "I just wanted to pull your leg, Mike. You know I wouldn't steal. I had ten dollars tuition money my mother gave me yesterday."

"Geez, Ralph, you almost gave me heart failure!"

We walked over the Braga Bridge in Fall River laughing and eating Table Talk blueberry pies in the pouring rain.

* * * * *

Ralph skipped school on Monday to caddy at Pawtucket Country Club. He needed to make up the tuition money he spent on the pies. He called the school from a pay phone at the Texaco gas station opposite Pineault's Corner.

When the school secretary answered, Ralph muttered, "Miss Truitt, I'm sick and can't go to school today."

While he was still talking to her, a car pulled into the gas station and ran over the signal wire at the pumps making a familiar sound…B–DING, B–DING, B–DING. The signal ran through the quiet morning stillness and continued over the telephone line.

Miss Truit asked, "Where are you, Ralph?"

"I'm home, sick in bed." Beads of sweat formed on his forehead. He said to himself, *"I'm dead!"*

The phone rang at Ralph's house. "Hello, Mrs. McGreavey?"

"Yeah."

"This is Miss Truitt at St. Raphael."

"Ooooh?"

"I understand Ralph's sick today."

"He is?"

The next day Miss Truitt informed Ralph that he was suspended for the last two days of the school year. She warned, "Ralph, if there's one more infraction of school rules, you'll be permanently expelled from St. Raphael Academy."

Chapter 3
School's Out for the Summer

Ralph and I needed to earn money now that school was out for the summer. We caddied at Pawtucket Country Club on Armistice Boulevard, just a couple of miles from my house. Ralph's Studebaker would get us at least halfway there most of the time. Ralph never seemed to be able to get serious about caddying or the game of golf, but appreciated the money and the exercise. I often thought that if fate hadn't stepped in and whisked away Ralph's chances, he would have been a country club member and had guys like me caddying for him. He was a doctor's son. The fickle finger of fate works in strange ways and can change your life in an instant.

We each carried two bags in a member-three-guest tournament on our first eighteen hole loop. Charlie Singletary was a new member, playing in his first tournament and his three guests were just taking up the game. Ralph immediately picked up on it.

"Mike, come here."

"Yeah, Ralph."

"Listen Mike, this guy's a newby...a real ham 'n egger...a novice. We'll spend most of the day kicking golf balls out of the woods. Look, his used Montgomery Ward clubs and white button-down shirt tells me that he doesn't part with his money easily. When it comes time for him to pay, let me handle it."

At the end of the round Charlie asked, "How much do we owe you guys?"

Ralph looked at the vinyl golf bag that held two putters and mismatched clubs and smiled.

Charlie pulled out a fistful of dollar bills. "Four dollars each, okay?"

Ralph moved closer and keenly said, "Let's see now," as he slowly peeled the first bill from Charlie's hand.

"Give me one dollar."

"Give Mike one dollar. Give Mike two more dollars. Give me three more dollars."

My eyes were bulging as the bills piled up in the palm of my hand.

"Give Mike two more dollars. Give me three more dollars... and you can give Mike two more dollars and I'll take one."

Mr. Singletary was so confused he just kept nodding with his mouth and his hand wide open. Ralph was in complete control.

He turned to Mr. Singletary. "Everything's perfect. Thanks a lot."

As we strolled out of the parking lot beaming, I said, "Ralph,

Charlie's still trying to figure out how much he actually paid us."

"Yeah, enjoy it while you can; that's the last time we'll ever get paid like this!"

On rainy days we played cards in the caddy shack and hoped the sun would break through the clouds. On tournament days, we hustled bags in the parking lot. When a guest opened his trunk to get clubs, we asked if we could carry them to the bag rack. Golfers liked this service and gave us a small tip. One day a guy opened his trunk and quickly put on a golf hat.

Ralph approached him, "Excuse me, sir. Can I carry your clubs to the bag rack?"

"Sure."

When Ralph picked up the golf clubs, his little finger hooked onto a soft, black furry thing. He reeled back. "Jesus, you have a rat in your trunk!"

The golfer whisked it off Ralph's finger and sheepishly stuttered, "Th-th that's not a ra- ra-rat, that's my ta-ta-ta-to-toupee."

We finished caddying early that day with five dollars burning a hole in our pocket. Ralph rested his back against a large boulder then lit a cigarette. He gazed out over the Ten Mile River. "Mike, do you know where this river goes?"

"Yes. It goes into East Providence."

Ralph's eyebrows raised up on his forehead as he flicked his cigarette, "First it goes by Narragansett Race Track. What do you say?"

"Let's go for it."

A shortcut through Slater Park got us to the track in five minutes. In order to save all of our loot for bets, we sneaked over a big fence and ended up near the paddock where the horses come out for the post-parade.

After two races, we were broke. "Ralph, we caddied eighteen holes for that money. Sure loses its value here!"

Ralph threw his losing tickets down on the cement floor and kicked them in the air. As his gaze lifted, he said, "Look! There's John Manning. Maybe he's got a few bucks we can borrow."

John heard Ralph's voice and walked over to us. "I was just about to ask you guys the same thing."

John's mother, Gladys, and Ralph's mother, Mary, were friends who worked together at various fabric mills in Central Falls and Pawtucket.

"How's your Mom, Ralph?"

Ralph whispered to me, "What the hell is he asking me about my mother for? Forget the pleasantries. We're at the racetrack."

He then said to John, "She's okay...How's yours?"

"Well, she's still working in the sweatshop."

Peering over his race sheet Ralph shook his head and said, "Yeah, what a raw deal those two got."

John Manning was a rugged guy with bowlegs. He was an all-star catcher in baseball and had a tough way about him. He was constantly whisking his disheveled hair out of his eyes. John's outdated clothes were wrinkled and whenever we saw him, he was wearing the same soiled, black sweater. Everyone in our neighborhood knew about the time he broke his index finger trying to catch a foul ball. The tip of the finger was on a ninety degree angle. He had a double header to catch the next day so he went home and put his finger in a vice and straightened it himself. John was a Mr. Fix-it. He thought he could fix anything, including his own finger.

Ralph lit a cigarette, took a long drag, pressed his lips together and let the smoke drift slowly out of his nostrils. "Son of a bitch, we'll have to go to plan B!" Then he continued, "Look, it's early. We can sell programs for half price."

John and I said in unison, "Right."

We spread out and looked for programs, picking up most of them from tables when people left to make their bets. Within a short time, we had enough race forms and resold them. We earned ten bucks from the late crowd. John was excited to have more betting money because he had a tip on the fifth race, a horse named Hugglescote. His barber, a racetrack tout, told him, "This horse can't lose."

Ralph was reluctant. "John, you want to bet the whole ten bucks on the nose? How good is this tip? According to this *Pawtucket Times* I just found, he's not the favorite."

I looked over his shoulder and interrupted the debate, "Hey Ralph, look at the picture on the front page. This guy looks like he's riding a chariot."

"Yeah, looks like the gravedigger finally got a riding mower at the cemetery!"

John looked up to the sky. The smell of fresh manure hung in the air as the horses came on the track to the call of the bugler.

He finally answered Ralph's question. "A thoroughbred like Hugglescote? Pat Knight? A great jockey? Absolutely!"

Ralph sauntered up to the window to place the bet, his shoulders more stooped than ever.

A muffled sound came over the track, "They're in the gate." The crackling speaker blared, "And, they're off!"

We rushed to the rail at the finish line.

The horse went wire to wire and the loud speaker blasted, "And, it's Hugglescote by three lengths!"

We all yelled, "Yeah, Yeah, Yippee, Yahoo!"

John danced around shouting, "It's gonna be big! It's gonna be big!"

Ralph jumped up and down cheering the loudest. He thrust his body high in the air, throwing his outstretched arms over his head. R-I-P...R-I-P...R-I-P. Pieces of the ticket he bought cascaded down from the sky.

John jerked in a convulsion and screamed, "RALPH! What are you doing?"

Ralph took a giant step backward. "Sorry, guys. I changed the bet."

John was fuming. "Are you outta your mind? Whadda you mean, you changed the bet?"

Calmly puffing on his cigarette, Ralph stated, "Sorry, John. Winterfair was the favorite. I thought he would win."

"BULLSHIT!"

John chased Ralph all around the clubhouse, out through the turnstiles, into the parking lot, down Newport Avenue and they were last seen entering Slater Park.

* * * * *

Ralph bought a navy blue golf shirt with a white alligator

46

logo on the front and wore it all the time. He rubbed his hand across the raised emblem and stated, "Boy, I love this shirt."

Jim Nichols, the caddy shack bully, strutted up to Ralph, "Hey McGreavey, nice ALLI–GATORE!" He squeezed Ralph's left nipple and his thumb twisted the alligator emblem.

Ralph turned white with anger. "This is my best shirt! Keep your hands off."

Nichols eyes widened, "What are **you** going to do about it?"

Ralph smoothed the alligator saying, "You'll see. I'm gonna take it off."

With a welcome gesture of his hand, Nichols said, "Be my guest."

As Ralph pulled the bottom of his shirt over his head, Nichols lunged forward with an uppercut, then two sharp jabs to the head. The caddymaster ran over, grabbed Nichols, and threw him aside. Ralph's mouth was bleeding and he gripped his lip quickly so his shirt wouldn't be stained.

Ralph glared at Jim and threatened, "It's not over yet, Nichols."

The next Friday night, a Dean Martin 45 record was softly playing *Memories are Made of This* at Warner's Dance Hall.

All of a sudden I spotted Nichols, "Hey Ralph!"

"I know, I know. I'll be right back."

Ten minutes later he reappeared wearing an old golf shirt and khakis. Walking through the crowd, he stepped in front of Nichols demanding, "Outside! Right now!"

Jim softened his demeanor squinting his eyes and pressing

47

his lips together said, "I'm sorry I sucker-punched you. C'mon! I'm here with a date. I don't want any trouble. Let's shake hands and forget it."

Jim extended his right hand.

Ralph put out his left hand, saying. "If we're gonna shake hands, it's gonna be left handed." Nichols removed his arm from his date's waist, as Ralph said, "I don't shake the hand that sucker-punched me."

Nichols face paled as he turned around and faded from view. I put my hand on Ralph's shoulder, "He got outta that one. You shoulda whacked him!"

Ralph just shook his head and said, "He got the message."

Ralph had another altercation that month when his cousin Paul invited him to fill in for an injured player on the Tiverton summer league basketball team. The next game was scheduled on the outdoor courts, under the lights in Westerly and Ralph agreed to play. Paul neglected to tell him that a fight broke out a week earlier when the two teams played in Tiverton. Unbeknownst to Ralph, there were hard feelings between the two teams. The game was rough; a hostile crowd jeered at the Tiverton players throughout the game.

When Ralph scored the winning basket in overtime, someone standing courtside yelled, "Who's this guy, McGreavey? Where's he from?"

When the game ended, Ralph left the court and entered the dark shadows of the alley leading to the street. A guy with slicked back hair in a box-cut style and long bushy sideburns blocked Ralph's path. He was dressed in a white satin jacket with a black and gold dragon emblem, turned up collar and sleeves pulled halfway up to his elbows. A big, gold belt buckle supported dungarees with rolled-up cuffs.

Ralph pushed him out of the way and asked, "What are you, a wise-guy?"

The guy pulled a lock blade knife out of his back pocket and retorted, "I'll give you wise-guy!" As the blade snapped open, he repeatedly snarled, "I'm gonna cut you."

Ralph was not intimidated as he backed up to a wall and motioned with his hands, "Come on. Come on and I'll stick the knife in *your* neck."

The guy backed off and darted into the darkness. Ralph calmly lit a cigarette.

I didn't have many fights myself, but my older brother had more than his share. He would fight Rocky Marciano if he had to. Joe lost some, but his opponent got everything he had and more.

When I was only nine years old, I tagged along with Joe to the golf course. I became a caddy when they were short of caddies one day and sent me out with Dave and Arlene Shore. They were wonderful to me and taught me golf etiquette. I was lucky to have them show me the ropes on my first time out. Most of the caddies played cards in the caddy shack while they waited to be assigned for the day. They usually played *High Low Jack*, but I only knew one card game my mother taught me.

One day I asked as I shuffled my new deck of cards, "Anyone wanna play whist?"

Bob Greenfield shouted. "Whist? That's a sissy's game." Then the jerk brushed some of the cards off the bench.

"Gimme my cards," I demanded.

When the big bully ripped them up, I was swinging and kicking wildly. He and his buddies hoisted me in the air and threw me in the Ten Mile River just beyond the caddy shack. Joe was furious and raised both fists ready to take them all on.

They just turned and walked away from him, but Joe grabbed me and sternly commanded, "Don't you **ever** bring those cards to this course again!"

* * * * *

When Ralph caddied for Smokey Gannon, known as the biggest drinker at the club, it was damp and rainy. Smokey put a fifth of anisette in his golf bag and took swigs after he got past the first hole to keep warm. Ralph started sneaking shots of anisette every time he went up the fairway to forecaddy. Watching from the Grill Room windows, the members realized that Ralph had discovered Smokey's secret for warding off the chill. It was quite a sight to see Smokey lumbering to the eighteenth green, his golf bag slung over his left shoulder and Ralph draped over his right arm.

Caddies knew the best tippers...they also knew the worst. Ralph was carrying a single bag for the cheapest guy at the club, on the hottest day of the summer. Ralph was irritated because blisters had broken out on both heels. He had trouble keeping up and the frustrated golfer had to wait on practically every shot for 'Gimpy' to bring him a club.

The cheapskate golfer gave him a nine cent tip....one nickel and four pennies.

Ralph hobbled after the guy, tapped him on the shoulder, and said, "Here, you need this more than me."

The guy shot back, "You'll never caddy for me again!"

Ralph mumbled under his breath, "My sentiments exactly."

Ralph limped to his car. Paul Oney and I were waiting for a ride. I hopped in the front seat and Paul climbed in back. As we drove out of the parking lot onto Armistice Boulevard, Ralph quipped, "Wait'll I tell you about the big tip I just got."

Our speed was picking up when we were opposite Slater Park. Oney asked, "Whatcha' get?"

Before he could answer, I yelled, "Ralph, slow down! You're driving like Winnie the Wheeler!"

Ralph turned his head to look at Paul in the backseat just as he went around a curve. The car skidded into the high sidewalk curbing at the edge of the road and the car flipped over.

"**Yow**!" We were all hollering.

Then the car went **BLAM BING BAM! CLUNK**! We landed back on all four tires, but not before tearing up a manicured front lawn. Clumps of grass were strewn all over the place and there was a gaping hole near the sidewalk. Ralph and I were okay. Oney was a little shaken after rattling around the back seat like a pinball. The strong odor of scorched tires encircled the area as we lifted the flat tire off the back wheel. A police squad car pulled up to us.

The officer asked, "Now where do you think you guys are going?"

I recognized his partner, Artie Wilson. He was a friend of my father's. Officer Wilson took the three of us aside and said, "Okay boys, think of a good story and all of you stick to it."

Ralph blurted, "It was the hubcap."

Thanks to my father's friend, the police report read, '*Front hubcap flew off, hit rear tire, causing vehicle to swerve into curb. No injuries reported. No charges filed.*'

The Studebaker's steering column was damaged, causing the front end to go thump, thump, thump every time the wheel turned. While the car was in for repairs at Manny's Garage, Ralph rode the bike he had built with parts from a junkyard. It was a rainbow of colors with different shaped reflectors of various sizes attached to rubber flaps and fenders and even the handlebars. A makeshift piece of cardboard attached with a clothespin vibrated on the rear spokes when he pedaled, making a motor sound.

One day Ralph spotted a kid stealing his reflectors. He followed him home and confronted the boy's father. He looked him straight in the eye and said, "I just saw your son take reflectors off my bike and I want them back."

"Not my kid!" the father vehemently retorted.

"I saw him take them," Ralph insisted.

The boy's father summoned his son, who looked like a miniature Mr. Milktoast with his angelic face. His father commanded, "Tell this guy you didn't take his reflectors, Sonny."

Slightly dropping his head, the boy said, "Ah gee, Dad, I took 'em—sorry."

"Get the reflectors!"

The kid returned with four jars full of reflectors. They were shining like rubies and emeralds through the glass.

His father's mouth popped open. "I can't believe this."

Shaking one of the jars, the boy sheepishly looked at Ralph and said, "Here...pick out yours! I think they're in this jar."

Ralph chuckled as he put his arm around the boy's shoulders and spoke to him like a counselor. "Did you ever think of spending your time doing something good, like maybe caddying, instead of stealing a bunch of reflectors?"

"Gee, I'd like to caddy, but I don't know how."

"No problem. I'll teach you."

The next morning Ralph and the young boy headed off to the golf course. Sonny rode on Ralph's handlebars and the reflectors shined, once again, as bright as Sonny's smile. Ralph took him under his wing. Sonny became a good caddy at Pawtucket Country Club and lost all interest in stealing reflectors, or anything else, for that matter.

* * * * *

We had more rain than usual in the summer of '55. There were a lot of days when we couldn't caddy. One rainy day, Ralph and I were sitting on my front porch, listening to the sheeting rain as it bounced off the roof above. I realized that caddying wasn't going to solve our bleak financial situation that day.

I said, "You know, Ralph, we need money like a church mouse needs cheese."

"There you go again with the clichés, Mike."

"I know, I know; they're half of my vocabulary."

Lighting up, Ralph beamed, "You know Mike, I've been thinking about that mandolin my brother Leo brought back from his Mediterranean tour in the Navy."

"Yeah, you said he got it in France."

"He paid 700 French Francs for it, *whatever* that means. Did you ever get it tuned?"

53

Strumming my fingers on my chest, I said, "Nah, I tried and tried, but I couldn't get it tuned. It's shoved way back in my closet."

"You mean it's just collecting dust?"

"Yeah, it just goes P L U N K, P L U N K. It's just collecting dust."

"But it's worth a couple hundred bucks, Mike."

"M M M, but to who?"

"The pawn broker down on Park Street."

We headed downtown and spotted the old, dimly lit 'C A S H' sign in the window. The neon letters flickered, and the 'S' was completely burned out. The grimy windows were streaked and splattered with rain. CREAK...CREAK. We made our way through the doorway and slowly walked over the rough wooden floor.

I whispered to Ralph, "Look at all these cast-off watches. They musta' been *someone's* treasure."

The seedy looking store smelled of burnt shellac. A guy wearing a dirty green visor looked up from behind the counter. Adjusting his taped glasses, he growled through gritted teeth clamped on an unlit juicy stogie, "What's that?"

Cradling the mandolin as if it was a Stradivarius, Ralph gently placed the instrument on the counter. "This mandolin comes from France. It's worth more than two hundred bucks."

The pawnbroker's beady eyes bulged, "Shit! This is a piece of junk."

His appraisal took us by surprise.

"What? No way!" Ralph insisted as the pawnbroker took it over to the only bright bulb in the place.

He said, "Look at this; glue is holding this piece of crap together. The pieces don't even match. Half of this thing is from a guitar. *Junk, just junk.*"

Dejected, Ralph and I looked at each other dumbfounded. The pawnbroker finally said, "I'll give you five bucks."

Ralph was desperate for cash and nodded, "I'll take it!"

On the way out, I quipped, "At least we got enough money to get a dimie hot dog and a glass of coffee milk at the White Tower."

"Can you believe that, Mike?"

"Augh, no one'll ever get that thing tuned."

Ralph methodically lit a cigarette. "That guy is gonna sell our mandolin for two hundred bucks some day. Somebody out there is going to pay good money for it. I've got a gut feeling."

Chapter 4
We Couldn't Even Spell Salezman Now We Are One

DIRECT SALES
$50/wk. Guaranteed–First Two Weeks
Apply in Person, July 6th   8–10 a.m.
Biltmore Hotel   Suite 321
Providence, R.I.

When my brother Joe and his best friend Jim Shanahan answered the sales advertisement in the *Providence Journal*, the room was filled with people. Everyone who showed up was hired. The advertised guarantee, however, applied *only* to those who were successful in recruiting four salesmen to work under them selling Catholic Bibles door-to-door. Joe and Jim were confident they could easily get four new recruits. They were the only two applicants to qualify for the guarantee. They were hired as a team and agreed to split the $50.

As soon as we stepped into my living room that night, Joe started in. "Mike, you and Ralph have got a chance of a lifetime! We're all gonna make a fortune selling Bibles."

Then Jim chimed in. "This is an easy sell for big bucks! No more carrying heavy golf bags for five bucks a day. One Bible sale for $29.95 and you earn eleven dollars commission."

Ralph, the reluctant caddy, enthusiastically agreed, "Count me in!"

"Hold on, Ralph. They think we're gonna sell Bibles like '*hotcakes.*' What if we don't sell any all day?"

Jim said, "It'll be like falling off a log!"

Joe said, "Look, we're gonna get Ted Gorman and Bobby Stanton to work with you as a team."

Well, that made the offer look pretty good. We liked the idea of working with Ted and Bobby.

The following week, we showed up at the Biltmore for an eight o'clock meeting, dressed in our jackets and ties and ready to tackle our first sales experience. We were ushered in by Homey Gladu, the local sales manager, who was hyper and a real wheeler-dealer. It seemed like we were at some kind of revival meeting, clapping our hands and stamping our feet in preparation for our first sales call. He was enthusiastic and so were we with all the hype.

On our first day in the territory, Homey had Ralph and me travel with Al Romano, one of his top salesmen. Al had curly brown hair, sharp features and a dark complexion. He resembled a tall, lanky distance runner. He was dressed in a light-weight gray business suit and shiny patent leather pointed Italian shoes with elevated heels. His assignment was to show us how Bible sales were made. He was a smooth talking ladies' man. We went door to door to quite a few houses that day, asking residents if they were Catholic and getting nowhere, fast.

As the temperature steadily climbed into the 90's, we were

finally invited in to make our first presentation to a newlywed couple. In the middle of his sales pitch, Al reached into his vest pocket and pulled out a handkerchief to wipe his sweaty brow. Out popped a packet of prophylactics that rolled on the floor and hit Ralph's foot. The young couple, Ralph, and I burst out laughing when Ralph put his foot over the Trojan. Al proceeded to remove the sweat from his forehead, continued his sales pitch oblivious to what had happened. Then he got frustrated, slammed the Bible shut and stormed out of the house.

"What the hell's wrong with you guys? You blew the sale! You can't laugh during a presentation! What's your problem?"

Ralph took the rubber out of his pants pocket and dangled it in front of his face as he smugly asked, "Could this be yours?"

Al shoved two fingers deep into his vest pocket. "Holy shit!" He turned beet red and then smiled and said, "Boys, one of the *first* lessons in sales is to be prepared." It took the three of us a good fifteen minutes to regain our composure from laughing before we could continue our '*Bible sales training*' with Al Romano.

The next day Homey told us that Bogart Farquardt, the big boss from Charleston, South Carolina was coming north for a major sales meeting at the end of the week. Homey said, "Mr. Farquardt likes to be called Bogie by his sales force."

Bogie arrived in Pawtucket driving a big, powder blue 1955 Cadillac Eldorado ragtop loaded with Bibles. It had rocketship tailfins and flashy sabre spoke wheels. The dashboard sported a shiny brass plate with 'Bogart Farquardt' engraved on it. He was an enormous man who weighed over three hundred pounds. Ralph and I mimicked the way he walked high on the balls of his feet. His thick, bushy hair was worn with an Elvis-style wave and was slicked back into a duck cut.

Ralph mumbled, "This guy's a piece of work."

Then he offered to help carry the Bibles up to the second floor rented office space. When he opened the door, Bogey was carrying an armful of Bibles and didn't see Ralph's foot in his path.

SLAM–CRASH–FART "OOPS…OOOOUGH." Bogie and the Bibles were spread all over the steps.

Holding a limp wrist, Bogie cried out, "You broke my wrist, you clumsy ox!"

Ralph said, "Sorry Mr. Farquardt. I was just trying to help." Then Ralph grinned at me, rolled his eyes and fumbled for a cigarette.

The meeting was delayed for a half hour while people applied ice to Bogie's wrist and debated whether or not Bogie should go to the hospital. Bogie's eyes were fixed on Ralph and he stopped talking to him. It was evident to the entire sales force that Ralph and Bogie had already developed a strong dislike for each other.

When the meeting finally got underway, Homey introduced Bogie. Bogie gave us a rundown of all the awards he had won selling Bibles. As the time went on he became more and more aggressive with his motivational speech. He finally ended his tirade with a rousing question directed to all of us. "How many Bibles will **YOU** sell today?"

Some of the salespeople had trouble selling one Bible a week but someone called out, "I can sell three."

Another person said, "I'll sell four today."

Ralph wasn't impressed by Bogie's hype and just shook his head in disbelief. When Bogie looked at him, Ralph lowered his head and whispered under his breath, "What a phony!"

Then he shot up, "ONE, IF I'M LUCKY!"

I quickly clutched Ralph by the arm, "You're gonna get us fired. You'd better lay off. This guy's the top boss, the kingpin."

"Okay, Mike, but I can't stand that fat bastard."

When the meeting ended, Bogie met everyone at the top of the stairs. He patted each of us on the back, giving us an inspirational send off.

When Ralph got to him, Bogie said, "Go out there and make those sales, tiger!"

I thought, *"Wow, the ice is melting."*

Ralph turned, and in a friendly gesture, flicked his wrist as Bogie leaned forward. In the quick, unexpected movement, Ralph's fingers hit Bogie on the side of his head. Bogie's hair slid off his head and completely covered his face. The duck-tail was now on his forehead. Ralph pressed his hand against the mass of hair and they both slid it back up onto his head. Without saying a word to each other, they turned on their heels and walked in opposite directions. Any chance of Ralph making points with Bogey just went down the drain.

Ralph grabbed me and asked, "Did I *do* what I *think* I just did?"

I shook my head in disbelief and sighed, "Jesus Christ, Ralph."

Ralph and I worked as a team selling the Bibles. We reported each morning at seven-thirty for a brief sales meeting and got our daily assignments, usually working with Ted and Bobby. Joe and Jim sold a lot of Bibles, along with the rest of the sales force they recruited for their territory. They also got a job at a Fiberglass plant in Ashton working the night shift from midnight until seven in the morning. On some days, they would caddy in the morning, sell Bibles in the afternoon and work at the factory at night. They found a way to rig the freight elevator to stop between the second and third floors, enabling them to take periodic catnaps on the elevator throughout the night.

On occasion Joe and Jim went from the factory straight to the morning sales meetings and then worked a full day selling Bibles. They were a great combination. Joe had good business sense and Jim was a mathematical genius. He could come up with figures faster than any adding machine.

Ralph and I were assigned to work with Joe and Jim on one very hot day in early July. As the car stopped in front of the Rumford Rexall, Joe instructed, "Okay, you guys work this Rumford section. Jim and I will be in Darlington. We'll pick you up here at four o'clock."

After going from house to house for a few hours, I suggested, "Ralph, let's grab lunch. I only made two presentations, but I *did* get a sale."

"I matched ya, Mike, but it took me three tries." Ralph lit a cigarette and blew smoke rings above his head. "Mike, did you happen to notice the movie playing at the Darlton?"

"Ya, I've had it. Let's go!"

Ralph didn't hesitate and stuck out his thumb. The second car to drive by picked us up. Boy did that air-conditioned theater feel good! We were engrossed in the movie and the great acting of Ernest Borgnine portraying 'MARTY', when two familiar silhouettes came walking up the dimly lit isle.

Ralph whispered, "Geeze! It's them; they're here. Get down!"

But Jim spotted us before we could duck down and bellowed, "All right, what the hell are you two guys doing here?"

Ralph put his finger up to his lips, "Shush, be quiet. People are watching the movie."

Jim gave him a curious look and continued in a hushed voice, "You're supposed to be working."

I asked, "What about you guys?"

Joe looked at me with a stern eye and said, "We're on the guarantee!"

* * * * *

In order to pump up the sales force, Homey devised little schemes that irritated us. One time he gave Al Romano's paycheck to Ralph and waited for him to see the large amount, which included all of the salesman's overrides.

"Oh, sorry Ralph, I made a mistake. This is your check."

Waving his small commission check, Ralph leaned into me and said, "Homey's so full of shit."

Homey often drove out to our territory to check on us and liked tooting his horn as a signal to meet him at his car. **BLALALA…BLALALA…BLALALA!** He sat behind the wheel and looked like Mr. Five-by-Five when his eyes peered through the large steering wheel. He tried to con us into thinking he had a special horn installed in his car, but we knew that the chrome circular ring on his steering wheel was broken and sounded an extended blast when he pressed it.

Homey knighted Ted Gorman as 'Crew Chief.' He was a good reliable salesman, and Homey trusted him. Ted enjoyed his title even though he didn't get any extra money in overrides from the other salesmen. Bobby, Ralph and I worked with him as a team, with Ted driving us to the assigned territory. He was a religious, serious perfectionist and was always on time.

One day he approached us and explained, "I got home from a date really late last night and I'm completely exhausted. Anyone want to drive today?"

Ralph fumbled for a cigarette, answering, "Sure. I'll drive."

Ted stretched out on the back seat. We were on our way to Warwick when Ralph noticed Ted dozing off. Each time Ralph glanced back, Ted's head nodded lower and lower. Ralph put his finger up to his puckered lips. He had a glint in his eyes. The car became silent. He turned the dial on the radio until he heard Brahams Lullaby. Before long Bobby and I were also dozing. Little did we know we were on a mystery ride, with Ralph driving on quiet, winding roads. Only he knew we were headed for Craigville Beach in Hyannis.

Bright sunlight bouncing off the water stung our eyes and the salty sea breeze tingled my nose as we rolled into the parking lot. Before long, the roar of the surf pounding the shoreline beckoned to us. We took off our jackets and shoes, rolled up our shirt sleeves and pant legs, then quietly exited the car. We left Ted in a deep slumber, snoring away in the backseat. Walking along the beach, the breaking waves trickled over the sand, soothing our bare feet.

Bobby said, "This sure beats pounding the beat with Bibles."

We were totally relaxed under a rented beach umbrella when we heard a maniac yelling over the sand dunes, "Get over here! Get over here right now!"

People on the beach stopped to watch this irate guy dressed in a business suit running through the soft white sand. Ted wearily stumbled into the umbrella and shouted, "Homey's gonna hear about this stunt, Ralph!"

I stepped between Ted and Ralph and calmly said, "You've been working too hard. We let you sleep."

He wasn't impressed and continued his ranting rage, "Gimme the damn keys, Ralph." We ran to the car, but couldn't stop this emotional basket case. The wheels squealed as Ted zoomed out of the parking lot.

Ralph observed, "There goes our ride–**and** our shoes!"

Walking barefoot on the hot pavement wasn't easy. We tried to avoid the tiny pebbles that became imbedded in the bottom of our feet as we thumbed home. We got a ride as far as Buzzards Bay and went into Lindsey's for fried clams.

Mr. Lindsey pointed to a sign, 'NO BARE FEET,' and said, "Sorry boys."

So we settled for coffee milk shakes next door at the Dairy Queen.

* * * * *

Ten days later we were back on the Cape. This time, we headed for Martha's Vineyard. We thought the island would be virgin territory for Bible sales.

The night before we left Pawtucket we saw Ted as he drove by Pineault's Corner. He yelled over, "Where are you guys going tomorrow?"

Ralph bellowed proudly, "Martha's Vineyard!"

With a casual wave signaling disbelief, he hollered across the road, "Ah, you guys are nuts."

But the next day, we were on the bus, headed for the ferry at Woods Hole, which is about two hours from Pawtucket. The island is the largest in New England and sits seven miles off the coast of Cape Cod. It's nine miles wide and twenty-three miles long. On the boat ride across the ocean, we could see the Vineyard in the distance. We felt the ocean breeze caress our faces. Ralph talked to a girl who was going to the island to visit her friend. He made a date for the four of us to meet later that night. When we docked near the main beach at Oak Bluffs, we walked along a circular drive to a stately guesthouse that faced a white gazebo on the town green.

A pleasant woman with blue tinted hair, wearing bright red lipstick and too much rouge explained, "People are in the process of moving out at the moment. You boys will have to wait for your room."

Ralph turned to me and whispered, "This woman looks like a feather duster and she smells like she just took a bath in a tub full of perfume."

We noticed a couple of guys, probably in their mid-twenties, bringing suitcases to a car. As we moved our things into the room they just vacated, Ralph asked, "Where's all the action on the island?"

One of them answered, "We saw a wonderful play last night." Ralph replied, "I mean, ACTION – ACTION – REAL ACTION!"

The fellow responded, "You're askin' the wrong guys."

Ralph wouldn't let up, "Okay, okay, are you guys Catholic?"

They both nodded so Ralph held up his Bible and started his pitch. "We're Bible salesmen; take a look at this beautiful masterpiece."

He opened the white leather Bible with gold lettering on the front. It was extremely well made and had easy-to-read large print. Many pages featured exquisite multicolored pictures, depicting the most sacred religious events.

Ralph turned to the picture of our Lord on the cross and repeatedly asked, "Would you deny Christ by not buying this Bible?"

I had never seen this approach before, by Ralph, or anyone else. I gave Ralph a long, quizzical look and noticed one of the guys was sweating profusely.

He finally said, "I don't know if I can afford it."

Ralph, the persistent salesman, quickly continued, "Look. It's only $29.99."

The prospect paced around the room for a few minutes, but it seemed like an hour to me. He eventually sat down and said, wringing his hands, "Gee whiz, I'd **love** to have it."

Ralph beamed, "Cash or check?"

The guy lit up a long, thin Tareyton cigarette, took a couple of puffs and thoughtfully said, "Out in my car…I have a briefcase." Turning to his friend he continued, "Henry, would you please get it for me?"

When Henry returned with a scruffy black case, he put it on the table. Fondling the case, the highly motivated customer handed it to Ralph. "How'd you like to have this briefcase? Give me the Bible and it's yours!"

"Are you shittin' me?" Ralph asked in a stunned voice.

I laughed and thought, *"If all the prospects are like this on the island, our virgin territory will remain intact."*

Early that evening, we got dressed in our corduroy sport jackets and pressed pants, as we prepared to pick up the two girls.

Ralph was with the girl he met on the ferry. She looked like Popeye's girlfriend, Olive Oil. She stood tall and thin, dressed in her long, straight skirt, plain white blouse and bobby socks with saddle shoes. Her friend, Mary Lou, was a pretty blonde girl with a pony tail. She wore a skirt, pink sweater, and a neck scarf. We decided to take a paddleboat ride in the bay at Oak Bluffs, just as it was getting dark. Mary Lou and I floated around for an hour and then returned to the dock, but Ralph and his Olive were nowhere in sight.

The boat owner was agitated. "I'm closin' up. Everyone's in but the *Hunky Dory*. Where the hell are they?"

An hour later he was ready to call the Coast Guard. Ralph finally came paddling in looking exhausted, with the girl in a state of shock.

Leaning forward at the edge of the dock, Mary Lou looked extremely concerned as she shouted across the water, "Are you two okay?"

I was also concerned, and a little more than a little curious, "Ralph, what happened?"

Ralph breathlessly exclaimed, "We got into rough seas outside the bay. The swift current swept us way out into the ocean. I tried to kiss her. She started crying and screamed. The boat plunged into a swell. Water splashed high over our heads. Olive got sick and threw up. I paddled and paddled like hell in the fierce high tide. It took everything in my power to get us back here!"

Olive shrieked, "I've had enough adventure for one night, Mary Lou!" In a huff she declared, "Let's go home."

I turned to Ralph and quipped, "So much for any chance of romance on this island!"

The next day, we went into town to rent a car. We were surprised to run into Peter and Paul Kelley, two brothers we knew from school. They lived in Central Falls and spent every summer on the Vineyard with their family. Paul worked at the drugstore and Peter gave out towels at the main beach. They both had the day off and wanted to show us the island. We decided to go to South Beach.

I reasoned, "Ralph, tomorrow we'll put in a full day with the Bibles."

"Ya, we've got the car, the Kelley's—and the whole island!"

The old '41 Plymouth Coupe headed toward Edgartown, with the radio blasting and the four of us singing the song about Davy Crockett and then *Sh-Boom*.

When we hit a narrow stretch of road with pounding surf in the ocean on our left and a placid salt pond on our right, we were drowning out Chuck Berry with our voices singing *Mabeline*.

The sweet salt air combined with the warm sunshine gave an intoxicating effect. We were on top of the world! Peter directed us through town right over to the *On Time Ferry* to Chappaquiddick. The barge could hold a few cars, but we were the only ones on it. In a few minutes we were on the other shore looking back across to Edgartown. We then drove through the quiet, serene island.

"There's not much to do here," Peter said.

We were anxious to get to South Beach and left Chappy the way we found it. The magnificent, long shoreline of South Beach stretched for miles. We gazed along the horizon. The ocean, sand and sky all seemed to meet in the distance. We noticed a group of college students partying behind a big sand dune. Their happy voices and laughter climbed over the dunes and carried out to sea. We enjoyed a few hours of leisure, like we had never experienced before. The sand and salt were baked on our bodies and our dry lips yearned for a drink.

Ralph faked a brogue, "Me throat is dry."

Paul returned from a walk holding a bottle of Narragansett Beer an inch from his face. He opened his mouth, tilted the bottle, and let the cold brew flow over his parched lips and tongue.

"Hey, where'd 'ja get that?" Ralph inquired.

Paul just grinned and said, "Their trunks are open."

Ralph's eyes glistened, "Any more where that came from?"

"Lots."

Ralph bummed a cigarette from Peter, then he slowly took his time lighting it.

"Mike, you and Paul, go get the car. Peter, **you** come with me."

When I looked into the rearview mirror before shifting into reverse, I noticed Ralph and Peter running toward us carrying a case of beer. They threw themselves and the bottles of liquid gold into the backseat. When I backed up, I hit a small street sign and knocked it over. It left a noticeable dent in the bumper.

Peter hollered, "Take off!"

I asked, "Where to?"

Peter looked back and yelled, "The cliffs at Gay Head!"

Luckily, Peter had a church key hanging from his belt, along with the keys to the towel shack. He used the key to pop open a couple of beers. When we got to the jagged Nashaquista Cliffs, we bounced along a narrow, winding path, down to the secluded beach. It was low tide. We lifted our heads a little higher to smell the fresh salt air wafting off baked seaweed on the exposed rocks. After a few beers, we talked about how the surf seemed calmer on this side of the island.

Driving by Menemsha with little fishing boats bobbing in the coves, Ralph said, "Boy, are we operating!"

We ate bowls of clam chowder at an outdoor clam shack on the wharf at Vineyard Haven and amused ourselves by watching people board the ferry.

Peter quipped, "Hey, guys. Look at the greyhound with the long neck. His owner looks like he was bred at the same kennel."

Paul pointed to a woman who was screaming at the ticket collector when he stopped her from boarding. She was trying to use a lower priced child's ticket, but he demanded she pay the adult fare. Her face was contorted in rage as she poked him in the shoulder. "Nobody ever checks my ticket."

"Lady, I'm just doing my job."

Paul sighed, "How'd you like to have that 'Quiet Sally' for a teacher?"

Ralph stood up, "Let's get to Oak Bluffs. We gotta get the car back."

I asked, "What about the ding in the bumper?"

"I've already taken care of it."

"Whatta ya mean?"

Ralph boasted as he lit a Lucky, "See this glue. I bought it at the A & P. Check the car out."

71

Ralph's imagination had really worked overtime on this one. After scraping off a big seagull dropping from the roof of the car, he glued it over the dent. It blended perfectly with the other bird droppings on the bumper. He called it his 'Picasso.'

Before returning the rental car, we stashed our unopened beer bottles behind a seawall by the dock in Oak Bluffs. When we approached the rental parking lot, I ran out of gas.

Ralph said, "We're outta gas? I can't believe you'd pull a Mike Ryan stunt like that even on this island."

"Yep. We're completely out of gas."

The four of us pushed the car onto the car rental lot then high tailed it out of there. We walked through the quiet back streets of the town to Trinity Park, site of the original Methodist colony. The streets were lined with tiny, gingerbread-style homes, which were all painted in bright colors. We rode the historic Flying Horses Carousel, which was brought to the island by barge in 1884, from Westerly, Rhode Island, where it was made. Steel rings were inserted into ring arms on each side of the carousel, but only one brass ring was loaded in each arm.

Everyone tried to catch the brass ring as the horses went round and round. If you were lucky enough to get the brass ring, you got a free ride. The Kelleys were adept at leaning off their horses and could quickly grab two, and sometimes, three rings at a time. They often got one of the coveted brass rings. Ralph and I could only grab one ring at a time and just kept getting the worthless silver rings.

As night fell, we headed back to the wharf and drank the remaining suds. Ralph got tipsy so we decided to go to the Captain's Table, a restaurant near the wharf, to get some black coffee. He was getting boisterous and kept yelling, "I'll have one egg-trillbie on a double decker! Hi, neighbor, have a 'Gansett!"

The proprietor firmly demanded, "I want you guys outta here–or I'll call the cops."

Peter and I picked Ralph up under his arms and carried him back to the seawall. Paul ran home and sneaked four blankets out of the house so we could sleep on the beach. The bright sun on the horizon woke us up early the next morning.

Ralph ran down the beach and began to yell, "Last one in the water's a rotten egg."

We all dove into the sobering, cool, crisp water, completely bare-ass. While we were frolicking in the water, the first ferry of the day approached the dock. The passengers stared when four pearly white moons popped up like porpoises, as we all did the butterfly stroke in unison. We raced back to the seawall, threw on our clothes, and disappeared from view. We avoided the authorities, but not Mrs. Kelley. When we brought the blankets back to her house, she grabbed Peter and Paul by the ears and pulled them inside.

With a stern face and pointed finger, she ordered Ralph and me into her car. "I want you two OFF this island."

She drove us to the Oak Bluffs ferry and waited until we went up the plank to get on the boat. We discovered, however, that this ferry was going to Nantucket, not to the mainland. When we were certain that Mrs. Kelley was nowhere in sight, we got off the boat and sat on a bench by the dock to wait for the next ferry going to Woods Hole. Two inebriated guys, appearing to be in their early twenties, swaggered over and sat right next to us reeking of booze. From our conversation, we learned that they were from Boston and were looking to raise a little hell on Martha's Vineyard. They each bummed a cigarette from Ralph.

Ralph told them, "We're Bible salesmen, but we haven't had any luck here."

One of the guys said, "We have to walk right by the church. Why don't you come with us?"

Ralph said, "Why not."

The priest was watering the grass in front of the rectory at Saint Augustine's Roman Catholic Church on School Street. A black Labrador was at his side. He gave the four of us a questionable look.

I said, "Hi, Father. Maybe you can help us."

Ralph interjected, "We're Bible salesmen. Do you know what our potential might be on the island?"

I thought, *What can the priest be thinking of us? We slept on the beach all night, we haven't shaved, and these two guys are drunk."*

Just then, one of our new-found buddies put his face right up to the dog's snout and nuzzled him saying, "HUM, BABE–HUM, BABE–HUM, BABE".

The distracted priest finally answered, "Oak Bluffs was originally a campground founded by the Methodists. There still aren't many Catholics living full time on the Island. The summer brings a lot of tourists. I'm afraid your prospects don't seem very good."

"Looks like we're outta luck on this island, Ralph. We'd better think about getting back to Pawtucket."

Back at the dock, Ralph looked at the posted schedule above the ticket window.

As he studied his round-trip ticket, he pondered, "Mike, we can thumb to Vineyard Haven and take a cheaper ferry. The refund will be enough for us to have…"

I cut in and we both said, "Lunch!"

We were the last ones to board the ferry as we ran with Bibles, hot dogs, soda, and our suitcases. We made it back to Woods Hole, but we were still a hundred miles from home. Exhausted, we dragged ourselves up the road to thumb to Rhode Island. Two sailors in white dress uniforms picked us up in a 1951 light blue Ford convertible sporting wide white wall tires. Once we were in the car, we saw them passing a bottle of Seagram's Seven back and forth. One of the sailors got off on Route 3 at the Rotary so he could head to Boston.

I leaned over to Ralph, "We should've gotten out when he did. This guy shouldn't be driving. The bottle's almost empty. He's starting to slur his words. His breath stinks. The car smells like a brewery."

Ralph commanded, "Pull over, we're getting out here." The sailor maneuvered to the curb and slumped over the wheel.

I said, "Ralph, we can't let this guy drive alone. He'll get killed."

We gently pushed him over to the passenger seat and I took the wheel. I drove directly to the Spa in Pawtucket with the sailor passed out cold next to me. We were able to sober him up with black coffee and donuts.

The grateful sailor said, "Thanks, guys. I really appreciate it."

Two good selling days had gone by and we only had one trade-in offer for a Bible. Now we had to face Ted and Homey.

Mary Ellen McDuff arrived at the Monday morning sales briefing and sat behind a large, brown plastic ash tray that matched her business attire. Her supple style reflected a low sales volume. Homey never reported her sales figures. He didn't want to embarrass her.

Al Romano, pinching his chin, approached Homey and suggested, "I've talked with the others, and some of us think it would be nice, if we sort of pitched in to buy a new outfit for Mary Ellen."

Homey closed his briefcase slowly, CLICK–CLICK. "Nooooooo! I've been telling her for a month how nice she looks."

Al nodded, "Yeah, maybe you're right. We don't want to hurt her feelings."

Mary Ellen was a member of Alfredo Bandeliero's sales team along with Adam and Eve Plouffe, a husband and wife duo. Adam was dapper, always dressed in the latest zoot suits accessorized with brightly designed neckties. He routinely had a toothpick in the corner of his mouth. Eve never sold a Bible. She just accompanied Adam on every call he made. She was six inches taller than her husband in her spiked high-heeled shoes. Her hair was bleached blonde and she had an attractive face, with oversized, seductive lips. She sported a different provocative dress each day. Her clothes clung to her slim body and looked like she bought them one size too small.

Fredo, the sales crew chief, had a 1948 battered Cadillac that burned oil and left a trail of black soot. Looking in his chrome side-view mirror, he would practice romancing women with his seductive accent.

We would ask him, "Meet any g–i–r–l–s today, F–r–e–e–d–o Bandito?"

With a smile of contentment he would say, "I ask them, 'You go for ride with me in my Cadillac?' They say, 'MMMMM.'"

Ralph and I would nudge each other and say, "Only you, Fredo, only you."

With raised eyebrows and tight lips Fredo always replied, "MMMMM."

Our sales team had a two dollar per person bet against Fredo's team each week to see who could sell the most Bibles. We only lost the bet one week—the week Ralph and I went to Martha's Vineyard. Our presentations got better and our sales increased as we became more experienced. We were making a lot more money than we earned caddying. Joe and I turned in a hefty paycheck to my mother each week, to run the household. My father was busy trying to keep his jewelry sales business going. Most of the money he made went right back into his company. Jim Shanahan's earnings were also appreciated at home, as he was part of a large family. Ralph needed his money to keep his old car up and running. The Rhode Island Bible sales teams were flying high. Little did we know that the briefing this morning was for a different purpose.

Homey addressed the attentive group. "You've done a great job and we're very proud of you. However, the Providence area has now been saturated."

The group reacted, "Augh, ooh." Someone asked, "What's next?"

Homey continued his obviously rehearsed speech, "Bogey's already rented office space in Boston. Anyone interested in working that area is welcome to join us."

One of the salesmen asked, "When are you going?"

Homey replied, "Next week."

It was now evident that they planned to work the northern

cities in the summer and head south in the winter. There were no takers for Boston.

Ralph put his Bible in the trunk of his car and said, "AMEN." He turned to me. "Whatta we gonna do now, Mike?"

"Well, the grass is always greener at the…" We both said together, "Golf course!"

Zeke interrupted me bringing me back into the present.

He leaned back against the tree, looked out over his manicured green grass that hugged the gravestones and said, "To me the grass is always greener at the cemetery!"

"It's easy to see where our thoughts go when we think of grass, Zeke. I think of golf, you think of the cemetery!"

"Yes—I even wrote a poem about cutting the grass years ago."

"No kiddin'! I'd love to hear it."

"Well, it's called *Within the Lawn* and it goes like this:

**"The sound of silence broken by steady wind created by machine.
Dandelion blow away as sun rays glow through silicon screen.
Ladyfinger ripped from stem and tossed to higher carpet.
Seed in cloud traveling high and far above destruction below.
Grasshoppers jump and fly with no direction home.
The toad on stone goes to ground and prays in earth below.
The blades above are spinning in a shadow that blocks the sun.
Caterpillar will curl in a ball, for he is too slow to run.
Butterflies are winging as the sun burns low.
For me, my work is done.
The grass was too long."**

"I'm speechless, Zeke. You've captured it all."

Chapter 5
The Pendulum Always Swings

Bill Tolland, the caddy master at Pawtucket Country Club, asked if anyone would like to caddy in the National Women's Amateur Tournament that was to be held at the Rhode Island Country Club in Barrington. Half of the caddies raised their hand, including Ralph and me.

Bill said, "A bus will pick you up here at seven every morning. Buses will leave the club in Barrington each afternoon at two o'clock and six o'clock."

The first day of the tournament was medal (score) play. The top sixty-four players qualified for three days of match play. Ralph and I caddied the first day for two women who qualified. In fact, we were in the same threesome.

I was caddying for Rachel Stein, a beautiful nineteen-year-old girl from Hackensack, New Jersey, who became the darling of the tournament. Ralph's amateur lost in her first match, but he still took the bus with me and watched Rachel play her subsequent

79

matches. She advanced to the quarter-finals, winning her first two matches as the underdog. She had a perfect, fluid swing, a marvelous short game and was an accurate putter. She possessed a poised attitude for the game of golf. She was charming. Ralph and I fell in love with her.

The day before her final match, Ralph and I took the last bus out of Barrington. We discussed how attractive Rachel was with her ponytail and wholesome facial features. We decided we would ask her if we could take her to Crescent Park. We figured we had enough money to pay for a cab to take the three of us from the golf course. We talked about how great it would be to take her on the roller coaster, ferris wheel, and dobby horses.

Ralph stated, "I'm sure we can win a prize for her. I'm good at knocking down the wooden milk bottles with a baseball."

By the time we reached the Pawtucket Country Club, we realized it would never happen. It would just embarrass her and us too, if we asked, but, boy it was wonderful to dream.

* * * * *

Jim Shanahan and my brother Joe were partners in business since they were young guys back in the days of our youth. Jim was always around golf at the Pawtucket Country Club and became an outstanding junior golfer at the club. The members realized his potential and paid for his junior golf membership. He was the best chipper at the club, using his old but trusty wedge. He hit shots high and they always landed soft, close to the rim of the cup. He played under control and was never overwhelmed. He played the game as a gentleman, but had a fierce desire to compete. In the spring, Jim qualified to compete in the National Juniors Tournament in Los Angeles by winning the New England Juniors Tournament. The club members chipped in to pay his air fare to California. His first opponent was the Junior Champion from Ohio....a fourteen- year-old from Columbus.

When Jim got back to Pawtucket, he told Joe and me, "This kid with a blonde crew cut was big and rugged. He cranked the golf ball. God, he hit superman shots—and boy could he putt. I lost the first two holes that were both par fives. The Ohio champion hit the green in two shots, birdying both holes. I was two down right off the bat."

Jim did win one of the holes with a birdie under unusual circumstances. His opponent hit over a high mound, cut the corner to this par four, and drove the green. He had trouble with the first putt because the ball was imbedded in the green and he ended up three putting.

Jim stated, "I thought I could beat any fourteen-year-old in the country, but not this kid. Nicklaus...Jack Nicklaus...He's gonna make a name for himself someday."

Years later Jim became a member at Baltusrol Country Club in New Jersey and volunteered to be a marshal for a major pro tour tournament held there. Jack Nicklaus was playing in the tournament and Jim got a chance to talk to him. Jim was amazed that Jack clearly remembered all the details of their match, just as he did, when they played each other in the National Juniors Tournament decades ago.

Jim asked me to caddy for him when he entered the Rhode Island Amateurs held at Pawtucket Country Club. He qualified for match play and his first match was against the premier medal player in the state, Angelo Margarilli. Jim was surprised that he was paired with the medalist in the first round because Angie had gone to the semi finals in the National Amateurs a few years earlier. Most people thought Jim would be ousted in short order, not realizing that he was brought up on the Pawtucket Country Club golf course. He knew every hole like the back of his hand.

Experience had taught him the best ball placement on the fairway for each hole and he had the capability of directing his ball to land just where he wanted it to go. He beat Angelo one up.

His second match was against 'Gordie' Goodson, the Club Champion at Pawtucket that year. They were all even going to the par four sixteenth hole. It's a long par four, over four hundred yards. 'Gordie' hit his drive down the middle of the fairway and had less than a hundred fifty yards to the green. Jim pushed his tee shot into the woods on the right side. His ball hit a tree and he was almost two hundred yards from the green. The ball was between two trees and he had to hit it under branches that were about ten yards out.

Jim surveyed the situation and finally said to me, "Mike, I've got to hit the ball low and hard in order to get to the green."

I nodded in agreement, "I know, Jim."

Jim calmly said, "I'll hit a two iron and hood the club face just a little."

"Okay."

Almost all of the club members and a lot of other spectators were silently watching the 'all-even match.' Jim hit a career shot. He hit the ball solid and it flew out of the woods just under the branches. The ball hit in the fairway about fifty yards from the green. It started to roll and didn't stop until it was two feet from the pin! The spectators gasped, then applauded. When I looked over at 'Gordie', he was looking at our pro, Wes Banner, and just shook his head in disbelief. Jim made birdie, giving him the lead. They halved the next two holes with pars. Jim had won his second match, one up.

In the quarter-finals, Jim was paired with 'Dutchie' Nevans. 'Dutchie' was a public course player and only played on weekends. He was, however, a marvelous player and a dogged competitor.

The more he played, the better he played. It was a tough match for Jim. 'Dutchie' played in a white T-shirt and khakis. His style was nothing pretentious; he just played hard-nosed golf. Jim had him down early, but 'Dutchie' fought hard to even the match on the eighteenth hole. Jim finally won on the first extra hole, but it was nineteen holes of pure grind.

In the semi-finals, Jim lost to the eventual winner, Bob Hoskin. Bob was a pro who got back his amateur status just before the tournament. He was the class of the tournament and went on to many more championships. Jim had a great year of golf as an eighteen-year-old, both nationally and in the state of Rhode Island.

* * * * *

Wes Banner, asked Ralph and me, "How'd you boys like to caddy for my foursome in a three day tournament on the Cape?"

I eagerly replied, "We'd love that, Wes."

Ralph mentioned, "We need transportation, though."

"No problem. You can drive my wife's car. Just meet us on the first tee each morning."

In this popular three day golf classic, professionals played with three members from their club. They played at a different course throughout Cape Cod each day. Our pro's team consisted of Lenny Jordan, Dan Garbecki, and Doctor Woodward. The first round was at Hyannisport Country Club. I looked out over the long, first fairway that was manicured to perfection and thought that this course was really plush.

Wes gave us some money for our hotel room that night and

said, "We'll meet you at the Woods Hole Country Club in the morning."

Wes and his guests left for dinner and we headed toward Falmouth when all of a sudden, a tire blew out on Mrs. Banner's 1949 Buick Roadster. I checked inside the trunk and found it empty.

I said, "Ralph, she doesn't have a spare tire. We've gotta buy one."

We didn't have far to walk before we found a gas station. With the new tire quickly installed, we were on our way once again, but I realized we were still in a pickle.

"There goes the money to stay overnight."

Ralph spotted the police station in the center of Falmouth and said, "Pull over here."

Ralph mumbled, "I'll be right out, Mike."

He went into the building and I sat in the car with the motor running. A few minutes later, Ralph bounded down the steps and was ecstatic. "I just made arrangements for us to stay here tonight. Get the suitcases."

When we walked into the small station, I noticed three empty cells in the back and thought, "*We're going to stay in jail? No way.*"

The police chief approached us and said, "Don't worry, fellas. The drunk tank is empty."

With a broad smile Ralph looked at me and said, "Put the stuff in the back cell, Mike. It'll be our room for the night."

The cell had two cots, with newspapers we could use for

covers. I sprayed our sleeping quarters with disinfectant I found in the washroom. It masked some of the stale smell of booze.

I grinned at the police chief and nervously said, "Please don't lock the cell."

Then Ralph had a request. "Could you please wake us at seven?"

With a chuckle the chief quipped, "What the hell do you think this is a motel?"

We slept without any interruptions. The police chief woke us up at seven the next morning and….the accommodations didn't cost us a dime. We washed up, shaved and headed to the golf course in Woods Hole.

Wes and Lenny won low gross in the Pro-member individual award, and the team came in second, in the overall tournament, representing Pawtucket Country Club well.

When we returned from the Cape, Wes asked me if I would like to work at his house digging post holes for a new fence.

"Sure. I can always use some extra money."

I ended up working ten hours a day for the next three days, only stopping for short periods to eat lunch and drink the refreshing lemonade that his wife brought to me.

Wes was pleased and said, "Mike, you did a good job. We could use some extra help at the golf course this month. How'd you like to work with the regular crew setting out sprinklers?"

Eager to make a few extra bucks, I answered with a smile, "Sure."

The heat of the August days was intense and the grass needed a lot of water. I worked on the golf course setting out sprinklers from midnight until eight in the morning. I worked alone, with a beat up '38 Hudson Terraplane cab truck that came equipped with a flashlight, alarm clock, and a baseball bat. The flashlight was provided so I could locate the sunken water connections for each green; the alarm clock was to wake me between sprinkler settings. The baseball bat was needed, I guess, in case trouble came during the night. I thought I'd never use the bat, but it was reassuring in my mind to know it was there, just in case.

I set out a sprinkler on each corner of six greens, slept in the truck for an hour, and moved the sprinkler to another corner, then slept for another hour. I did this four times each night until the six greens were completely watered. The next night I took care of six more greens, and the third night the final six, until all eighteen putting surfaces were wetted down. Then the sequence started all over again. At night, the golf course had its own distinct smell. The sweet smell of the fresh cut, sun-drenched grass, gave way to a heavy, damp, musty odor.

I never used the bat but I got a scare one night when Ralph paid me a surprise visit. It was three in the morning. Ralph waited to see my truck lights coming toward the thirteenth green in the pitch black night. He hid near the faucet that was deep in a hole by the green. He was screened by the shadows of big oak trees. I had to stick my head and half of my body into the hole to turn the sprinkler on. When the water spurted out, Ralph grabbed both of my ankles and yanked me out of the hole.

"YOOOOOOH! YOOOOOOOH!"

"Mike. It's only me, it's only me. Damn it, Mike, you probably woke up all of Pawtucket and half of Seekonk."

"Don't you ever do that to me again! You scared the livin' shit outta me!"

Ralph doubled up laughing so hard he fell to the ground.

Who would think I was capable of that scream? My first thought was, *"Where's the bat?"* I didn't have to check my underwear to know my reaction to that prank!

On occasion, when they were shorthanded, I was asked to work on the golf course during the day with the maintenance crew. Our pro, Wes Banner, also served as the head greens keeper at our club. John Barnum was his assistant, maintaining the golf course. Their friendship was strong and John's loyalty to Wes was immense. John's whole life was the golf course; he married it at a young age. Now in his fifties, his days were spent nurturing the course. He knew every blade of grass on every green and fairway. Barnum had a rugged build, deep brown, weathered, leather-like skin and sad looking, misty eyes. He had a wonderful set of tooth. His pants were always slack-ass off his butt and he trudged rather than walked.

He was the kindest man I had ever met. I always liked working with him because his views on life were plain and down-to-earth and he responded to whatever problems arose with fresh and innovative approaches. I connected the hoses next to the greens so John could spray them with a strong chemical. If the chemical got into your eyes or face, it would burn like hell. He sprayed each green while trudging through a mist of this powerful chemical and his leather face and eyes never showed any signs of discomfort.

I often looked at him in amazement, closed my eyes, and thought to myself, *"Oh boy, how can he do that?"*

John loved root beer. On our break, we often went to the pro shop and he ordered two roots, one for him and one for me. He always chewed a plug of tobacco. Juice ran by his one tooth, over his lip, and down the left side of his chin. Before he took a swig of soda, he pushed the tobacco plug with his fingers, up into his gum.

After taking a gulp, he would say, "Michael, nothing like a good root." I knew that half the swallow was tobacco juice and thought maybe that's why he loved his root so much.

John gave me my first and last experience chewing tobacco when he asked, "Wanna try some?"

"Sure," I volunteered as he broke off a small piece from a plug he had in his pocket.

My first reaction was that it was very sweet and I thought, *"Gee, it really does taste pretty good."* After a few minutes, however, the sweetness turned grossly bitter, and I spit it out.

"Michael, you having trouble?"

Spit, spit, spit, "YUK! Do you really like this stuff, John?"

Laughing he said, "You think I've been enjoying myself all these years?"

"Why do you do it, John?"

"Ever hear of Babe Ruth or Ty Cobb? They were my idols."

I tried candy, soda, toothpaste, you name it, but I couldn't get that awful tobacco taste out of my mouth for a week. Never again did I chew tobacco, and I stopped drinking root beer, too.

One day, John approached me and lamented, "Michael, I took my shoes to the cobbler this morning. The holes were so big he said it would take a week to fix them."

I thought, *"He must think that the size of the hole justifies the length of time it takes to fix a pair of shoes."*

John said, "Michael, go get the hoses."

Still clowning around, I said, "Why don't pigs fly?"

I liked kidding John just to get his reaction. In all seriousness he looked at me in his deliberate way and said, "Some pigs fly, in a airie plane."

I shook my head and chuckled, "John, you mean some pigs fly in an airplane."

He just smiled and said, "Let's get back to work."

"I'm out foxed again," I thought and picked up the hose.

The other members of John's crew were Johnny, Big Bill, Walter, and 'Lieutenant Jack.' Johnny was Barnum's sidekick, a little roly-poly Irishman. His red nose had pinholes all over it. You knew he didn't get *that* nose from drinking soda pop. Johnny and John seldom went inside the clubhouse. They were both well liked. Members would befriend them by offering drinks and asking questions regarding the maintenance of the course. After work each day, Johnny and John rode together down Armistice Boulevard to The Pub for a little libation.

One day Johnny mentioned, "Michael, my father was a pitcher. One day he pitched right-handed and the next day he pitched left-handed."

I said, "Oh, he was ambidextrous."

Johnny looked puzzled, then said, "Call it what you like, but one day he pitched right-handed and the next day he pitched left-handed."

Walter was a loner. If he couldn't get the lawnmower to run, he kicked it and started swearing. He was quiet, but explosive, and you knew instinctively not to bother too much with him. 'Big Bill' was a huge bald man and a hard worker. He put in a good days work and then went straight home. 'Big Bill' was never seen anywhere after work. He showed up the next morning, always on time to start a new day of steady, hard work.

My favorite crewmember was 'Lieutenant Jack,' a fireman who worked part time at the golf course. He was a gray haired, handsome man with movie star looks and a mischievous twinkle in his lively eyes. He always had a new joke to tell and some kind of scheme going on. 'The Lieutenant' was friendly with the chef at the club. The chef prepared two sandwiches with ingredients from the *Special of the Day* and then put them behind the hedges outside the clubhouse kitchen. We would wait until after one o'clock in the afternoon to slip past the pro shop without being seen. This freebie was a treat when I worked with 'Lieutenant Jack.' Oscar, the caretaker and clubhouse tattle-tale, didn't like 'Lieutenant Jack' and because I was the 'Lieutenant's' friend, he didn't like me. He was envious of the popular 'Lieutenant' and acted like he owned the place. He was constantly watching 'The Lieutenant.'

'The Lieutenant' kept asking me, "Why's this guy clocking me?"

I surmised, "He's just jealous."

'The Lieutenant' told me a joke about the Fug-ar-wee Indians the first time I met him. He said, "They got their name when the Indian Chief looked out over a part of the land that was to become Rhode Island. With his right hand cupped over his eyes, he said to his tribe, 'We're Fug-ar-wee!'"

From that time on, every time I saw 'Lieutenant Jack,' he would pose like a cigar store Indian. The last time I saw him, Ralph and I were at Sunday Mass at St. Theresa's Church across from the fire station on Newport Avenue.

Just before Pastor Fazzol came out on the altar to begin Mass, Ralph suggested, "We're early, let's go get a cup of coffee."

When we got back to the church, we had missed half of the Mass and there were no seats left, so we stood in the outside aisle.

I glanced at the parishioners standing along the opposite wall and noticed 'Lieutenant Jack' at the end of the line. When he spotted me, he cupped his right hand above his eyes and looked out over the pews. I burst out laughing and thought, *"We're Fug-ar-wee."*

* * * * *

Every weekend, if I wasn't working on the golf course, I was caddying. One Sunday, an Electrical Manufacturing Golf Outing was held at our club. Some of the golfers had never played the game before and came to the outing to drink and enjoy the clambake, and to try to play golf for the first time. Ralph arrived early, and was assigned to caddy for two guys who had never been on a golf course. One of the hackers showed up with three new golf balls he had just bought at Mike's 5 & 10. The discount balls were x'd out Mary Jane's, but to him they were as good as the top brands, because the price was right. His friends called him 'T-T' or 'Two-Ton,' which accurately described his girth. Heavy downpours delayed the start of the tournament for an hour and puddles were still visible on parts of the fairway. On the first hole 'T-T' hit two x'd out balls into the pond in front of the tee.

After the first shot, Ralph said, "Take a Mully."

With a quizzical look 'T-T' innocently asked, "What's that?"

"You're allowed a Mulligan, that means an extra try," Ralph explained.

When 'T-T' got to the water, he noticed one of the balls close to the edge of the pond. He took out his long-handled retriever and leaned over, but couldn't quite reach the ball. Directing Ralph, he said, "Stand here and grab my hand....just a little further, and I'll get it."

Ralph was wearing rubbers over his shoes. With his feet close together, he held on for dear life as 'Two-Ton' stretched further for the ball. S–L–I–I–I–P! **SPLASH!** The rubbers slid in the mud and they both plunged into the pond.

Treading water, 'Two-Ton' screamed at Ralph, "What's the matter? Couldn't you hold me?"

Ralph retorted as he dragged himself out of the pond, "Obviously not!"

When they started up the first fairway, 'T–T' grabbed his nine-iron, which is usually used for short distances, but they were three hundred yards from the hole. Ralph realized that 'Two-Ton' thought that using the club with the highest number made the ball go further.

Walking to the second hole, Ralph explained, "Excuse me, sir. The higher numbered irons are used for the shortest distances to the pin."

'T-T' looked a little embarrassed, but was interrupted when his partner found a ball in the rough and hollered, "Who's Tit–less is this?"

Ralph informed him, "The correct pronunciation is Titleist."

Then the golfer shanked his next shot, which hit 'Two-Ton' in the left buttock.

Ralph muttered to himself, "That was a bum shot!"

On the fifth hole, 'T-T' hit the ball deep into the woods on the left side of the fairway. His partner was already on the green on this short hole. When Ralph and 'T-T' got to the ball, it was nestled next to a huge boulder.

After assessing the situation, he asked Ralph, "Is it all right if I move it?"

Ralph looked up and down the fairway, checked the green, and determined that no one could see him move the ball.

He shrugged his shoulders and said, "Go ahead."

Much to Ralph's amazement, 'Two-Ton' knelt down, put his arms around the boulder and started to grunt as he attempted to move it. Ralph knew the humungous rock couldn't be moved with a derrick. He had trouble facing 'Two-Ton' without laughing during the rest of the round.

There was one foursome still waiting for a caddy when I arrived late for the Electrical Manufacturers Tourney that day. The caddy master said, "Mike, carry two bags. Two guys will have to carry their own clubs."

I said, "They all have light weight bags. I can carry the four of 'em."

I ran all over the golf course giving each man the appropriate golf club for the first nine holes. On the back nine, however, I was tired and walked straight down the fairway and let each guy come to me. By the time we reached the eighteenth hole, I could just about make it up the hill beyond the green. I let out a deep sigh of relief and thought how lucky my brother was to be working in the locker room that day rather than carrying heavy golf bags. Joe worked in the locker room on tournament days. Members and their guests got a strong whiff of fresh shoe polish whenever the door was opened. Small fragments of dried grass and dirt, previously stuck on cleats, sometimes littered the floor and polished golf shoes were lined up in front of each locker.

Pip, the locker room attendant, was always smiling and dressed in a colorful shirt from his native Hawaii. He liked to sing Hawaiian songs while the steamy showers ran in the background,

Joe came outside wearing his wax–smudged apron and approached us as we came off the eighteenth green. He told the four golfers, "You guys had the best caddy in the club."

When I got home, I was proud to give my mother the crisp new twenty dollar bill I had earned that day.

* * * * *

Monday was designated as 'Caddies' Day' and we were allowed to play the course. Some of the members let us use their clubs and they were instrumental in teaching us the fine points of the game. They set a good example, gave us advice, and tried to help us any way they could. We enjoyed their stories and overheard conversations about world travel and business deals. We gained valuable knowledge and insight to help us later in life. One 'Caddies' Day' the Pawtucket Country Club had an individual challenge match with eight caddies from Newport Country Club. I was teamed with Packy Doyle, a very good golfer and outstanding basketball player at Pawtucket East High School. Packy was a tremendous competitor who was often overheard saying, "I'm a very gracious winner, but a hard-ass loser."

This philosophy seemed to be prevalent throughout our Darlington neighborhood. Packy was in a close match against Lenny Lancaster, an outstanding player and a real gentleman from Newport. Packy knew he had to do whatever it took in order to win. This included bending the rules, every chance he got. He and his caddy, Bulgie North, moved his ball in the rough. Packy spit out a lifesaver on the fairway then propped up his ball on it. Shattered white mints were all over the course.

Bulgie wedged a low branch in a tree so Packy could hit his shot unimpeded. When he reached the greens, Packy placed his marker in front of the ball. When he was ready to putt, he put the ball down in front of the marker. This subtle procedure put him an inch closer to the hole on every putt. Bulgie gave little fake coughs during Lenny's back swing and jingled change in his pocket during Lenny's putting stroke. The match was dead even going into the last hole. Lenny had to know what was going on, but he just continued to play his game and never said a word, always the perfect gentleman. On the eighteenth green, Lenny needed to sink a twenty foot putt for the win.

When the putt dropped into the hole, Packy yelled, "Foul!" and stormed into the pro shop complaining, "He just tapped down a spike mark before he putted. This guy should get a two-stroke penalty!"

Even though two officials standing on the patio overlooking the green had watched the putt and disallowed the complaint, he still contended that victory was stolen from his grasp. A two-stroke penalty levied against Lenny would have given Packy the thrill of victory instead of the agony of defeat!

Chapter 6
A Little More than a Little Luck

Devastating hurricane Dianne hit Rhode Island in mid August and left severe damage in its wake. Rain-swollen rivers burst their banks, flooding coastal towns and blocking roads and properties. Fallen trees and downed electrical wires were everywhere. At Slater Park, a tree fell over the moat at the Monkey Island. All the monkeys escaped by running across the tree and scattered all over Pawtucket. Clean up work was desperately needed after this tumultuous display of nature.

Ralph observed, "There's money to be made. I've got a two man saw in my garage."

"Well, I guess that qualifies us as tree surgeons. This could be our bread 'n butter."

Our first job was for 'Old Man Weeden' over on Harcourt Avenue. A huge tree had become uprooted and left a deep crater in the middle of his yard. We were elated to get the job. Mr. Weeden was thrilled by the prospect of getting the tree off his property, without having to pay top dollar for a professional tree service. After negotiating a price of a hundred dollars, we attempted to remove the tree. We cut the tree at the trunk…big mistake….no leverage for removing the stump. The thick tree separated from the gigantic trunk and the heavy root clump fell back into the hole. We used saws, shovels, and axes, and finally cut all the roots.

"Ralph, how are we gonna get this enormous stump out of the ground? Did we bite off more than we can chew? We're between a rock and a hard place."

Ralph was exhausted. He leaned on his muddy shovel, gazed at the hole, and slowly looked at the sky. The clouds were lifting as he carefully lit a cigarette and blew oval smoke rings lazily into the air.

"Pulleys. We need pulleys."

Quizzically, I said, "Pulleys?"

"Yeah, I learned how they work in physics class. Mr. Farley said you get a nine-to-one pull-strength ratio with pulleys."

Still not convinced, I sighed, "Well, I guess it's worth a try."

The drive to the Darlington Hardware Store gave us a little relief from the humidity with the warm breeze blowing through the car windows.

I told Ralph, "You're lucky, Pierre. They actually *rent* pulleys here. All we need is some heavy rope, and we're *back* in business."

We wrapped the rope around the old stump. Then we ran it through several pulleys that we had attached to trees in the yard. The end of the rope was fastened to the bumper of Ralph's car using a clove hitch. Ralph called out, "Let 'er rip!" As I stepped on the accelerator, a postman stood with hands on his hips, watching this engineering feat in action.

He sighed, "It'll never work."

But, Ralph's idea *did* work and the stump was dragged right out of the hole on the first try. I was thrilled. "Ralph! That was great!" The postman shook his head in disbelief.

Ralph grinned and said, "Now we have to get it to the dump. Let's drag it with the car."

The stump was like a dead elephant and it began to flip over. Ralph climbed on top of the stump and holding onto the largest roots, he sat on the back end to weigh it down. He had now become a human ballast.

"Drive as slow as you can, Mike. Don't give it too much gas." Ralph laughed as passing motorists gave him the thumbs up.

I yelled back, "Are you okay?"

With a broad smile he hollered, "I'm a gladiator riding my chariot; sound the trumpets! Onward, ho!!!"

* * * * *

Armistice Boulevard was always quiet, early in the morning. Ralph was standing on the corner when a turquoise 1953 Corvette convertible, with a white interior and rooftop, pulled into an empty parking space on Pineault's Corner at the intersection of Armistice Boulevard and Newport Avenue, just as it did every morning. The stones snapped and crunched under the weight of the fat whitewall tires. The driver's door slowly swung open and out stepped a tall man with long legs and an athletic build. He looked like he just bought the clothes off the mannequin at Shepard's Department Store. He wore a tan sports jacket and a herringbone soft hat that highlighted his square jaw and high cheekbones. With his massive hands, he held the passenger door open and let out a short whistle. Out sprung a spirited, well groomed boxer. The dog's tan coat appeared golden in the low morning sunlight. It was Dominic 'The Duke' Moradian and Rocky.

Daily rounds started with Rocky relieving himself on the telephone booth at the corner. His territory was then marked on the fire hydrant, the drainpipe in front of the fish & chips store, and then the flowerbed at the florist shop.

Duke called out, "Come on, Rocky! Atta boy, Rocky!" as he rounded the corner.

The front seat was Rocky's. He rode shotgun and 'The Duke' consulted with him as if he were a co-pilot. Dominic liked to put the top down and cruise around Pawtucket. Rocky, with his nose in the wind, must have considered himself 'King of all dogdom.'

Ralph and I planned to play in a golf tournament in Barrington at one-thirty that day. Our opponents were from Metacomet Country Club and Rhode Island Country Club.

When Ralph met up with 'The Duke' that morning, 'The Duke' asked, "Would you like to take a ride?"

"Sure, why not?" Ralph shrugged.

As Ralph opened the passenger door, Rocky put his head down on the dash and spread his body across the seat. Ralph crammed himself into the back seat and said tongue in cheek, "Got enough room up there, Rocky?"

They cruised around downtown Pawtucket past the bus stop in front of Shartenburg's Department Store. Duke smiled,

"Rocky likes to check out the girls at the bus stop. Right, Rocky?" Rocky lifted his head and drooled on the front seat.

The next stop was the home of the Coney Island hot dog, Ziggy's Grille, and Rocky's favorite. Ralph's back had endured every pothole and road heave in Pawtucket like a bottomed out shock absorber. 'The Duke' pried Ralph out of his confined quarters as Rocky tugged on his pants leg. When Ralph took his first step, he doubled up like a twisted pretzel.

"Oh my achin' back! How'm I supposed play in the tournament? Mike's countin' on me."

Lighting up his Camel cigarette, 'The Duke' said, "I've got just the guy to help you."

'The Duke' helped Ralph into the back seat, where he waited in agony while Rocky finished eating two chili dogs.

Ralph grimaced and finally yelled out, "Let's go!" After driving twenty minutes over bumpy roads Ralph said, "Duke, are we almost there?" We're already over the Massachusetts border. We're in the sticks of Seekonk!"

Duke tried to keep Ralph calm while speaking softly, "There's the sign now."

Ralph's eyes widened, "Damn it, Duke! That sign says, 'VETERINARIAN'!"

Duke snapped back, "What's the difference? He knows what he's doing. And besides, he's done wonders for Rocky."

Ralph just moaned, "Ugh."

The receptionist stated, "Mr. McGreavy, you'll be next after Fluffy." Ralph was seated in the crowded waiting room between two high strung Siamese cats waiting to be neutered.

When the vet entered the room, he said, "I'm Euclid Poupart; you can call me Dr. Clyde. What's the nature of your problem?"

Ralph could hardly bring himself to answer, "My back's killin' me." Dr. Clyde positioned Ralph on a long table with rollers on the top then climbed up onto a trampoline. Ralph said to himself, *"What the hell is this?"*

The doctor proceeded to jump up and down on the trampoline until his head almost touched the ceiling. Finally he sprung up, flipped off the trampoline, and landed with his two knees, square in the middle of Ralph's back. "Augh Yeaough! You son of a bitch, Duke!...Duke! I'm gonna kill this horse's ass!"

Ralph went into Dr. Clyde's office listing to the left...and when he came out, he was listing to the right! Now Ralph was really desperate. The pain had become horrendous and our tee time was quickly approaching.

Ralph was anxious to get out of Duke's car and said, "Drop me off at the Spa."

The owner, Soupy Campbell, noticed Ralph's unorthodox posture and said, "Ya know, Ralph, years ago I was a waiter at the Biltmore Hotel. We had to carry heavy trays, loaded with silver teapots. We wore eight inch rubber belts to give our waists support. Why don't you try something like *that*?"

When I appeared at the door, Ralph said, "C'mon Mike. We're going shopping."

Ralph and I were still riding around an hour before tee time, looking for *anything* to relieve his pain. He finally spotted Mona's Corset Shop on Main Street in downtown Pawtucket and said, "Ah hell, what have I got to lose?"

The teenage sales girl squinted at us as we walked into the shop and then politely inquired, "May I help you?"

Ralph held onto the glass display case and leaned forward, "Maybe you can. I'm looking for something to give my back support."

Holding back a smirk, she continued, "Would you like something plain or trimmed with lace?"

Ralph squirmed and managed to hold his composure as he answered, "I don't care...as long as it fits." He tried on several corsets of different styles and finally found one with beads and sequins that fit his masculine physique. "Can you take out the stay near the crotch...and cut off the garter straps?"

The nice young girl lilted, "That could easily be done."

Ralph managed a sigh of relief, "Okay...I'll take it!"

Clad in his new girdle, Ralph arrived at the golf course strapped up like a tight shoelace. Rushing to the first tee, he quickly teed his ball up, and took a big swing at the ball. He let out a yell that could be heard on all the fairways around him. "EEE–yoh! That's it, Mike. I can't hit another shot. You're on your own. I'll give you moral support, but I can't play."

I started out playing exceptionally well, but then fell behind and ended up two down after nine holes. I got lucky while playing the back nine and finally got even with our opponents going into the short seventeenth hole which ran parallel to the ocean. A strong, stiff wind was blowing. Buddy Smiley and 'The Great Kazoo' Bobby Kareemo, both hit on the green. My first shot hooked far left and landed in the water. My second shot also was swallowed up by the ocean.

"Look, Ralph. We're going to lose this hole unless you try to hit a shot!"

"But, my back, Mike!"

"The hell with your back. You're tighter than a bull's ass at fly time. Take a seven wood and tee it high. Just try to make contact."

Taking my advice, he teed the ball up higher than usual. When he swung, he let out a grunt and almost collapsed. It was a low liner that took a big hop over the edge of the trap and ran up onto the bank, just shy of the green.

I exclaimed, "Great shot, Ralph! Maybe you can chip close and give us a half!"

"Geez, you don't want much." He closed one eye as he lined up his chip. The hole got in the way of the ball and it rolled smack dab into the middle of the cup for a birdie.

I was dumbfounded and said, "Lucky shot, Magoo! Real lucky...I love it."

"That's it for me, Mike! I'm one under for the day. My back's killing me. I can't take another swing."

Ralph's forty foot chip gave us the win on the hole. I halved the last hole, which gave us the victory. I won my individual match. Ralph, of course, lost his, but when we won the team match one up, we ended up with an overall two to one victory.

When we returned to our club, Willie 'Luck Box' Roverson asked, "How'd you guys make out?"

Ralph proudly responded in a loud voice, "WE WON!"

'Luck Box' shook his head and surmised, "I knew I shoulda' bet the farm on you guys."

Roverson was a caddy turned gambler. He didn't like to caddy and only wanted to play cards. He always showed up with a deck of cards to ply his trade. When the caddies came off the course, some of them would take their chances with 'Luck Box,' but every week, he was the big winner. Willie was handsome, with sparkling eyes. He was a sharp dresser, wearing buttoned down dress shirts and pressed khakis. He was a seasoned card shark, always ready for action. Whenever someone challenged him, there was a very good chance they would lose some hard earned money. Everyone knew this, but he was still able to entice players into his gamblers' web.

There was always some kind of commotion in the caddy shack—card games, various competitions, and arguments that sometimes led to fights. If challenged, you fought. Whether you won or lost, the argument was settled and the dispute was over when the fight was finished. Al Falcone, a new caddy, joined our ranks. He had a reputation as a fighter and boxed at the Pawtucket Boys Club. He was a tall, wiry guy who always had a scowl on his face and for some reason he usually directed it at me. I knew by the way he looked at me, that sooner or later, we would go at it.

One day my brother and I arrived at the shack and I walked over to sit on the bench next to my friend, Joel Goldman. Falcone was sitting next to him and as I approached them, he moved closer to Goldie, making it impossible for me to sit down. I politely asked, "Could you please move over?"

He didn't budge, but took this opportunity to swear at me. Then he stood up and threatened me with a sneer. I grabbed him by the shoulder and smacked him hard in the face with a clenched fist. He stumbled out of the shack. Then he positioned himself on the high side of a hill. In a rage, I charged up at him. He threw straight jabs at my face. I turned beet red. *He* was winning and *my face* was losing.

Joe yelled to me, "Get on the high ground! Get on the high ground, Mike!"

Facing Falcone, I moved sideways until I was able to get

higher than him. Then I charged like a bull with fists flying. I overpowered him and knocked him to the ground. We fought until I got him in a headlock. I squeezed as hard as I could until he almost passed out. When I was pulled off him, he said, "Enough! Enough!"

Falcone told my friends that he'd be back with brass knuckles. Joe saved my face from becoming a punching bag during that one. Falcone never made good on his threat.

A few days later, Falcone and I were paired up to caddy with Tom Hudson. We carried single bags for three members. When we went ahead to forecaddy, Falcone started to slap Hudson around on every hole. It infuriated me, because I knew he was just trying to bully and intimidate Tom.

I hollered, "Fight him, Tom; fight him!"

Tom just shook his head and said, "Nah, let it go."

But when Falcone slapped Tom on the back of the head on the eighth fairway, I couldn't ignore it any longer and shouted, "If you touch him one more time, I'll smack you in the mouth!" He swore at me, but he didn't touch Tom again during the rest of the round....and he completely ignored me.

The next day, Ralph and I were assigned to caddy for a new member, Donaldo Radinski and his brother-in-law, Louie Commotozzi for a four-ball match against two long time members. Donaldo was a terrific golfer and a good guy. He had a slight build and a Charlie Chaplin mustache that suited his face to a T. He had a compact swing and hit the ball a long way. Donaldo had been on the waiting list to join the club for years and he was elated when an opening finally became available. Louie was six-four and weighed about two seventy-five. The guy was solid muscle. He sported a bushy crop of black hair that made him look like a wild man. His dark eyes were set deep and his ever-present five o'clock shadow cast a dark pall over his face.

On the first tee Donaldo reminded his partner, "Look Louie, watch your temper. The only reason I invited you is because of your wife, my sister."

"Donaldo, you have my word. I promised Gloria I'd be a perfect gentleman. I'll make you proud I'm your brother-in-law."

They approached the first tee with confidence, but Louie put two balls in the pond just in front of the tee. Showing no emotion, he just shrugged his shoulders, confident his game would improve once he settled down. On the second hole, his tee shot hooked left out of bounds. He moaned a little expletive that could hardly be heard, but kept his cool.

After they lost the first two holes, Donaldo looked a little frustrated. "Come on, Louie, let's get with it!" On the third hole, Louie hit two balls out of bounds again. When the second ball careened over a fence, he quickly turned and in an intense rage, let out a yell. "Ahhhhhh!"

He swung his entire body around and around in a circle. His golf club flew out of his hands. The head of his driver hit Donaldo right in the crotch! Donaldo keeled over, clutching his groin. As he hit the ground, he passed out cold.

Ralph turned to me and gasped, "Oh my God—I think he's dead!" He ran into the clubhouse to call an ambulance, while everyone on the golf course huddled over Donaldo.

It took fifteen minutes for the ambulance to get out to the third tee, but it seemed like forever. Donaldo was taken to Memorial Hospital. The next day Ralph and I went to the hospital with a basket of fruit. As we approached Donaldo's door, we could see him in the bed near the window. He was lying on his back with both legs in stirrups. His two testicles were packed in ice, swollen like bruised melons.

Ralph and I glanced at each other as Ralph mumbled under his breath, "Looks like Donaldo *already* has a fruit basket."

We heard Gloria whimpering inside the room, "Louie's awfully sorry."

"I'll give you sorry. When I get out of this contraption, I'll kill him! I'll never live this down. The whole city of Pawtucket knows about this!"

Donaldo missed out on the remainder of the golf season and we never saw Louie at Pawtucket Country Club again.

* * * * *

The summer was flying by and football season would be starting up at the end of August. We had spent most of the summer trying to make money any way we could.

Ralph said, "Mike, we need a break. Let's go to the Cape for the weekend." Ralph's car, however, needed a new transmission after pulling the tree stump. It took some convincing before Joe agreed to let me borrow his car. After getting last minute instructions from my brother, my father intercepted us on the porch, "No drinking boys."

"We promise," Ralph replied.

As we pulled around the corner, Ralph surprised me when he said, "Stop at Laverty's Liquor Store, Mike."

I blurted, "Are you nuts? We just promised my father we wouldn't drink!"

"We promised your father we wouldn't drink–ON THE PORCH! We're drinkin' ON THE CAPE!"

Ralph looked a little older than the legal drinking age of eighteen and was never questioned in the package store. Whistling *The Yellow Rose of Texas,* Ralph sauntered out of the store, clutching a quart of Smirnoff's Vodka in a brown paper bag tucked under his arm. Then he ducked into Zaccachini's Variety Store for a bottle of orange juice and two packs of Lucky's. Armed with his necessary provisions, we headed for Hyannis. As we drove through the *'Gateway to the Cape,'* we passed the welcome lighthouses on each side of the road. Ralph was singing along with the radio, which was turned up as loud as it could go. His all time favorite song was playing. Mitch Miller's *The Yellow Rose of Texas* blared throughout the car.

Once we reached Buzzards Bay, we were anxious to get into the salt water at Onset Beach. Two girls sat on a blanket nearby, but we were a little reluctant to start a conversation. Ralph relaxed for quite a while, unlaced his shoe, and said, "Okay, watch this." Approaching the girls he asked, "Have you ever seen a ship shank with a square knot?"

Ralph's brother, Leo, recently showed him how to tie knots like they did in the Navy and Ralph was starting to get a lot of mileage out of his newfound knowledge. I winced, doubting the Navy ever used a knot like that one, but Ralph was in his glory. His hands maneuvered like a magician, as he wove intricate knots with his shoelace. Before long, the girls were giggling and all four of us were sharing one blanket. We made plans to meet them again the next afternoon.

"Ralph, I don't think you know the right names for the knots, but if the Navy is as successful as you were with those girls, maybe they should use *your* terminology."

Flicking his fingers he explained, "It's not the name…it's all in the hands, Mike. It's all in the hands."

As the sunny, relaxing day faded into dusk, we continued down the winding road toward Hyannis, getting deeper into the Cape…and Ralph continued drinking his Vodka and orange juice. I concentrated on the driving.

"Hey, Ralph. There's the Mill Hill Club."

"That's where all the *action* is, Mike. Pull in."

The place was jammed and jumping with loud music blaring from the juke box. *Shake, Rattle, and Roll* was playing. Ralph walked up to a table where five guys were drinking beer. They looked like they were football linemen, or wrestlers for a college team.

Ralph slurred, "'Scuse me," as he grabbed a bottle of Schlitz off the table in front of the biggest guy. After taking a long gulp, he banged the bottle down on the table with a loud thump and said, "Thank you."

The guy was irate and stood up. His buddies stood up too. They were ready to pounce on Ralph. I muscled my way through the volatile guys, holding my hands up, "Sorry. He had too much to drink. Sorry; he didn't mean it."

I calmed them down before they turned the place into a slaughterhouse. Before we reached the door, Ralph did a one-eighty and leapt up onto a table. He hollered at the top of his voice, "I can take on anyone in the house!" The five guys circled the table. Moving his arm back and forth, Ralph yelled, "I don't mean fighting. Come on, who wants to arm wrestle?"

Two burly bouncers grabbed Ralph by the shoulders and threw him out the door. I stuffed Ralph into the back seat and said, "Jeez, Ralph, I can't take you anywhere."

I drove to Craigville Beach, where we slept in the car. All I could smell was the strong odor of Vodka, as I listened to the waves pounding the shore. Warm sunshine, streaming through the car windows, woke us up early the next morning. With a severe case of hiccups, Ralph groaned in the back seat as he rubbed his eyes, "I've got wicked heartburn. Where's the Vodka?"

I replied, "I threw it in the woods last night."

"What? I need it for my heartburn." Leaves and twigs crunched, snapped and cracked under Ralph's footsteps, until he stumbled over the bottle. He finished off the Vodka, and within seconds, his heartburn….and the hiccups, disappeared!

We drove to the center of Hyannis for breakfast at the Mayflower Restaurant, where we used the Men's room to freshen up and change clothes. The sign on the hostess podium read, '*Hello, please wait to be seated.*' By the time *we* were seated, it read, '*O Hell, please wait to be seated!*'

Ralph winked at me and said, "Move one single 'O' and everything changes." Ralph loved to express his creative, humorous thoughts, whenever an opportunity arose. People noticed Ralph's little prank, but the hostess was not amused as she corrected the sign.

"Ralph, did you see the reaction to your sign? Remember Howard Johnson's Hotel in Providence? Their marquee said, '*Welcome Helix Stop Nut Company.*' I bet they had a fit when they saw what you did."

"Yeah, I moved the "S", so it said, '*Welcome Helix top NutS Company.*'"

"Ralph, you crack me up. The best, though, was the sign you changed the day the scouts had a raft race on the Ten Mile River."

"Yeah, the sign said, '*Rafters This Way*' and I transposed the R and the F."

We sat on a bench outside the restaurant after breakfast and watched a steady parade of people walk by. The smell of bacon and eggs emitted from the restaurant and was captured in the air above us. Ralph enjoyed his cigarette while we tried to decide if we should stay in Hyannis or go back to meet the girls in Onset. Two girls slowly walked to the corner and looked at us as they passed by.

The oldest one turned around and walked back, "Excuse me, fellas. My cousin and I missed our ride home with a friend. Now we're stranded here on the Cape. By chance, are you going anywhere near Malden?"

I asked, "Up near Boston? Boston? No. We're going back to Pawtucket...near Providence."

Ralph blew out a few smoke rings and interrupted, "Now, wait a minute. If you chip in for gas, we'll take you to Malden."

One of them said, "No problem."

We were always ready for an unexpected detour. I said, "I'll get the car, Ralph."

I stepped off the curb into the oncoming traffic without looking to the left or right. Ralph bellowed in a voice I had never heard before that knocked me right off my feet.

"WATCH OUT MIKE! THAT'S HOW MY FATHER GOT KILLED! JESUS!!"

Shaken, he grabbed me, then thrust his arm around my shoulders. We walked together in silence across the busy main street.

I pulled the car up to the curb in front of the restaurant. Joan, the younger cousin, swung open the front door. She motioned, "Marilyn, you ride in back. I want to pick the radio stations. I know all the good ones."

Now Joe's car was on the road toward Boston! The girls treated us to pizza at Tiny Tim's Italian Restaurant at the Bourne Bridge Rotary, in Buzzards Bay. Joan called her mother. "We'll be home in a couple of hours. We got stranded, but now we're getting a ride all the way home." She hung up the phone and said, "My mother's gonna have spaghetti and meatballs ready for all of us."

As we approached the three story tenement building, the aroma of Italian spaghetti sauce tinged our nostrils. Angelina's spaghetti dinner was the best we'd ever had. We each ate two huge helpings. Rubbing his meatball-stuffed stomach, Ralph politely said, "Thanks for the delicious meal, Mrs. Piantidosi."

She handed us five dollars as she replied, "Remember to stop to fill the gas tank, boys. Drive carefully."

CHUG, CHUG. Approaching North Attleboro, we ran out of gas. Ralph was exasperated and moaned, "Augh, not another Mike Ryan deal. We have the five dollars."

"How'd I know Joe's gas gauge would malfunction?"

Ralph said, "Right. You should tell your brother to always have a gas can in the trunk for this kind of emergency."

I said, "Right."

Heading down Route One toward Pawtucket, Ralph's eyes widened when he spotted someone replacing the words on the sign in front of The Wilde Goose Restaurant in South Attleboro. It read, "*Welcome Ducks Unlimited.*"

"Pull in here, Mike."

We followed the manager into the restaurant. When he left the alphabet on the bar, Ralph spread it out and took one letter from the pile. We ran back outside.

"Hoist me up on your shoulders, Mike."

Ralph took down the 'D' and inserted the letter 'F' in its place. We no sooner finished, when there was a commotion on the highway. We could hear brakes squeal as truck drivers blared their horns. Then the front door flew open and the manager stormed out into the parking lot, briskly waving a letter in his hand. He changed the sign then stood under it with crossed arms, guarding it like a sentinel.

As we drove off, we could hear him yelling after us, "I got your number....I'll know that car anywhere!"

Ralph quipped dryly, "Gee, Mike. I hope Joe has a good alibi."

"Sure he does. *His* car is down the Cape!"

* * * * *

Throughout the summer, we found time to catch several movies at the Darlton Theater. One rainy Sunday afternoon, we wanted to see *Rebel Without* a *Cause,* starring James Dean. Once again, we found ourselves flat broke. Blowing smoke rings into the air outside the theater, Ralph came up with a new idea. "Mike, when the matinee lets out, we can walk in backwards; they'll think we're coming out and we'll be lost in the crowd."

"Great, but what'll we do when the ushers clear the theater?"

"We can hide upstairs in the baby room."

"Yeah, we'll be there like the sleeves on a vest. I think your scheme might work, Ralph."

"Quick….up the steps, Mike. The room is soundproof and they can't see in through the one way window."

The movie started and we could tell it would be a great one. "Okay Ralph, the coast is clear. Let's go down and get some choice seats."

We had just settled into the packed theater, when Bulgie North crammed into our aisle. He tripped over some guy's feet and spilled an extra large Coke and a huge box of hot buttered popcorn all over Ralph.

"Great! This clumsy ox is worse than Bogie."

"Shush…quiet in front…shush."

Ralph and I brushed the soggy popcorn from Ralph's alligator shirt. Ralph squirmed in his seat. He smelled like a buttered popcorn stand throughout the entire movie. Bulgie stepped over us again, when he went to get another Coke and more popcorn. He finally settled down in his seat in the middle of our row. He hoarded his big box of popcorn as if it was his last meal.

We used another ploy that worked like a charm when we went to see *The Rose Tattoo* and *Blackboard Jungle.* We had a bunch of guys wait at the back door, which was always locked. We all chipped in to buy one ticket. Shemp used it to enter the theater. As Lenny, Pokeye, Packie, Ralph and I waited outside the back door, Shemp made his way down the aisle and positioned himself in the end seat of the first row. When the lights dimmed, he dropped to his hands and knees and crawled toward the wall. Then he slipped behind the curtain. He dashed up the concrete stairs and unlocked the door. We all piled in, one by one taking turns emerging from the curtain, then scattering to random seats throughout the theater. We all met in the Men's room five minutes later, then came out and sat together. We tried it one more time, but were foiled by the manager. Shemp was barred from the theater.

Ralph assured the manager, Ed, "We'll make sure he doesn't do it again."

Just then, Earl the usher, in his red jacket and black slacks, came up the aisle. He shined his lone high beam aluminum Eveready flashlight directly at Ralph's creased face and said, "What do you mean, *you'll* make sure? You're the ringleader. Who's gonna watch you?"

* * * * *

The only time my family had a vacation, was when we rented a cottage at Indian Mound Beach, in Buzzards Bay on Cape Cod. We had the place for a week at the end of the summer. Joe and I wanted to stay home, but thought we would be able to caddy at some of the nearby golf courses. So we agreed to go. The weather was nice at first, but then it turned rainy. After some coaxing, we were allowed to go back to Pawtucket to be with our friends. The weather improved a few days later, so we headed back to the Cape.

When we got to Indian Mound Beach, we stopped to talk to the girls we saw sitting on a bench at the triangle intersection, near the entrance to the beach. I started playing *Side by Side* on my ukulele and everyone sang along. Then we swung into *You Are My Sunshine*.

Now the vacation was getting interesting. My eyes were riveted on the girl with long, curly blonde hair. The next day, I recognized the girls on the beach. I found out that they were cousins from Taunton, Massachusetts.

Later, as I sat on the bench with Patty, the one who had caught my attention, I asked, "Would you like to go to the movies tonight?"

She declined my invitation explaining, "I promised my parents I wouldn't go out with boys while I'm visiting my aunt. I'm going roller skating with my cousins in Buzzard's Bay tonight."

I made a mental note, "*That's where I wanna be!*"

Later that afternoon, Patty and I took a walk to Lindsey's for fried clams.

She said, "These are my favorite....we come here all the time."

Pointing to Mr. Lindsey's homemade sign, I told her, "I was here once before, with my friends Ralph and Bobby. We got thrown out because we had bare feet."

When we finished eating the salted clams dipped in tartar sauce, we walked hand in hand back to her aunt's cottage on Fearing Street. There we joined her cousins who were playing softball in the yard.

I convinced Joe to go roller skating that night. I wore my favorite white silk dress shirt, with vertical red stripes and rolled up short sleeves. My hair looked blonde with my pompadour wave combed high above my forehead. My head was on a swivel until I finally spotted Patty wearing a white angora sweater and short white skating skirt, with her gleaming roller skates gliding beneath her. Her shiny, suntanned face and curly blonde hair were a nice contrast to her outfit.

I thought, "*She looks like 'good huggin'.*"

I noticed she was an advanced skater as I walked over to try on my rentals. I got the last pair of skates left in my size. They were completely worn out and had frayed laces. When I attempted to tighten the right skate, the lace broke and Joe had to secure a new one for me. Of course, they had a brand new pair of skates in Joe's size.

Joe scolded, "That's what you get for taking so much time fixing that pompadour, Mike. I waited an hour for you."

I decided to take a test run before I greeted Patty and her cousins. The lively carnival-type music made it easy to acquire skating legs after a few solo practice revolutions over the solid wooden floor. It didn't take long for me to get enough confidence to ask Patty to skate. I liked the way she skated backwards as we glided around the rink together while Johnny Maddox and the Rhythmasters played the *Crazy Otto Rag*. When I took a break with Joe, it was "Ladies Choice," and *she* asked *me* to skate. As we skated on the shiny surface, I noticed glowing blue lights around the building next door.

I said, "The *Blue Moon* looks like a great place. People are dancing outside on the back patio. Some day I'd like to dance out there with you."

"That would really be nice."

"Can I give you a ride home?"

"Oh....my cousin's boyfriend Whitey is picking us up...but if you want to ride with us, we'll take *you* home."

Joe skated up to me and said, "Let's go, Mike. I've got a couple of '*townies*' and we're going to the root beer stand."

I replied, "I'm all set. I'm going with Patty and her cousins."

"Okay, I'll see you at the cottage."

One cousin was in the front seat and two more were sandwiched in between Patty and me in the back seat. I hung onto the left side door and Patty was crammed against the other door in Whitey's 1949 Chevy. It only took five minutes to get to Indian Mound. They dropped me off first. Here I was, already home, and my brother and the '*townies*' were at the root beer stand. I sat on the fence in front of the house gazing up at the stars reliving the whole night and finally focused on the *Blue Moon*.

The next day Patty was on the beach, wearing a beautiful green bathing suit. She really dazzled me with her perfect figure. I loved her in that green bathing suit. It was a once in a lifetime first impression that stayed with me all my life. The summer ended without me seeing her again. Her address, in her handwriting, lived in my wallet. Every holiday, I unfolded that note and sent a Hallmark greeting card to '*Someone I Seldom See.*'

For a moment, I lost my thought. Zeke was still staring into 1955. His eyebrows were arched in anticipation. "How're you doing, Zeke? Would you like to take a break?"

"Yeah, I'm gonna get a soda. How 'bout you, Mike? Can I get you one?"

"Sure."

As he was leaving, he called back over his shoulder. "But I want to make sure you finish the story."

The sun began to toast the fertilizer behind Ralph's grave. Blackbirds were picking at the pile. I sat down beside the gravestone and leaned back against the cool granite. I stroked the mandolin and smiled, knowing it would never stay in tune. I sang the words, "I'm Irish and I'm beautiful" to the tune of *When Irish Eyes are Smiling*.

"Isn't that the way you sang it, Ralph?

Zeke returned with a cold bottle of soda. I took a quick gulp. "Ahh, smell that root beer! I almost forgot how good it tastes. I haven't had one of these since I was seventeen, when I had my last plug of tobacco." I sniffed the bottle one more time and remembered John Barnham.

119

Chapter 7
Along for the Ride

That summer Ralph was put in charge of security for Pokeye's kayak. Pokeye built the kayak in his cellar. He had to dismantle it when he tried to get it out the door and put it all back together again in his garage. After a tremendous amount of thought and consideration, Pokeye had come to the decision that Ralph would be the best man for the job because he was a little older, more experienced and had more resources than any other guy he knew. Besides, Ralph was the only one who would do it.

"Follow me, Ralph."

Ralph stepped in front of Pokeye, pushing branches in front of him as a maple branch snagged his shirt and slapped Pokeye across the cheek.

"Jesus Christ, Ralph! I said to follow me. You almost poked me in the eye."

The camouflaged kayak was secretly hidden, fifteen feet off

the Ten Mile River. The kayak, resting under a bush, was Pokeye's pride and joy. Months of work, attention and detail went into every part. He said, "I sanded all the wood. I double shellacked the canvas. I carved the paddles out of beech wood. If I could take this kayak to Maine with me, I'd have a ball. But, I know it will be safe with you, Ralph, until I get back. Don't let anyone know about it."

Ralph lit a cigarette, as he exhaled, "Double shellac, huh!"

The next morning dust rolled off the dirt road as we drove to a rugged dead end. "Ralph, where does this road go?"

Ralph's eyes shifted to me. The car struck a rock and slammed to a halt. "We're there now. Just follow me."

The hinges groaned as the car doors flew open. Ralph headed down the trail. A stick snagged his sweater and whipped at me. SWISH.

"Jesus Christ, Ralph, it almost poked me in the eye."

When we got to the hiding place, I was surprised and exclaimed, "Wow! A boat? How'd you know about this boat?"

Ralph boasted from the corner of his mouth, "A kayak... double shellacked and built for adventure...and...it's ours for the week! Grab the other end." We struggled up the steep bank. Ralph said, "When we hoist it up on the roof, make sure you tie it down with a ship shank and a square knot. This is Pokeye's double shellacked masterpiece; we don't want to wreck it."

The next day Ralph slouched at the table in his kitchen. "Supper was great, Ma," Ralph said as he kissed her on the cheek.

She looked up at him and said, "Ralph, Sal wanted me to ask you if you could give him a ride to Newport tomorrow...

something about a fishing trip with his buddies. I don't know why any of them can't pick him up, but I told him I would ask you if you can take him. Can you do it, Ralph? Do you have other plans?"

"Sure, Mom. I can take Sal…and pick him up, too!"

"There's a beach nearby. Maybe you and Mike could have a beach day."

Ralph sauntered to the window and looked out at the kayak strapped to the roof of the car. He pondered, "Okay."

She put her arm around him, "I know Sal can never replace your father, but he does think of you as his son."

The next morning when the car rolled up in front of my house Sal rolled down the window and said, "Good morning, Mike. Hop in. Glad you can make it."

I sat on one of the paddles and pulled it out from under my rear end. Tapping the ash from his cigarette out the window, Sal said, "Are you boys going to tell me the story about the kayak on the roof?"

I peered out the window and watched the trees whizzing by. Ralph just smiled and looked at me as he mumbled, "Yeah, no one's gonna find this kayak under the bushes."

Ralph rambled, "Well, it's like the guy with the duck on his head." Sal looked up.

"A duck?"

"Well this guy had a duck on his head, so he went to the doctor. The doctor asked, 'Do you want to get that duck off your head?' Before the guy could answer, the duck said, 'No! I want to get this guy off my ass!' "

Sal rolled his eyes and shook his head.

The Studebaker found its place in the parking lot at Second Beach in Newport and sat idling. Sal stepped out of the car and pushed his black, windblown hair from his eyes and peered into the car window. "Hey, guys. Looks pretty rough out there. You're not really going to take this 'duck' here too far out are you?"

Ralph, with his right hand on the pearl shift, looked up at Sal and said, "It was built for the sea—all sanded and double shellacked."

"Yeah, but you've got canoe paddles; they're not designed for a kayak. In the ocean, it'll be like peeling an apple with a spoon."

Ralph said, "Hey, Mike. Does applesauce go with pork chops?"

I said quizzically, "Yeah?"

Ralph lit a cigarette as he talked to Sal, "Have fun fishing and YOU be careful out on those rocks."

As the ropes were untied, the wind got under the kayak and we struggled to keep it from flying away. We stopped to rest in front of the clam shack. The beach was empty, except for the last of the boats that were secured to the docks, hunkered down for a violent storm. The wind grabbed the corner of a small craft advisory poster and ripped it from the tacks on the bulletin board. I looked at Ralph as the rain started to pelt against my face.

"You think we otta' go?"

"Look, Mike. Once we get beyond those big waves, it'll calm down, and we can ride the swells." The surf thundered and two gulls zoomed by us low and fast, as he shouted over the wind. "Hold on tight, Mike! Get it straight to the surf!"

I yelled, "Look out!"

CRASH! Another wave pounded the boat and rolled it like a waterlogged barrel. The wind furled a salty spray in our eyes.

"Faster! Run into the waves!" Ralph shouted, "Faster–to get over the top!"

We ran with the kayak as if it was a battering ram. SMASH! CRACK! The frame was beginning to buckle. We managed to jump over the next wave and sit in the boat.

"Paddle, Mike, paddle!"

The top of the kayak lifted on the next wave. The canoe paddles threw us off balance. The tip of the kayak then slammed straight down and threw us into the violent water. The next wave rose high like a mountain so tall, and the wind blew the foam from the top as it crested.

"Look out!" I shouted.

The rumble from the wave pounding down was a sound I would never forget. Then **CRACK!** The boat was smashed. Surf pushed the limp craft far up on the beach. Like a tent with no poles, it sloped in the sand. We dragged the heavy waterlogged canvas, with its double shellac, through the sand to the car. We fastened the battered kayak to the roof. People driving by shook their heads. Who would believe that we would attempt to weather *this* storm in *this* boat?

We kept the car heater on full blast, but we were still shivering as we waited in the car for Sal to finish his beer with his buddies. "I knew it was going to be rough out there for you boys," Sal groaned when he finally approached the car. "It looks like you need to do some maintenance work on that kayak."

I cranked down the window a notch and quipped, "Yeah, the USS Pokeye is now a submarine."

Sal threw his gear and himself into the back seat and soon started to snore as Ralph headed back toward Pawtucket. The radio was playing *Moments to Remember* by the Four Lads. Ralph looked at me sitting in the passenger seat and said, "My Goddamn cigarettes are soaked, Mike. Why the hell didn't you remind me to take them outta my top pocket?"

"I still have a pound of sand in my bathing suit liner irritating me enough. I don't need to be told I'm the keeper of your lousy cigarettes."

"You know, Mike, you're starting to get to be just like your sister."

"Whata you mean? What do you mean?"

"I thought she'd be the first to wear my class ring."

I looked at him and the hair on the back of my head stood straight as my eyes turned dead on him. "Your what?"

"You know how much I like her. I wanted her to be the first to wear my ring. I even had it hanging from a baby blue piece of yarn. You know that's her favorite color."

"What the hell are you trying to say, Ralph? What the hell are you trying to say?"

Ralph took his saturated pack of Lucky's and threw them onto the dashboard. It blocked the flow of the air vent as a patch of fog fell on the corner of the windshield. "Look, Mike. Before you're Nancy's brother, you're my friend. That's the way it's always been. Right?"

There was a deafening silence. We sat motionless and outside the wind and the rain were pelting the car furiously. My jaw was paralyzed. My teeth were clenched. My anger was torn between what Ralph had said and the fact that it blindsided me so quickly.

"Blood is thicker than water, McGreavey...and Nancy's blood!"

"All I know, Mike, is she should have been honored to wear my ring. If you and Nancy are so close, then why doesn't she wear YOUR ring!"

"Pull this car over. I'll ring your damn bell."

Ralph jerked the wheel to the right. The kayak bounced on the roof and a cascade of water spilled out of the canvas as he slammed on the brakes. "One more word outta you Mike...and I'll knock your damn head off."

The doors of the Studebaker flew open and our anger ejected us from the seats. Sal popped up from the back and squeaked the fog from the side window with two fingers. He didn't know what was happening and probably thought we had a flat tire. Ralph was swinging at my head. The car dipped and rocked as he knocked me over the front fender. Sal's hand streaked across the window to gather a full view and make sense of what was happening. I swung at Ralph with a left hook and missed. He smirked and S M A C K! I hit him so hard with my right fist that Sal heard it with the doors closed. It was a shot in the left eye that sent him head over heels rolling down into a muddy drainage ditch.

I could smell the mud and dirty water. Running down the bank, I slipped, and slid into Ralph with my knees. I was on top of him. He was stunned and helpless. I could see his wide eyes looking into mine. I went into a frenzy, swinging with both hands, punching and ripping at Ralph as I hollered over the rain with every swing, "Blood is thicker than mud! Blood is thicker than mud."

From the top of the embankment, Sal shouted through cupped hands, "HEY! Hey, knock it off!" I've never seen Sal so mad. I kept swinging my arms. We wouldn't hear him...we wouldn't stop. Sal ran down the embankment. He grabbed my cocked right hand and draped his body over my right arm and kept me pinned down.

First the smell of fish, then beer hit my nose, then two sharp punches from Ralph. **WHAM! WHAM**! Right in the nose.

Sal had to stop this. He became desperate. He knew we were out of control. He started clutching his hands across his chest. He shouted, "I'M HAVING A HEART ATTACK! I'M HAVING A HEART ATTACK!"

We froze and looked at each other.

Ralph's usually ruddy face turned an ashen white color as he kneeled down over Sal, "Jesus Christ, Sal! Are you all right?"

With a look of helplessness, Ralph pleaded, "Quick, Mike, we've gotta' get him to the car." With the rain pouring down on us, we carried his exhausted stepfather out of the ditch and deposited him in the back seat like a wet rag. I don't know who was in the worst shape–me, Sal, Ralph or the kayak! We drove in silence.

Sal groaned, "Let's stop at the next gas station."

Ralph stood in the cold night air, holding a cold bottle of coke on his reddened, closed eye. I splashed freezing water on my swollen lip and bruised nose. That fake heart attack put a scare into us and made us stop fighting. We learned something that day. That blood *and* friends are thicker than water.

Everyone at the Spa wanted to know what happened. We said we were playing sandlot football, but they all knew that we had a fight.

We spent the next few days quietly repairing the kayak. A few screws, paper mache, and another coat of shellac were applied to the sad looking craft before the kayak was ready to go back into the Ten Mile River. Ralph was excited about the prospect of another new adventure as the kayak slid into the water like a cigar on a puddle.

Daggett Avenue waved as the summer sun cooked the pavement creating an optical illusion. Neighborhood kids swam in the Black Beauty swimming hole under the *Second Tarzan Tree* in the murky waters of the Ten Mile River.

"Ralph, let's paddle toward the *Second Tarzan Tree*. It's at the best swimming hole around."

"*Second Tarzan Tree*? What happened to the first one?"

"The cops cut the rope down, so Pokeye and some of the guys just went further up the river to Black Beauty and put up another one. C'mon, let's check it out!"

We glided in the now triple shellacked kayak like two swans on a placid lake. "Mike, look at the size of that huge oak tree. It's pretty incredible that a tree that big started in a nutshell."

"The guys put up a stronger rope this time, Ralph. It's thicker and a lot better than the last one!"

"Yahoo! Let's go, Mike!" We grabbed the rope together like Tarzan and Cheetah, swinging out over the river yelling, "YE ALL–EIAYA." Splash!

The muddy bottom got stirred up and the water became very murky. It was pretty scary down there, but the excitement of swinging like a wild monkey and plunging down into the water like skydivers was exhilarating.

"That was a blast, Mike,"

We headed toward the small falls in the kayak and then fished along the river's edge. The current began to get stronger as we moved downstream. Before we knew it, we were being carried swiftly through the water and we reached the falls sooner than we expected.

"Watch out for those falls, Ralph. They're really swollen today. The water's rushing over the rocks faster than I've ever seen!"

We tried to turn the kayak, but it stayed right on course. All of a sudden I could feel the current pull us right over the waterfall in rapid decent. I could hear Ralph's distorted voice trying to warn me, "Hang on, Mike. We're in for the ride of our lives!"

The kayak plunged hard into the swirling, gushing force, nearly crashing into the protruding rocks. It tumbled over and over, but floated upside down when we reached the bottom of the falls. We struggled to get the kayak upright. We were lucky that people were fishing near the falls and rushed to help us.

Huffing and puffing on the bank of the Ten Mile River and completely out of breath, Ralph asked, "Mike, did you grab the paddles?"

"You've gotta be kiddin'. They're gone! Gone with all the tackle and fish, but we did save Pokeye's super duper triple shellacked kayak!"

As soon as he got back to Pawtucket, Pokeye ran right over to check on his pride and joy nestled in its hiding place. Then he confronted Ralph. "Where are my paddles?"

Ralph took a long drag on his cigarette and said with an innocent look on his face, "Do *I* look like *I* know where your stupid paddles are?"

Pokeye turned on his heels and disappeared through the thick reeds. Later, we heard through the grapevine, that the next time Pokeye took his kayak into the river, it sank.

* * * * *

We enjoyed swimming in the State Line Quarry when we finished caddying on hot summer days. We crossed the street by the eleventh hole, cut through the parking lot of the Ice Cream Parlor, and headed deep into the woods. The aura created by the clear, cool water moving over light-hued stones evoked an impression of coolness in the deep pit. A small shack at the adjoining pumping station served as a high dive tower. We would climb on top of the slanted roof, run down it, dive out over a cement wall that was about six feet from the shack, and plunge into the deep water. The water got much colder deeper down in the pit. It was a dangerous thing to do, but, oh boy, what a thrill! Rumor had it that old cars were at the bottom, but none of us ever got down far enough to see them.

Unfortunately, a death took place there when I was a kid. Joey McNeil, the Boy Scout advisor for my Cub Scout Den Pack, drowned when he was fourteen years old. My troop, comprised of ten-year-olds, attended his wake together. We were all deeply affected by this tragedy. It was the first time any of us had ever seen someone in a casket. It was especially hard, because Joey worked closely with us, guiding us as we earned our Cub Scout badges. I thought he was the greatest kid in the neighborhood because he devoted so much time to scouting. He was an inspiration to me. I earned my *Wolf Badge*, but lost interest in scouting after his death. I never completed the requirements for the *Bear Badge*.

131

When I got home from the wake, my father and my uncles were sitting on the porch listening to the Joe Lewis–Jersey Joe Walcott fight on the radio. I just went straight to my room. I cried and felt completely overwhelmed. I could hear the men cheering for hours as they listened to the long fight. Joe Lewis finally knocked out Walcott in the eleventh round. I never left my room...after all, the brother of my best friend at Cub Scouts had just died, and he was about to be buried in the morning.

I sat in silence for a few moments before Zeke said, "Terrible things happen during our lifetimes. I live with sadness every day. We have to learn that life goes on and remember the good times. We can't dwell on the sad ones."

* * * * *

A few of the jockeys and hot walkers swam at the quarry and hung out at the Darlington Spa. Ralph and Dominick were at the spa when they overheard Red Maguire, one of the top riders, talking on the phone.

"A friend of yours asked me to call you, Dr. Sommerville, 'cause I've got a great tip. I'll be riding *Thompkins County* in the third. You can bet the farm on this one, Doc...and tell your bookie to put a hundred on the horse for me. Yeah, it's a sure bet. I'll be at your office at five o'clock to pick up the money." Listening, with the phone pushed close to his ear, he answered, "Ah, you won't have any trouble recognizing me, Doc! They don't call me Red Maguire for nuthin'!" Replying to the skeptical doctor, Red continued, "Ah, don't worry about this horse winning. *It will win*! I'll be 'a ridin' him and I'll make sure of it!"

Red hung up the phone and dashed out the door just as our four foot nine friend Shemp walked in. Rocky barked and ran toward the door. Dominick poked Ralph. They BOTH had the same idea as soon as they saw Shemp.

132

Ralph leaned his cigarette on the edge of the ashtray and announced, "Here's OUR Red Maguire!"

Shemp was all for the idea of impersonating the jockey. His ears perked up and his eyes almost popped out of his head as he listened to the scheme. "I'll do it as long as I get my cut!"

Ralph left the Spa and came back with some red hair dye he picked up at Pineault's Drug Store. They dyed Shemp's hair in the bathroom at the Spa. The toxic smell made Shemp nauseous and the dye rolled down his forehead and stung his eyes. He complained, "This better be worth it!"

Thompkins County won by a nose. At four-thirty sharp, Shemp briskly walked into the doctor's office on Broadway and returned to the Spa shortly afterwards waving a fistful of money. He divided two hundred eighty seven dollars among his cohorts. Shemp rubbed his head and sighed, "I'll have to lay low for at least a month until my hair grows out!" Ralph tried to rush the process by bleaching Shemp's hair blonde the next day, but it turned orange. We often wondered, but never heard what happened when the *real* Red Maguire showed up at Doctor Sommerville's office at *five* o'clock.

When I met Ralph at the bowling alley on Central Avenue the next day, he was in the midst of playing the '*honesty game*' with John Manning and a bunch of other guys. His cigarette butt smoldered in an ashtray. They had stuffed an old wallet with paper, cut the size of dollar bills, to make it look like the wallet was bulging with money.

The wallet was then placed on the floor near the entrance to the men's room where someone was sure to spot it. I stood at the back of the room and noticed the stale smell of lingering smoke as I watched them make bets among themselves. I could hear Ralph's voice as he said, "Now we'll see who's honest around here. If a guy turns the wallet in at the front desk, he's honest.

If he takes it into the men's room, he's dishonest." Ralph held up a modified score card and continued, "I'll keep a chart." They amused themselves all afternoon. At five o'clock, Ralph announced the results in a loud voice:

"Honest–5, Dishonest–4." Then he bellowed, "It's just about fifty–fifty!"

When the manager checked to see what was going on, Ralph told him, "We're getting a better education doing this than anything we could learn in school."

The manager gave him a quizzical look and said, "Quit horsing around. Get back there and tend to your job, or we'll have to get someone else to set up the pins tonight."

Ralph retorted, "Okay, okay. I was just taking a survey." He rolled his pack of Lucky's into the sleeve of his T-shirt.

When I met Ralph at the bowling alley the following week he said, "I met *two hot numbers* who were bowling a couple of days ago. They were in Pawtucket, visiting their cousin, Martha Stuvinski. They're sisters who live in Jewett City, Connecticut. I have their home address, Mike. See if you can borrow Joe's car on Friday so we can go to Connecticut. My car is on the fritz."

Shrugging my shoulders, I said, "Why not."

Friday night we were off to Jewett City, a trip that took over two hours. Along the way, Ralph kept singing a song he made up about Jewett City sung to the tune of *Kansas City*.

By the time we got there, we were full of enthusiasm and expectation, but the house was in darkness. Feeling let down I observed, "Looks like there's no one around, but knock on the door again Ralph, just to make sure."

He turned to me as his face flushed, "Oh, geez, I thought they'd be home."

There was no singing on the way back. A heavy fog rolled in and it was hard for Ralph to see the two lane highway on Route Six. I spotted blue lights approaching from behind. The cops pulled Ralph over, just before we reached the Rhode Island border.

"License and registration."

Ralph obliged, taking out his dog-eared license and I got the registration from the glove compartment. Ralph inquired, "What's the matter, officer?"

Staring at me, the Connecticut State Trooper inquired, "Are you Joseph Ryan?"

"No, sir, this is my brother's car—I'm Mike."

The officer stated, "You boys were stopped for straddling the line."

"Straddling the line?" Ralph asked in disbelief. "It's hard to see tonight. I was trying to follow the line in the road, but then it disappeared."

"Well, just stay on your side of the road and have a safe trip home, boys."

"Yes officer," Ralph said in a pleasant tone.

When the cruiser drove away, I said, "Ralph, this trip was a bust! We can't win for losin'."

Ralph nodded, "Just our luck."

I said, "Yeah. The anticipation always ends up better than the event. This was just another wild goose chase!"

After the disappointment we experienced in Jewett City, I don't know what possessed me to suggest we try another 'road trip' to pursue two girls from Revere, Massachusetts. We met Carla and Gina at Jack Witchies' Arena in North Attleboro when we went to see the country and western singer, *Eddie Zack and his Hayloft Jamboree.* I told the girls we'd see them in Revere in two weeks.

When the time came, Ralph didn't want to go. "Mike, why do you want to attempt this again? How do you know they'll even be there?"

I frowned, "Look, we told them we would see them tonight and I think we should go."

"Oh, for Christ's sake."

Ralph reluctantly put on his new rusty colored suede jacket. Then he laced himself with his unmistakable, highly scented Aqua Velva after-shave lotion. I threw on my tan corduroy sports coat and we took off for Revere.

It was difficult finding the house on the narrow streets with cars parked on both sides, but we finally located 983A Rotondo Street. Gina answered the door with a surprised look on her face when she saw the two of us standing there. "Please wait in the parlor while I call Carla." When Carla arrived a few minutes later, the girls went into a huddle, and started to giggle.

"What the hell is this, Mike?" Ralph whispered to me, holding his hand as a shield close to his mouth. Then he said out loud, "How about letting us in on the joke, girls."

Gina explained, "We didn't think you guys would *actually* drive all the way up here."

Carla chimed in, "We go out with Eddie and Frankie every Saturday night and they'll be here any minute now."

Ralph looked at me and said, "I told you, Mike. I *knew* it would be a dry run."

Then he addressed Gina and Carla as we stood at the open door, "It's just as well, because *this* would have been a very short date. We were going to take you for a soda. We're supposed to meet Kelly and Megan for a big date later tonight in Pawtucket."

Ralph wouldn't speak to me all the way back to Ziggy's Grill. We each chowed down two Coney Island hot dogs, dripping with sauce and washed them down with coffee milk. Ralph finally broke the silence and said, "Have you learned your lesson now, Mike?"

"Yeah, let's not go around chasing rainbows when we've got a pot of gold in our own backyard. I didn't want to stand *them* up, but I never counted on *us* being booted out! I wish there really was a 'Kelly and Megan' waiting to meet us."

Ralph let out a dejected sigh; "It's too late to do anything now. Let's just go home and get some shut eye. We've got a big day tomorrow."

* * * * *

Lois Quackenbush was a friend of Packy Doyle's aunt. She had a house that needed to be painted on John's Pond in Mashpee, on the Cape. Packy, Ralph and I agreed to tackle the job for twenty-five dollars each. She provided free room and board for three days and expected us to work from sun up to sun down until the job was finished. Upon rising each morning, Packy would go outside, raise his finger up to feel any breeze in the air, then say, "No work today, fellas…too much wind."

Ralph would confirm his weather report by saying, "Feel that humidity. We can't paint on a day like this!" Then we'd all pile

137

into Packy's car and head for Falmouth Heights to spend the day at the beach.

'The Duke' showed up to help on the second day we were there and presented Lois with a bag of delicious red tomatoes. He had just bought them at the roadside stand around the corner. He put his hand on Lois' shoulder and said, "I just picked these beautiful tomatoes especially for you. They're from my mother's garden."

Lois, thrilled with his thoughtfulness, smiled brightly and said, "You're sweet, Dominick."

Dominick bowed from the waist in a genteel manner as he said, "I'm taking you all out to dinner at the Coonimessett Inn tonight."

We enjoyed a fantastic dinner at the expensive restaurant. We devoured clam chowder, steamers and two-pound lobsters. As 'The Duke' was wiping his chin with his fancy dinner napkin, the bill arrived. He immediately dropped the napkin to his lap and swiped the bill off the table with a swift, brushing sweep. "I'll get that," he flamboyantly announced.

He started patting all of his pockets. Then he moved his hands quickly over his body feeling for his wallet. He looked under the table and all around the room. We all looked for the wallet. Then Duke said, "Oh, boy. My wallet must have fallen out in the car!" He looked at Ralph square in the eyes. "Would you please go out to the car and take a look? It probably fell behind the seat."

Ralph obliged and started searching the car from top to bottom, before he realized what was going on. *What the hell am I looking for? He doesn't have any money!*

In the meantime, Dominick sat at the table looking sad and stated, "It's not the wallet or the money. My favorite picture of Rocky is in the wallet!"

Ralph dashed back into the restaurant. His face flushed as he explained, "I looked all over. Sorry, Duke. Your wallet's not there!"

Duke continued to look under the table and got up to glance under all our chairs. Finally, Lois said in an understanding whisper as she patted 'The Duke's' hand, "Don't worry, darling. Tonight will be my treat. You can get it the next time."

When we got back to the house she said, "Dominick, you can have the special purple guest room upstairs tonight."

With a big grin on his face, 'The Duke' stood at the top of the steps, picked his teeth with a toothpick, and closed the door to the luxury suite.

Leaning against a newel post on the porch, Ralph took out a cigarette, then shook his head, "That was a new one on me, Mike!"

I concurred, "That guy's a real piece of work!"

In the morning, Dominick yelled from his room, "Good morning, breakfast lovers. Mother, oh Mother, I'll have tea, toast, duck eggs, marmalade and crumpets–and don't forget to butter the corners of the toast!"

After a hearty breakfast, the four of us worked until dark, slapping on a thick coat of paint until the quaint Cape Cod cottage was as fresh as new. It was picture perfect, sitting among the beds of sweet smelling lavender that surrounded it. We sat under the bowers of pink roses that grew on an arbor. The roses flourished in the seaside air.

Counting our loot, Ralph quipped, "Pay thee well." Then he took a long drag on his cigarette.

Chapter 8
You Can Smell It in the Air

The night before football practice started, I walked out onto the porch, shaking a Chicklet into my mouth. The screen door creaked as I pushed it open. A crisp breeze softly announced that the season was changing. It was in the air! Football Season. It was in the air! As I stood there, in the coolness of that late August night, deep inside of me, a band began to play, *'When the Saints Come Marching In.'* My heart pounded as I stared into the starry night. Even now, crisp late summer nights still take me back. The scent of the season returns to me every year at that time.

In '54, a Rogers half-back snapped my thumb and a Cranston tailback's cleat flattened my nose and blackened my eyes. Oh, yes, 1954 battered me around. The injuries faded and healed. '55 had arrived and the enthusiasm rocked the locker room with a new beat–louder, stronger, tougher. This veteran team was more seasoned, quicker, smarter, and ready.

Coach Farley was a chemist. He taught chemistry and physics

and was also the head football coach. He had formulated our team like a powerful chemical potion utilizing our strengths in all the right places. The backs were more explosive; the line was solid. The chemistry of the team was based on respect–players to players, coach to players, and players to coach. Coach Farley had a special feeling for this particular team, because most of the players were also honor students. He along with Vin McDonald, the assistant coach, worked on all of the plays and strategies. Together, they were seen as the Einsteins of the X's and O's. The split T was drawn on a blackboard. This formation would prove to be a trademark of Farley's creativity and talent. We were the first to use this offense in our league. Defensively, Coach McDonald took us to a new level. He custom fit defenses to each team we played. Working together, like a motor and transmission, we had the capability of a bulldozer.

Football season started out great, but I still had a few problems with new injuries. I sprained my left ankle against Bristol in a scrimmage. Then just before the season opener, I sprained my right ankle. Coach arranged to have me go to Brown University before each game to get my ankles taped. I was treated by a master trainer. He was an older gentleman, past retirement, but he still loved to help athletes. He used his large hands to wrap ankles quickly, in a pattern all his own. When he finished, my ankles felt like they were in firm but flexible casts. I thought he must have taped over a million ankles in his lifetime.

Jackie Shannon was our quarterback. The players knew it, the school knew it, all the newspapers knew it. He was an outstanding all-around athlete. A Pawtucket hero, of sorts, he was All-State in football and baseball, and a great basketball player. Coach Farley pitted me up against Jackie during our first practice.

"Mike Ryan and Jackie Shannon–on your feet and over here!" Coach dragged his low spiked cleats across a bald spot on the field as he pulled up the waistband of his sweat pants. "Stand behind this line, guys." The other players sauntered over, gripping their helmets tightly. They knew this would be a good one. "Fifty-yard dash," Farley yelled, while straightening his baseball cap. "I'm gonna count, 'one, two, three Saints.' When I say 'Saints', that means go!"

"One, two, three…" and the whole team yelled at the top of their lungs "SAINTS!"

It was like a shotgun went off. Immediately, I felt myself taking the lead. The adrenalin kicked in, and I jetted over the finish line–first by a few steps. The surprised team members cheered and threw their helmets high in the air. Me, Mike Ryan, especially to *my* surprise, beat *the* Jackie Shannon.

I always wanted to carry the ball. I thought the coaches might give me a shot if they saw that I had some speed, but my chances were actually slim to none. We had three tremendous backs on the team, but Coach decided to put in a new play that would give me a chance to get more involved in the offense. On a goal line play, he wanted Jackie to step up on my rear girdle pad after he took the snap from center, and leap into the end zone as I dropped on all fours. When he leapt into the end zone, I was supposed to lunge forward from the right guard position.

The first time we tried this play in a scrimmage, Bob Castle, the rugged defensive guard opposite me, came across the line and threw his head and shoulders into Jackie. It stopped Jackie from leaping into the end zone, so he tried to *run* into the end zone instead. Bob held him in the air and Jackie's spikes dug into my back inflicting long, deep scratches as he pumped his legs up and down. Coach Farley immediately blew his whistle. He scrapped that play! Vinnie McDonald ran over with the first aid kit and applied Mercurochrome to my back. It smelled like ether and stung like hell.

Hope High had high hopes, especially after trouncing us the year before. They even tried a forty-five yard field goal on the last play of the game, just to rub it in. We all wanted to cream them. We did so by beating them 19-0 in the Injury Fund Round Robin game in Providence. This short contest was played each year to kick off the season. All of the teams in the state played and it gave everyone a chance to scope out the teams they would be playing. The proceeds from the Injury Fund games were divided up between the schools.

After half-backs Hennessy and Riley scored our first two touchdowns, we missed the extra points on running plays. Coach Farley had me kick the nineteenth point after Hennessy's final touchdown. It sailed end over end right through the center of the goal posts. I kicked extra points in all of the early games until I missed several points in a row against Pawtucket West. We went back to running or passing for the point after touchdown. We won our first four league games against Woonsocket, Mount St. Charles, Classical, and Pawtucket West–without being scored upon. In fact, our lowest score was 40–0. Everyone thought that this team was the best they'd ever seen representing Saint Raphael.

* * * * *

"Ya know, Zeke–Ralph got kicked out of St. Rays during the football season."

The week of the Stonington game, Ralph happened to be standing next to Wally Ossinchowski, one of our funniest class members. As a gag, Wally mimicked a shifting car during the after lunch announcements. The last announcement blared over the loudspeaker, "Ralph McGreavey–report to the office."

Ralph was dumbfounded. He stood in front of Brother James, "I heard you making loud noises during the announcements."

Ralph quietly said, "It wasn't me, Brother." But he knew he was behind the eight ball again.

"Those sounds came from your direction, McGreavey. If it wasn't you, you know who did it."

"It wasn't me, Brother."

"If you don't tell me who it was, you're out of here."

Ralph looked him straight in the eyes and said, "I didn't do it, Brother."

"Pack up your books, McGreavey; you're Tolman's project now!"

Ralph had incidents at Saints that got him in trouble, but his character was always to be admired. He had scruples and could be relied upon to back you up in any situation. He always stood on his own two feet and displayed courage no matter what the consequences.

The 1955 football season was a fun time for me, even though Ralph was now a Tolman Tiger. He was my greatest fan, attending all of our games and cheering me on to victory. While I was concentrating on the opposition's running backs, Ralph encountered his own trials and tribulations. A few days before the Thanksgiving Day football game, Ralph and I were walking down Armistice Boulevard and we ran into Saint Raphael's baseball coach, Bernard. He glared at Ralph and said, "I don't want you to hang around with Mike now that you're going to Tolman."

Ralph was astonished and said, "Are you nuts? Now that *I'm* going to Tolman, I can tell *you* where to put your fungo bat! Go pound sand!"

Coach mumbled, "McGreavey, you'll never change, you'll never change," and walked away.

Ralph shook his head and said to me, "Mike, I may have gotten kicked out of Saints, but how could he think a little thing like that could break up *our* friendship?"

"You're right, Ralph. You're right."

Chapter 9
The UN–UN–UN Saints!
(Unbeaten–Untied–Unscored Upon!)

We played Woonsocket on a Friday night in our first league game of the season. Ralph hurt his shoulder during practice the week before and couldn't suit up for the game. He was disappointed that he couldn't participate, because he played baseball for Woonsocket's Legion Team a few years earlier and knew a lot of the townspeople.

Coach Farley requested, "Ralph, I'd like you to '*spot*' up in the press box for Saints tonight. You can help the announcer identify our players."

Ralph was elated. "Right, Coach." He ran over to tell me.

I said, "That's great, Ralph. It's the next best thing to playing. You'll feel like you're right in the game."

Jim Hennessy, our right half-back, came to Saints as an

147

outstanding prospect. Jim and end Charley Mont and I had a lot of playing time together because we were the only three football players from Goff Junior High to enroll at Saints. The rest of the Goff team went to Tolman, which was called Pawtucket East until 1955. Jim was injured in both his sophomore and junior years. After having knee surgery, he returned as a senior.

Seated together on the bus heading for Woonsocket, I said, "Geez, Jim. Those damn injuries prevented you from realizing your full potential the last couple of years."

With a determined look on his face, he answered, "The first time I carry the ball today, I'm gonna refuse to be tackled!"

On the opening kickoff, we returned the ball to our thirty yard line. Jim got the ball on a dive play, called the forty-two. He ran through the hole between the right guard and tackle so fast that he smacked into Woonsocket's linebacker, who didn't even react as Hennessy bounced off him. Jim ran seventy yards for a touchdown. I watched him dash into the end zone as I cheered from my offensive right guard position.

Remembering his prediction, I ran toward him pumping my right hand in the air, shouting "Atta way to go, Jim!"

On defense, I played outside linebacker against Woonsocket's strong side. They had an unbalanced line; they over-shifted players to my side, and ran most of their plays toward me. I made a lot of tackles, but the loud speaker blared, "Tackle by McGreavey! Tackle by Ralph McGreavey."

Ralph was beaming up in the press box as his name resonated throughout the stadium. Then it dawned on me, *'Ralph has the announcer thinking my name is McGreavey!'* He joined me in the locker room after the game. I just stared at him. He gave me a big wink and smiled. We left together, only to find a group of people waiting outside for *him*. They cheered and patted Ralph on the back and completely ignored me.

"Great game, McGreavy!" I heard a voice bellowing, **"You were all over the field, McGreavy!"**

Ralph beamed and chuckled, "Yeah, they were tough."

The West Warwick Wizards had a legendary coach, Frank 'Turk' Lewicki. His teams were unbeatable. With Turk at the helm, they won fifty-two league games without a loss, over a seven year period. 'Turk' was a former West Warwick All-Stater, and an All-American at Boston College. He played for the Chicago Bears in the pros, and in 1946, he played in the Bears National Football Championship. They beat the New York Giants, and in that game, Turk kicked three extra points and a field goal. He was also, in my opinion, an *All American Coach*. In 1952, West Warwick was chosen to play against a high school team in Florida. As a young teenager, I enjoyed listening to the game on the radio.

Both Saints and West Warwick were undefeated going into the fifth game of our season. As we sat in the locker room under McCoy Stadium, we could hear the people cheering in the stands. Coach Farley said, "I'd like you all to be quiet and think about your assignments. This will be the biggest game of your life." Our school band was playing '*When the Saints Come Marching In*,' but you could hear a pin drop in the locker room as we waited to go out on the field. When that moment finally came, we almost tore the doors off the hinges. We were ready!

Coach McDonald initiated a special defense to use against West Warwick. We lined up in a six-two defense (six men on the line...with two linebackers behind the tackles). Their center called out the defense, and when he called six-two and put his head down, we switched to a six-three defense. Our defensive half-back, Tom Conroy, played the left side and came up to the outside linebacker spot. At that point, I slid over to the middle linebacker position, but hid behind our guard. Their center didn't realize we had a six-three defense. Ray Riley played the outside linebacker position on the right side with his brother, Ed, an outstanding defensive half-back, behind him. They were both tough football players.

Charlie Palumbo, our best defensive end, was always placed on the end that was on the wide side of the field. With Palumbo forcing the West Warwick ball carriers into the middle, and with no one blocking me, I had a field day tackling the runners during the first half.

Steve Almeida, their best running back, carried the ball 80 percent of the time. Their quarterback, Tilo Priminese dislocated his shoulder in the first quarter when our tackle Ron Kornfeld sacked him. Almeida had to carry most of the offense alone. We blitzed West Warwick and had them 19–0 at the half!

When the second half started, their center was looking for me and played a lot tougher. We beat them 25–0, their first league loss in seven years. It was the lowest scoring game and the toughest contest of our first five games. Coach Farley was right when he said this would be the biggest game of our lives. Coach Lewicki congratulated our coach.

Coach Farley shook his hand and said, "You are to be congratulated 'Turk.' You set a record that never will be broken."

I thought, "*Coach Farley always shows a tremendous amount of class.*"

Years later, Steve Almeida told me that Coach Lewicki wore the same 'victory necktie' to every game. When Saints beat West Warwick, he threw the tie out the bus window on the trip back to West Warwick. He was a tremendous competitor and losses were tough for him to accept. Steve also remembered me tackling him on every play, even when he didn't have the ball.

I told him, "The percentage was on my side. Chances were that you'd be carrying the ball."

When I got home my father greeted me at the door with my two uncles, Ed and Paul, who were at the game. The four of us hugged in a small huddle for a long time. I was able to control my overwhelming emotions, but when I got upstairs to my room, I sat alone on my bed and cried. I was overcome with joy. The victory was ours and this was one of the happiest days of my life. Up to this point we had won the round robin and our first five games without anyone scoring a point against us! The next day the *Pawtucket Times* sports page headlines read: "Un Un Un Saints! Unbeaten, Untied, and Unscored Upon."

It was during the following week that Ralph was thrown out of Saints, but that didn't curb his enthusiasm for our team and his friends. We originally had a 'bye' after the West Warwick game, but our coaches scheduled an out of state game in Stonington, Connecticut. Earl Marceau, a former coach at Saints now lived in Stonington and arranged for our two teams to meet. The Stonington Bears were also undefeated after their first five games in their tough Southeastern Connecticut Conference. This was the second week in a row that we played an undefeated team.

It was pouring when we got to Stonington. Their Junior Varsity Team was on the field and they looked small to us.

Coach Farley checked with the officials, "Will we get this game in?"

Some of my teammates chanted, "We want to play! We want to play!"

After a short delay, it was decided that the game would be played. When their Varsity Team came on the field, they looked like a college team. The linemen averaged well over two hundred pounds! I walked onto the field for the coin toss and faced their captains, Chesterfield and Arthur. They were both six feet four. Feeling like a midget in a land of giants, I looked down to see if I was standing in a cleat hole! By kickoff time, the rain had let up for a short time. Then, it started coming down in pounding sheets. It didn't dampen our spirits even though we played the whole game in a sea of mud.

When Ralph came into the stadium, he called out to me, "I made it, Mike. I made it!" Just then his foot hit the side of the bleachers as he waved his arms at me. He slid into a puddle of mud, splattering the wet turf all over his white zip pocket painter's pants. "E-yeoh!" his voice bellowed throughout the stands. He watched the whole game looking like a brown and white jersey cow.

I usually played outside linebacker in a six-two defense, or the middle linebacker in a five-three, but I played on the defensive line in this game. Coach McDonald put me in the gap between the two guards in their right over-shifted line. It was the only time I played this position all season. It didn't take long for us to know that we would be in a barn burner. Chesterfield was at tailback in their powerful single wing offense. He ran, passed the ball, and punted. He was a bull of a runner and it took a good defensive effort to bring him down.

In previous games, our right half-back, Hennessy, scored most of his touchdowns on the right side with straight dives, between guard and tackle. If Ron Kornfeld, our tackle and I didn't move our men out of the hole, Hennessy would run right up our backs. We knew Stonington had scouted us when their biggest and best linemen lined up with a man in front of me, a man in the gap between Ron and me, and a man on Ron's head. The 42 dive wouldn't work this game.

Tom Conroy and Ray Riley scored touchdowns for Saints. Tom, our fullback, scored on a play Coach Farley adjusted during the game. We had a great 'game day' coach. He was adept at adjusting plays as the situation arose. Coach Farley noticed that Hennessy and Jackie Shannon were having trouble going outside. Also, Stonington had shut down the dive play. He told Tommy to line up to the right of Hennessy and counter off his tail. As Jackie faked the dive to Hennessy, he reversed with a pivot and gave the ball to Tommy. Tom sliced into the zero-hole over the center. This counter play allowed us to pick up a lot of yardage. Tom went on to score with this play in the first half, giving us a 7–0 lead at intermission.

The second half was a tremendous battle. Our opponents finally scored in the third quarter on a pass from Chesterfield to Arthur. Hennessy tipped the ball in the end zone and Arthur picked it out of the air. With the score at 7–6, they were attempting the extra point. Chesterfield took the deep snap from their center and quickly ran toward his right tackle. Stonington's tackle and guard double teamed our tackle. When their offset guard missed a block on me, I found myself in the hole, facing Chesterfield. He smacked into me with his legs grinding, his right knee driving high into my facemask. This was the first year we were issued facemasks. They were made out of thin plastic, about three or four inches wide. The force broke the right hinge attached to my helmet. I was lucky it didn't get pushed into my nose or mouth. The contact was intense at the three yard line. Chesterfield finally dropped down in the sloppy mud, just short of the goal line.

When I ran to the sidelines to get another helmet, Coach McDonald said, "Nice tackle, Eddie." Then, realizing his mistake, he chuckled, "Oh, Mike, I thought you were Eddie Hulton. I forgot *you* were on the line this week."

I played the rest of the game wearing sophomore Lenny

Menard's helmet. Ray Riley scored on a reverse, to ice the game for us in the fourth quarter. We beat them 14–6. This was the only game all season that Hennessy didn't score a touchdown, but he did score two extra points. Stonington finished the season as Southeastern Connecticut champions. Our game was their only loss for the year. Chesterfield and Arthur got full scholarships to Colgate.

Zeke remembered the 1955 season right along with me. He finally said, "Mike, I saw all of Saints' home games that year. The Un, Un, Un Saints were causing quite a lot of interest with Pawtucket sports fans. The *Times* gave Saints a lot of publicity in the sports section almost every day. It sparked all kinds of interest all around town."

Our next game against Westerly, at McCoy Stadium, was a blowout...45–0. The following Saturday, we traveled to Newport to face DeLaSalle Academy, another Christian Brothers School. It was a beautiful day and a large crowd filled the stands. The Brothers from both schools were seated together, each rooting for their respective teams. The DeLaSalle coach, Andy Pozzulo, always produced a good team. They were big, but we quickly took a 49–0 lead by the end of the third quarter. Coach Farley didn't want to demoralize them. He took out the first team and put in the second string. In the fourth quarter, every Saints player got in the game. DeLaSalle quickly scored three touchdowns. Our reserves were no match for them.

After their third touchdown, Coach Farley said, "Mike, you're always bugging me to carry the ball... so here's your chance. Go out there and play at the single return spot." Coach told the rest of my teammates, "If you get the ball, lateral it to Mike."

Ron Kornfeld, at 230 pounds, lined up in front of me and hollered, "Follow me down the right sideline."

Ray Riley got the ball on the kickoff and tossed it to me. I took off down the right sideline with Ron in front of me. He threw a block that knocked out three defenders. When I hit our forty-yard line, it was clear sailing all the way to the end zone. Out of the corner of my eye, I could see that their kicker was lagging back. Instead of running hard down the sidelines, I turned quickly and ran right at the kicker. We both went down in a cloud of dust.

When Ralph saw me at single return he knew I was going to get the football. He ran fifty yards down the sidelines with me. But, when I got tackled, he continued running all the way down the field until he reached the end zone with both arms raised high in the air.

Coach Farley shook his head and said, "You're a true lineman, Mike. You'd rather have contact than score a touchdown. I have you in the right position!"

I laughed and said, "Ya," as I patted the dust off my uniform.

After they scored three touchdowns, and my kickoff return, coach Farley put the first team back in. Jackie ran the option play. He faked to Conroy off tackle, ducked inside the end, and ran forty yards for a touchdown. DeLaSalle's coach started waving a white towel. The score was 56–21. They had enough and were ready to surrender!

When I met Ralph after the game he said, "I scored, but you didn't."

* * * * *

Thanksgiving Day! Tolman High School! City Rivalry! The Big Game!

Art Marchand held the school scoring record for nine years,

with 126 points, in 1946. He gave the team an inspirational talk about sportsmanship at one of our last practices. Jim Hennessy needed only eight points in the Thanksgiving game to tie Art's scoring record and nine points to beat it. There was a lot of hype at school and around the city as game day drew closer. Anyone who has ever played football knows the spirit and pride we felt playing in this final game of the season.

The gymnasium shrieked with unbridled enthusiasm at our pep rally with the entire student body in attendance the day before Thanksgiving. Everyone was caught up in the excitement as Jim Buckley led the cheerleaders in skits, hanging the Tolman Tiger in effigy.

I often think about how proud I felt leading my team into the gymnasium as everyone stood up and cheered while the school band played '*When the Saints Go Marching In.*' I still get goose bumps whenever I hear our school song. Trumpeter Ron Lavalley led the band with our fight song, '*Cheer, Cheer for St. Raphael,*' sung to the tune of the Notre Dame fight song. When we came into Saints as sophomores, the Athletic Director, Brother Luke, told us that Notre Dame stole the song from us!

McCoy Stadium was filled to capacity every Thanksgiving for this city rivalry. Both teams put in a great effort all season. All of the players knew each other. In fact, many of Tolman's players played with Hennessy, Mont, and me at Goff Jr. High. We won the city championship in 1952, defeating Sayles, Slater and Jenks Jr. High Schools.

Tolman had a very good team that year with many outstanding players. Bobby Nolan and Al Langlois were exceptional running backs and Alan McDay was a tough and smart quarterback. Ends 'Duckman' Molloy and Clarence 'Be-Be' Sparrow along with their two captains, center Ken Collins and guard George Dempsey, excelled. Dempsey was an All-State defensive lineman.

Our quarterback, Jackie Shannon, had a terrific year running, passing, and punting. Our ends, Charlie Mont and All-Stater Charlie Palumbo were excellent. We had an undefeated team comprised of talented players, like tackles Ron Kornfeld and Doug O'Toole. Left guard Jigger Burns and center Ray Shawnier were terrific blockers. On defense, Bob Castle replaced Burns and Ed Hulton and Ed Riley replaced Mont and Shannon.

The first half was fiercely competitive. Jim Hennessy scored a touchdown and we took a 7–0 lead at half time. Tolman was playing us tough, but just before the fourth quarter, Tom Conroy scored our second touchdown. Hennessy still trailed the school record by two points and needed one more touchdown to break it. With only four minutes to the end of the game, we were on our forty yard line. Jackie Shannon ran the nineteen double reverse. That was my favorite play and I asked Jackie to run it a lot. He would always say, "Wait 'till I set it up." Jackie would flip the ball to Hennessy, who would hand it off to Tom Conroy. Tom then handed it off deep, to Shannon, who was coming back toward the left end. If no one was on my head, from the right guard position, I ran off into the secondary. If someone was on my head, our center, Shawnier, blocked him, and I would cut off his rear and head down field. I would run deep down the field and then peel left and start running up the sideline toward Jackie. The play took a while to develop. When Jackie appeared around the left end with the ball, the other team would start to react. The opposition's defensive player never saw me coming up the sideline and I was able to pick off the first defenseman coming toward Jackie.

On this Thanksgiving Day, Jackie ran the nineteen double reverse play, taking the ball down to the two yard line. Coach Farley, always ready to adjust and adapt, realized Tolman would be stacking our right side to stop Hennessy from getting the record breaking touchdown. He told Shannon, "Switch Riley and Hennessy and run the twenty-three dive."

Sure enough, almost all of the defensive linemen and linebackers were lined up in front of Riley. Hennessy broke the school scoring record on the next play, by running the dive from the left side. It was his only carry from that side all year. His new record, a hundred thirty points, topped off a championship season for Saint Raphael.

We were undefeated State Champions, with nine wins and no losses. Tradition was to give the Thanksgiving Day game football to the captain of the winning team. For over fifty years, I have cherished that pigskin football with 'SRA 21 THS 0' painted on the side.

Chapter 10
Three Strikes and You're Out

Zeke spoke in a nostalgic voice, "In 1938, I captained Pawtucket East. I still remember all the players. There was Billy Rutland, our quarterback, and a tough little end named George Patrick Dooley...and Big Tommy 'Tangerine' Tatro. We beat Saints 7 to 6. I caught a Turkey Day pass for the winning point. *That* game football is on my mantle. Oh, yes, old Pawtucket sure has seen a lot of heart. Most of those kids were tougher than football pigskin."

My eyebrow lifted as I reflected, "The neighborhoods had phenomenal athletes with competitive spirit. Yes, Zeke, they had a lot of guts–guts and character; character and guts–that's what it was all about."

I thought back. Sayles and Slater Jr. High School students started high school in the tenth grade at Pawtucket West. (The name was later changed to Shea High School.) Students attending Goff or Jenks in junior high went to Pawtucket East.

159

(It was renamed Tolman High School.) Those electing to attend Catholic high school chose Saint Raphael Academy. That's when the city rivalries became fierce.

We played Pawtucket West in all sports during the regular season. Tolman was our biggest rival because the two schools were within walking distance of each other and football fueled the fire. The neighborhoods were like a full fishnet from two different schools, each proud to have their own colors–the red and white of Tolman and the purple and gold of St. Raphael. The annual Thanksgiving Day football game between them was a tradition that started back in the 1920's.

Doug O'Toole was the only junior on our all senior first team. His younger brother, Dennis, was our water boy. Dennis later captained another terrific Saints team, and then became a respected Saint Raphael coach with several super bowl victories.

One of my biggest thrills was seeing my son, Mike, thirty-three years later in 1988 score three touchdowns against Tolman on Thanksgiving Day. One of the touchdowns was a seventy-five yard run. Quite a few former players gravitated back to Saints to coach. They knew the spirit and pride that was instilled in the students and passed the same winning attitude on to their players. I love Saint Raphael Academy. It has wonderful spirit, great teachers, and marvelous tradition.

Zeke spoke up with a melodious twang. "Tolman is a great school, too. Fig Patnaude was a marvelous coach there for years and years and years. The Thanksgiving Day games at McCoy Stadium brought out the whole city in those days."

I pointed to an area on the far right of the cemetery now covered with headstones. "Zeke, that's where we played sandlot football when I was a kid. I can still hear the crack when I broke my nose playing right there. You never forget that sound. I was playing against a gang of scrappers from Central Falls. Ray Oney threw a block on one of our opponents. The wily kid spun off him and his head slammed right into my nose."

Zeke looked bewildered. "Hey wait a minute. Hey…wait a minute. It was you who broke his nose. I remember that day. It was 1948, my first summer working at this graveyard. It was you I helped carry across the street to the home of the Darlington Braves Baseball Coach, Roy Norman."

"I don't remember *who* carried me to Mr. Norman's house, but it was Ralph McGreavey's head that broke my nose. I remember that!"

Zeke looked at Ralph's tombstone, "I remember that boy. I remember that look. I remember how he looked up from the ground, with blood streaming from a gash on his forehead. He asked me, 'Is he going to be all right? I mean, is he *really* going to be all right?'"

I mused, "Yeah, Zeke, I was all right, but I didn't see Ralph again until our sophomore year at Saint Raphael Academy."

Zeke shook his head, "Well wadda ya know, wadda you know!"

That day Mr. Norman drove me home and explained to my mother that I was in the car with a broken nose. In disbelief, she looked past him, "Oh, Mr. Norman, Michael's upstairs sleeping."

"You'd better come with me, Mrs. Ryan."

I was in the front seat of Mr. Norman's Dodge, holding a bloodied towel on my nose.

She gasped and turned to Mr. Norman. He shrugged. "Sandlot football." She looked at me and said, "Oh, Michael."

"Sorry, Ma, I climbed down the trellis."

Zeke chuckled, "Why on earth did you leave your house that day, Mike?"

"My mother sent me upstairs to my room when I told her that I wanted to go back to the cemetery to play in a sandlot football game. I didn't sleep much the night before. I kept the whole family awake because I was constantly turning on the light to go to the bathroom. I left early in the morning for a baseball game between the Darlington Braves and Central Falls. We won a close game and after the last out, the Central Falls players challenged us to play a football game scheduled for two o'clock.

"After lunch, my mother said, 'You're not going out now. You're exhausted. You go upstairs and get some rest.' I went to my room protesting vehemently. I wasn't going to let my team down by not showing up to take Central Falls on in football. There was no way I would miss that game. I sneaked into the spare room, climbed out the window and walked across the narrow roof over the porch. As I grabbed onto the rose trellis, I got a strong whiff of the red American Beauty roses. The rose stems pricked my hands until I finally dropped to the ground. I hopped on my bike and peddled to the cemetery as fast as I could."

Zeke said, "Those pickup sandlot games could be rough. No one had the right equipment."

I sighed, "I know; the rest is history. I ended up in the hospital and sported a couple of black eyes. When the Darlington Braves picture with our coach, Mr. Norman was taken, I looked like a raccoon."

I shifted my position, pulled my legs up to my chest and leaned my elbow on my right knee as I cupped my chin. "You know, Zeke, when we were in our early teens my brother Joe was the best sandlot player in our neighborhood. He was a fierce competitor and a crunching tackler in football. He always organized our teams to play other neighborhoods at Slater Park or the Daggett Avenue Field. One Saturday at Daggett Avenue, he tackled a star running back named Charlie Reynolds. Joe hit him so hard that Charlie quit and went home. Charlie was a good running back at Goff Jr. High, but after a few hard tackles by Joe in that sandlot game, he never played another game against our neighborhood."

Joe got a group of sandlot players together and formed a pickup baseball team. He arranged to play my Pony League Team comprised of thirteen to fifteen-year-olds. Mr. Belvedere was our coach and I played shortstop. It was a close game until Joe hit a homerun in the eighth inning for them to take a two run lead. It was a long fly ball that went over the third base line. It soared all the way to the high grass in the outfield. Mr. Belvedere had asked our relief pitcher who was not playing to umpire the game. He called the ball fair. Mr. Belvedere tried to overrule the call, and got into a big argument with Joe. Mr. Belvedere finally picked up all the bases and told everyone to go home.

Joe called him a big baby and then said, "Go ahead! Take your bases and go home, you sore loser."

The next week my father was in his jewelry store when Mr. Belvedere came in to buy a gift. My father called Joe from the back room to meet my coach. Joe looked at him and grinned, "I believe we've already met. Mr. Belvedere used to supply the bases for our sandlot games."

Joe went out for high school baseball. On his first time at bat, he hit a line drive single. He then proceeded to steal second, third, and finally home plate. The coach was irate because he never gave the steal sign. Joe was always best in an individual situation. His sandlot instincts were the best I've ever seen. Joe also was an outstanding half-back in high school. He was known more for his defensive tackling ability. However, on Thanksgiving Day, as a sixteen-year-old senior, he had a great game offensively.

With the game scoreless in the fourth quarter, he bolted twenty-five yards to a first down on the three yard line. When Saints failed to score, the game ended in a zero-to-zero tie.

I remember one overcast evening, when the sun slid behind Pawtucket's skyline; Joe held my arm firmly with a grip and spoke softly, "Mike." His grip tightened, "Mike, playing football takes a lot of guts. You can't show any fear."

The innocence of my youth began to lift. I was a newly enrolled, fifteen-year-old sophomore at Saint Raphael. **Football was everything!** My ears were ready for my brother's advice. I was sharp.

"Yeah?"

"Mike, I'm gonna run at you as hard as I can with my knees high. You give me your best tackle and we'll see if you favor your nose."

Lawton's lawn was lush green and turning darker. Joe paced away at ten yards and turned sharply. Our shadows were cast long against the clapboard house. He started running in place, pumping his knees up and down like pistons. I snapped quickly to a position that resembled a bear cub standing up on his hind legs.

"Mike, here I come."

He squinted slowly as his eyes burned. We ran at each other like locomotives. We collided. The momentum carried us high in the air and sideways, into the side of the house. **OOH! BLAM**!! With the smell of turf in the air, we lay stunned in the soft grass. I slowly moved to feel my nose and quickly put my hand back to my side. He looked at me and put his arm around me as we walked down our street. A big smile came over his face. "You're all right, Mike! You're all right!"

* * * * *

I could see Zeke positioning himself to sneak a peek at my nose. "How many times did you break it?"

I ran my index finger and thumb down my nose and answered, "Three times, Zeke. The second time was in my junior year playing against Cranston."

Zeke interjected, 'Oh, the Green Wave.'

"Uh, huh. Their powerhouse team came to McCoy Stadium on Friday night. They were all dressed in green, with bright green helmets. They ran strong around the ends. As an outside linebacker on defense, I didn't make a tackle all night. Their blocking back and two guards came at me like a 'green wave.' I thought, *"Now I know where they got that name."*

"Our coach said, 'Mike, you're doing a good job of stripping the interference.'

"I was, however, taking a terrible beating and they were grinding me into the turf. On one of the running plays, I lifted my head, after being blocked to the ground. The running back hit me square in the nose with the toe of his cleat. I remember walking down Walcott Street in the rain on my way home that night. My whole body was aching, my nose was broken, and I had a dislocated thumb."

Zeke winced his eyes, "Your thumb? What happened to your thumb?"

"I dislocated it a few weeks earlier in a game against Rogers in Newport. A fast little back was right in front of me. In an instant, he tried to jump over my head. In the fury of the moment, I raised my arm, and my right thumb somehow jammed into his cleat."

In the next game against Central, my thumb was throbbing, swollen and stiff. The coach tightly taped a boxing glove to my hand to protect the injury. I ran out onto the field and a whistle blew. A ref motioned to Coach Farley. Coach tracked the powder from the lines as he darted to meet with the whistle blower. He returned shaking his head and motioned for me to come back.

"Off with the glove, Mike. We will have to come up with something else."

The assistant coach came to me with a block of foam and a roll of duct tape. After that, I guess you would say I stuck out like a sore thumb.

My nose was broken for the third time when I was a senior. I caught an elbow just above my facemask on the second play of the Thanksgiving Day game. I swallowed some blood, then shook my head from side to side, spraying blood all over Dr. Slocom's beige cashmere coat. He didn't care one bit about his coat. My injury was his only concern. Dr. Slocum stuffed cotton swabs deep into my nostrils to stop the bleeding. Then he gave Coach Farley the 'okay' signal and I was able to go back in the game.

Ralph drove me home after the game and said, "I'll stop by after dinner."

I climbed the steps and sprung onto the porch. Millie Crawley was standing in the doorway with a tall drink in her hand. She said, "Mike, I listened to the game on the radio. The announcer said you broke your nose. It's really swollen now."

"I'm fine, Millie."

Raising the glass on high, she handed me a highball (VO and ginger ale). "Congratulations on your Thanksgiving Day victory! I think you're old enough to have one good stiff drink!"

Raising the glass up high to salute her, I gestured, "Thanks a lot, Mil."

166

Millie lived next door to us on Sixth Street in Providence at the time when Joe and I were born. We moved to Lowden Street when I was two years old and Joe was three and a half, before my parents bought the house in Pawtucket. There were two things about Millie–her smile and her hairdo–they never changed. She was a teacher at Hope High School in Providence. She started teaching back in the late '30's and never changed her job. She never married. Millie and her mother were constant companions to my mother. We considered them part of our family. Millie spent most of her free time at our house, even after we moved to Pawtucket. She had a special fondness for us kids, as we did for her.

Millie was so tiny, she couldn't see over the steering wheel. She had to sit on two pillows to look through the space in the middle of her oversized steering wheel. Millie puttzed along the back roads at slow speeds and led a parade of frustrated motorists behind her. She avoided the new highway, Interstate 95, when it was built.

"Zeke, I'll never forget August 11, 1948. Millie took Joe and me on the train to Braves Field to see the Boston Braves play the Brooklyn Dodgers. I was almost ten years old. During the eighth inning, I nudged Millie and whispered, 'Do you realize that Vern Bickford has a no-hitter going?'

"She slowly nodded. I looked down and saw her holding her rosary beads as she twisted them with her fingers, silently saying the rosary. Her prayers must have been answered, because Vern Bickford ended up pitching a no-hitter for the Braves that day. What a thrill it was for us to be there. The Braves won 7 to 0, but the fans got a scare in the last inning. Roy Campanella, the Dodgers catcher, hit a long ball out to center field. Sam Jethroe, the National League Rookie of the Year, caught it on the dead run. Years later I saw the winning baseball from that memorable game. It was showcased in the Baseball Hall of Fame, in Cooperstown,

New York. Gazing at that ball, I relived every moment of the great day we had with Millie."

Zeke said, "I listened to the game on the radio, Mike, and remember it as if it was yesterday. Alvin Dark, the shortstop, also made some tremendous plays."

"Yeah, that was one of the all time great games in baseball."

Millie also took us to a Red Sox game that year. They played the Cleveland Indians and Joe and I talked to Satchel Paige, the Cleveland rookie. He was the second black player taken into the major leagues, right after Jackie Robinson. Some people said he was forty years old, others thought he was fifty years old. I remember looking at his spikes. He had the biggest feet I'd ever seen in my life. Millie's favorite player was Babe Ruth. She saw him play many times.

Millie came to our house on Thanksgiving every year. Her car always carried homemade Irish Bread. She'd also bring apple, blueberry, and mince pies for dessert. My favorite pie was blueberry, and I would swear I could smell it baking a week before Thanksgiving. Everyone else enjoyed the apple pie, but the mince pie was always left untouched at the end of the meal. Millie always took it back home with her. Ralph liked to kid me after she left with her mince pie. "Millie will be sharing that pie with her cat from now 'till Christmas!"

Thanksgiving was a memorable occasion. The family was always in good spirits. We reflected about football games, past and present, while enjoying the feast prepared by my mother and our unrelated family member, Millie. My younger brother Gary liked to recite a poem he learned in school:

TANKX GIVIN'
"Tankx given is the time for liven'.
Tankx given is cheerful and for given'.
Tankx given is when you eat a lot.
Tankx given is when the turkey's in the pot.
Tankx given's when you get fat.
Tankx given's when you take off your hat.
Tankx given is fun, for a seven-year-old."

Gary was a track star at Saints in the mid sixties. He could run. He set the school record in the hundred yard dash, at ten seconds flat, one tenth of a second faster than Jim Hennessy's track record, ten years earlier. Gary went to the University of Rhode Island on a track scholarship and graduated with an engineering degree, as did our older brother Joe.

Upon graduating and landing his first job, Gary felt he didn't want a career in engineering. He enjoyed playing the piano and realized that music was his first love. He enrolled in Rhode Island College, and took a four year course in Theatre. He was named in 'Who's Who in College'. After graduating with his second college degree, he formed a children's theatre company with Robert Zanni. Gary wrote, produced and performed in plays for children, focusing on productions for the handicapped. He won many awards for his work over the years, including 'Rhode Island Citizen of the year.' Gary is certainly the most artistically talented member of our family.

Chapter 11
You Can't Put an Old Head on Young Shoulders

My father was asleep in a soft rocking chair. I could hear the distant sound of running water in the kitchen sink. The dull clatter of Thanksgiving dishes being stacked away in the cupboard reverberated over the low static coming from the Motorola television. As Groucho Marx rolled from the top to the bottom of the screen, I realized that no one was watching the show. Even I was dozing off. I could hear my mother and Nancy talking about how delicious Millie's pies were, as they tried to unravel her baking secrets.

BEEP BEEP–BEEP BEEP! Five seconds later the front door flew open–It was Ralph. "Come on, Mike–Let's go!"

My father slowly peered through his heavy eyelids. "Where 'ya going, Mike?"

I perked up. "Where we goin', Ralph?"

"Downtown to see what's goin' on."

171

I threw on my corduroy sports jacket. It was cool from hanging near the door as I slid my arms in. As we pulled away from the curb, a chirp came from the tires. "Where we goin' Ralph?" I asked.

He replied, "*Roma Italiano.*"

"The Italian Club?"

"Ya, we can get a drink, and we've got a plan to make. We've got a big plan to make."

We galloped down the creaky stairs of the dungeon-esque club. As we pushed open the heavy door and entered the dimly lit room, we were greeted by the heavy aroma of cigarette smoke and pasta sauce. We slid silently past the bar and found a corner table. Muffled conversations were all around us. Ralph lit a cigarette and exhaled as he looked me in the eye.

He leaned forward and said, "Football season is over. It's party time, pal. It's party time!"

A serious excitement gripped me. "Yeah?"

A waiter appeared. "What are you guys having?"

"Cutty Sark on the rocks. Mike, here, will have a highball." The waiter walked briskly away from the table. "Thanks, Ralph. That's the only drink I know."

"Well, Mike, Saturday night we're gonna change all that." He took a drag of his cigarette. "Parents are gone." He took another drag. "Beach house in Florida." He snapped the ash from his cigarette. "I convinced Digger Leary that this party will go down in Pawtucket history as a colossal event. It'll make Digger famous with the fillies. It will set the standard for all future parties!"

"For Christ's sake, Ralph; he lives in a funeral home!"

172

"Yeah, a very big funeral home. Perfect for a party." Ralph continued, "So far, we've got ten guys that are in."

The stoic waiter slapped heavy, oak coasters onto the table in front of us. "Highball?"

"Here," I said as my voice cracked, then cleared my throat and repeated deeply, "Here." Ralph took a gulp of his Cutty Sark as the waiter drifted away.

"Girls?" I asked.

Ralph's grin began to grow, "Oh, ya...oh, ya."

A guy in the back of the room with a loud stammering voice bellowed above all the other sounds, "Happy Tanksgivin'–Happy Tanksgivin'."

"And beer and hard stuff, Ralph?" Ralph finished his scotch quickly, then slowly and deliberately placed the glass directly in the center of the coaster. Methodically, his finger tips released the glass. "Booze...oh, ya....but of course! With ten guys chipping in, we've already got enough liquor stockpiled to fill the Ten Mile River!"

"Sounds as if you've got everything worked out."

"Yeah. We're all set for a big night of action."

On the day of the party, Ralph's liquor catch was ready for transportation to Digger's house. He spent the morning loading up his trunk. But at noon, Ralph got a frantic call from Digger.

"I'm sick as a dog. The party's off!"

Ralph's panicked voice blasted into the phone. "No! No! You can't do this to me!"

Digger responded in a hoarse voice, "I can't help it. Sorry, Ralph."

Utterly disappointed, Ralph sighed a deep breath and phoned the girls, one by one. He was surprised to learn that most of them didn't plan to show up when they found out that Ralph had an overabundance of liquor for the party.

"Mike, what a bummer this has turned out to be!"

All the guys were disappointed but assured Ralph that they could do it another time, when the opportunity presented itself.

Later that evening, I was at the Spa with Jim Buckley and a couple of other friends, Biggie Bloom and Lorne Moore. Ralph walked in, looking dejected. He slid into the booth next to me, and tapped his cigarette against the back of his hand. He kept his head down and didn't speak for a while, then his face brightened, "Why don't we just stop by to see how Digger's feeling? Maybe a shot or two will cure his cold!"

Buckley casually mentioned, "Yeah, after all, Ralph still has all the liquor in his trunk." Biggie and Lorne nodded in agreement, as Buckley continued, "Yeah, maybe he already feels better!"

When Digger answered the door, he looked awful. His neck was tilted to one side and his red nose was running. His argyle socks extended five inches beyond his toes and he was wearing his father's white, monogrammed bathrobe. He smelled like he had just consumed a whole bottle of cough medicine.

Buckley said, "Geez, Digger, this place smells like a hospital!"

In a muffled voice Digger said, "I feel like I'm going to die. Hey guys, you don't have to go home, but you can't stay here."

Ralph said, "How 'bout if we just stay out on the porch?"

Digger straightened up, "NO!"

"Oh, come on, Digger."

Rubbing his sore throat, Digger wearily answered, "Well, okay, but stay out of the house, so I can rest."

Ralph shot back with a smile and a flick of his wrist, "No problem!"

We emptied Ralph's trunk and then we all piled onto the screened porch. Disturbed by our voices and unable to sleep, Digger joined us, and before long, the cough medicine combined with a few drinks, sent him reeling. He was drunk as a skunk.

Carloads of gate crashers started to pull up to the house. 'Buzz' Harris, a Tolman dropout, said, "We overheard you at the Spa. Mind if we join you?"

Ralph answered, "No problem."

The scratchy blast of a Raytheon portable transistor radio was now at maximum volume and everyone had to speak in a loud voice. Digger was having the time of his life.

Ralph hollered, "Feeling better, Digger?"

Digger snapped an argyle sock off the end of his foot and swung it in the air. "YA HOO, YA HOO!"

All of a sudden, **SMASH**!!! A bottle of beer broke on the porch...then another...and another...until brown glass was all over the floor. The smell of beer hops filled the porch. The mixture of beer and glass carried into the kitchen and all through the carpeted rooms as everyone sloshed around. One of the Tolman guys wanted to fight Buckley. When his belligerent harassment finally got to Buckley, he was ready to take him on, but the aggressor backed down. It's a good thing they didn't end up in a fight. It could have been a disaster with all the broken glass.

One guy ran upstairs, emptied all the dresser drawers, and completely ransacked one of the bedrooms. Then he found the brand new, automatic, two-tone green RCA 45 record player. He threw *that* out the second floor window. It bounced off a shrub and landed on the lawn in pieces. Candles were broken over the piano. Every glass in the kitchen was broken. A bottle went flying through a living room window, and curtains were torn down. Overflowing ashtrays were tipped over, and the smell of stale cigarette butts and cigars stunk up the whole house. To this day, I thank God that the four funeral parlor rooms were locked.

Digger was really feeling his oats and started doing pushups...99, 100, 101. When he couldn't lift his body another time, Buckley and some of the other cheerleaders hoisted him on their shoulders then ran through the house, and cheered him as if he was a hero, yelling, "Yeah, Digger! Yeah, Digger!" as a Tolman guy danced by with a lampshade over his head.

A loud crash came from the kitchen. It was the first of several to follow. Guys were running across the kitchen floor and diving on the table, knocking beer bottles over like bowling pins. A motor roared in the garage. It was Mr. Leary's 1955 Porsche 360 Carrera. Fine china rattled behind glass doors as the rumble peaked.

Somebody yelled, "Lenny–Lenny–Nooooo...," as the tires smoked and screeched down the street. The keys from the kitchen hook along with the Porsche and Lenny Wilkinson were gone.

I raised my voice, "Hey Ralph! Get over here! This is getting wild!" People left to try to find Lenny.

Zeke thought back and said, "You know, Mike, everyone in

Pawtucket knew that car. It was the only one like it in the city. It sure was a beauty! That guy caused havoc in it that night. He tore around the graveyard and did a lot of damage here. In fact, this very plot was dug up the most, and it took me weeks to get it looking good again. The ruts were so deep I had to reseed the whole plot."

"Gee, Zeke. I didn't know *that* happened during his joy ride. Lenny returned the car to Mr. Leary's garage and hightailed it outta there."

Jim, Ralph, Digger and I had to sober up *fast*! I wasn't about to take any excuses when I said, "We need to get our act together."

Ralph said, "Okay, but let me have some coffee and a smoke first, then we can fix up this place."

Buckley assessed the situation and said, "Holy smokes! We musta' done a couple a thousand dollars worth of damage."

Looking around I knew someone had to take control. I said, "Ya, we'd better all stay here 'till we figure out what we should do."

We gulped black coffee and threw cold water on our faces in an effort to sober up. Ralph sat up in a plush chair smoking one cigarette after another while the rest of us tried to get a little shuteye, sleeping off and on through what was left of the night.

At daybreak, Digger slowly woke up in the corner. As he lifted his head, his hair stood straight up as if he had slept in an electric chair. His father's white bathrobe now looked like a tan beer stained bar rag. He popped himself to his feet like a newborn calf and with horror in his eyes looked around at the destruction that surrounded him. "Oh, boy." He said looking around again, "Ohh bouy." The silence of the dawn was broken by Digger when he saw his new record player in pieces on the lawn. He bellowed, slurring his words, "YOU SONS OF BITCHES! I TOLD YOU I WAS SICK!"

Ralph admonished, "Digger! Digger! Calm down and get over here. We've got work to do! Now get in here! Cut out screaming like a jackass. For Christ's sake, Digger, what'll the neighbors think?"

Digger slumped his way into the house with his broken record player under his arm. Ralph looked around and slowly pulled his last cigarette out of his wrinkled pack. He blinked sharply and looked around with the unlit cigarette dangling from the corner of his mouth.

"Break out the mop, the broom, the dustpan and brush, and the sewing kit. Get the scrubber, the stain removers, the bleach, the vacuum cleaner and any kind of glue that you have in the house. Mike, split the house up into separate zones and get movin' on whipping this place back into shape. Wake up Buckley and tell 'im to get his ass in gear. I have a phone call to make."

I heard Ralph say, "Yes, yes. This is an absolute emergency. Please get here as fast as you can."

Ten minutes later, a van with "La Glass" painted on the side panels came to a screeching halt in front of the house. A man with curly black hair rushed into the house. His white jump suit had the name 'Lucien' embroidered on the pocket. He looked around. "Whew," he whistled. "HOLY COW! You boys really had a time last night! How many windows are we looking at here now?"

I piped up, "One on the porch, one in the kitchen and one in the living room behind the piano. How long you figure?"

Lucien looked at his watch and said, "I should be able to do it in about an hour."

We worked in the house all day. The floors and rugs cleaned up pretty darn good, although a few beer stains didn't come out. We became adept at hand sewing and hanging drapes and Digger did a superb job gluing his record player back together...It even worked!

I glanced around the room and said, "Looks pretty good!"

Ralph added, "Mr. and Mrs. Leary will never know we had a party!"

"Oh, I don't know about that, Ralph," I said in a pessimistic tone. "The Leary's will still know there was trouble brewing while they were gone. The piano's marred, the record player's glued together, and slivers of glass glitter every now and then. There's no way we're gonna get out of this one scott free!"

Digger scuffed his slippers along the soggy carpeting, "Thanks a lot. I told you guys I was sick."

Ralph put his hand on Digger's shoulder. "Don't worry, Dig. You'll be fine. I'm only a phone call away."

The funeral home was now quiet, except for the chug of warm water splashing in the white porcelain tub. A cracking hiss echoed from the hallway and then, softly, the voice on Digger's favorite new record began to sing *Tweedle Dee*.

Digger carefully lowered his aching and sore body into the tub. He closed his eyes and continued singing along with 'Her Nibs', Georgia Gibbs. He squeezed a yellow rubber ducky. Shampoo had been lathered to make his hair stand straight and he began to feel the healing effects of the warm bubble bath. The world had seemed to slow and the steam from the water calmed the room with a soft fog. Then slam! The door flew open! "DAD! Da–Dad!" Digger stammered.

Mr. Leary was blocking the doorway like an over stoked

179

furnace. His fury energized the room. "You're–you're home er–er early Dad?" Digger gasped. It was apparent that Mr. Leary had a walk through the house. Our clean up efforts and the disinfectant had failed.

Two days later, I saw Ralph at the Spa. Ralph's tanned complexion had turned a pasty white when I greeted him. "Mike, Digger's father cornered him while he was in the tub. He got a wicked whipping with a strap. His folks were so mad they left the house and haven't been back."

I said, "I bet they're at their summer house at Bonnet Shores. My God, Ralph, this is bad, real bad. How's Digger now?"

"Not good, Mike, and Digger's father visited my mother at work and told her I had a party at his house. Mr. Leary said there was extensive damage done and he has decided to press charges."

But Ralph never did hear from Mr. Leary. They must have had a change of heart when they realized their son was as much to blame as anyone else. He was at the right place at the wrong time. My name was never mentioned. I don't know why. Jim was also off the hook and so were all of the other guys. Digger must have taken the whipping for all of us.

Buckley was concerned because he had just been in trouble with his parents, the school and Reginald 'Miggs' Hallihan, the Pawtucket Chief of Police. The school reported him missing, along with the chief's son, Howie. They skipped school and headed for Boston in Howie's car to see the Burlesque Show in Scully Square. When they reached the Rhode Island border on their return, they were greeted with a police escort, right back to Chief Hallihan's house. Buckley's parents were notified and he knew one more incident like Digger Leary's party would cause hell with his parents.

When I got home, the dull lingering hangover mellowed my spirit. Soon the house began to smell like fresh brewed coffee. My piano teacher, Mrs. Danning, was poised next to me on the piano stool teaching me classical music. A nervous disorder made her shake. A cup of coffee rattled as she attempted to place it on top of the piano.

My father would always say, "Mike, give us a little tune. Go tickle the ivories."

That's when I would play boogie woogie. Mrs. Danning, however, wanted me to play like Liberace, but I wanted to play like Fats Domino. The prim and proper lady handed me a new sheet of music.

"Oh, Mrs. Danning, I think I'll really enjoy playing this song—*Two Garters!*"

She pounded her fist on the keys and whacked my fingers with a pencil, and yelled, "Mrs. Ryan. MRS. RYAN! PLEASE COME IN HERE!"

My mother dropped her ladle into the pot of pea soup she was making and rushed in. My head was still pounding from the night before, as Mrs. Danning gushed, "Where is your son's mind? He's talking about garters! The name of this song is *Two Guitars!*"

My mother gave me a quizzical look as I winked at her through a bloodshot eye. She shrugged and returned to the kitchen and added the ham bone to her boiling pot. Beep, Beep. Mr. Danning was waiting outside for his wife as he did at the end of each lesson. Beep, Beep.

"Is that pea soup with the nice ham bone ready, Mrs. Ryan?" Ella, the seasonal cleaning lady asked. With a pleasant smile, she took a whiff and said, "Umm."

She was a tall woman with sharp German features and a plump figure. Boy, did she enjoy my mother's homemade soup. A monocle attached to a chain hung from her neck and was submerged between her large bosom. She searched for it when she wanted to read the newspaper during her lunch break. She loved to hear me play the piano.

"Michael, do you know any romantic French songs?"

I answered, "I sure do, Ella." But the only thing *French* I knew was the name Letourneau; the Letourneau family lived on our street. I sang, *"Latourneau La La La Tourneau Le Tourneau."*

I just repeated the words over and over while changing a few chords on the piano. Ella gasped and put the newspaper down and dropped the monocle, which was immediately devoured by her cleavage. She put her head back, rolled her eyes, and wagged her tongue, as she sang along with me *"La La La Latourneau, Le Le Le Tourneau."* She wiped her eyes and said, "Oh Michael… that's so beautiful!"

I smiled and thought, *"I guess I just made her day!"*

The phone rang. It was Ralph. "Mike, meet me at the Spa."

I quipped, "I'm off, like a pair of honeymoon pajamas!"

182

Chapter 12
Let's Take It and Make It

Ralph and I were talking to Dominick 'The Duke' Moradian at the Spa. His brown pork pie hat and herring bone sports jacket gave him the look of Gene Hackman as *Popeye Doyle* in the movie, *The French Connection.*

"Hey, Duke, Duke," a voice called out from across the Spa.

It was Chet O'Dell, in his Pawtucket West Rangers jacket. He scurried up to 'The Duke,' in anticipation.

'The Duke' said, "Hey, Chet! You look pretty sharp in that new jacket." Smiling, he answered, "Well, Duke. A captain has to look good for his team. Any news?"

"Looks like Hofstra is very interested in you pal."

'The Duke' was a fixture, leaning against the west end zone goal post at all our home games. He was well liked by everyone and helped a lot of high school athletes get into top colleges. In my class alone, we had several players who received scholarships that they would not have been awarded without his help. Ron Kornfeld went to Northwestern, Charlie Palumbo was a star end at Brown University, Jim Hennessy entered Boston College on a football scholarship, Bill Allwood enrolled in Providence College and then Xavier University. Jackie Shannon went to Brigham Young University and Cal Poly in San Luis Obispo, California.

There were many other athletes in our city who benefited from 'The Duke's' help. He took players to colleges and set up meetings with head coaches. He presented detailed information on each player's ability. He brought films of games and recommendations from the high school coaches. He knew the background of each college and was an expert on their sports programs. 'The Duke' never received any money for doing this, he just loved helping athletes.

During the fourth quarter of one of my Saturday morning games, he asked Coach Farley if he could take me to Boston. That afternoon Boston College would be playing the University of Detroit at Fenway Park. We were beating Classical 40–0 and I was on the sidelines. Our reserves were playing the fourth quarter, so the coach allowed me to leave before the end of the game. Soon after we arrived, 'The Duke' scanned the game program. He noticed the name of a Detroit tackle, John Moradian. Boston College won in a tight game, but we headed straight for the Detroit dressing room. 'The Duke' found Moradian and introduced himself.

"My name's Dominick Moradian. They call me 'The Duke,' he boasted in his best Howard Cosell voice. "You played *one hell of a game*, Moradian." As the big football player stood up to shake his hand, 'The Duke' said, "Two great hands meet." Dominick continued with his imitation of the famous sports announcer. Chomping on an unlit juicy stogie, he said, "Meet lineman Mike Ryan. He's from Pawtucket, Rhode Island."

We went to the Boston College locker room and met Head Coach Mike Novak. Then we had dinner in Brookline at Jack and Marion's Restaurant. He treated me like a king. It was one heck of a great day! 'The Duke' had no formal training or credentials. It's amazing how convincing he was to the coaches. He was certainly a colorful figure around Pawtucket. He was quite a prankster and a jokester, but he was also suave, capable and persuasive.

'The Duke' strutted into the Darlington Spa early one Saturday during football season and helped Rocky take off his wool knit sweater. "You won't be needing this inside, Rock."

Rocky shook his matted fur and licked 'The Duke's' hand. 'The Duke' sat down and told us he ran into George LaValley, a former St. Raphael quarterback and Boston College linebacker. George told 'The Duke' that he was now coaching for St. Mary's High School in Brookline, Massachusetts and was scheduled to play a key game against Brighton.

Ralph suggested, "Why don't we go up there and give George a little support?"

Billy Swanson and Ron Kornfield kicked open the front door of the Spa and headed to the car. We played on Friday night against Westerly, so Ron and I were free to go. St. Mary's won a thriller (14 to 7) and George was elated to see us there.

Ralph, Ron, Billy, 'The Duke,' Rocky and I drove back from Brookline on the Fenway. Cars whizzed by like bullets. Ralph suddenly yelled out "STOP THE CAR!"

I jammed on the brakes and yelled, "What's the matter?"

He repeated, "STOP THE CAR NOW!" I pulled over and the idling motor rumbled. Ralph flung the door open and vanished.

185

Ron let out a big sigh. "For Christ's sake, where's Ralph going now?"

'The Duke' yelled, "Shut the door before Rocky jumps out and gets hit by a car." Rocky leaped from Duke's lap and crashed into the window as I slammed the door shut.

I could see Ralph on a porch gathering up a huge pumpkin. I said, "We're parked on the side of the road so he can steal a pumpkin."

I glanced in the rearview mirror and saw Ralph huffing and puffing as he ran toward the car. I took off slowly keeping just ahead of him so he couldn't catch us. We heard someone yelling. Ralph looked back and saw an irate man chasing him. All of a sudden, Ralph just stopped running and came to an abrupt halt. He caressed the top of the pumpkin and then carefully placed it on the ground. I stopped the car just long enough for Ralph to jump into the back seat. Then I stepped on the gas pedal and high-tailed it out of there.

Billy and Ron were in hysterics and I said, "I can't believe that pumpkin didn't get smashed, Ralph."

Ralph countered, "Auh, I couldn't ruin Halloween for that guy's kid. I was just tryin' to have some fun with you guys."

We all chimed in together, "Ralph, we can't take you anywhere!" Rocky barked in agreement.

I remember the day 'The Duke' told Ralph and me he went out with the daughter of the president of the Stetson Hat Company when he was in the Navy.

Ralph said, "You're full of crap Dominick!"

Unfazed 'The Duke' said, "Believe me, Mac; it's true."

186

"Ah, it's baloney. I'll bet 'ya twenty bucks," Ralph countered.

"Make that another twenty!" I added to sweeten the pot.

Dominick stretched his neck up. "Everyone in the car!"

Ralph lit a cigarette, "Where we heading, Duke?"

"Philadelphia, Pennsylvania!"

"You're on!" Ralph retorted, as we closed the car door. We made sure Dominick didn't leave our side when we stopped for gas and a soda. Ralph watched him like a hawk so he couldn't make any phone calls to set up a scheme. After eight hours on the road, we pulled up to a big mansion near Villanova University. Dominick rang the doorbell.

Ralph said to me, "Boy, this guy's got balls!"

A pretty girl in her late twenties answered the door. When she saw Dominick, she yelled, "DADDY, DADDY–'THE DUKE'S IN TOWN!"

Ralph's mouth popped open in disbelief. We were invited in for the night. The elegant house featured walls of glass that revealed a panoramic view of a beautiful golf course. We were in luxury. Dominick related story after unbelievable story.

The morning sun shone through the sliding glass doors in the palatial guest room. I stood looking out at the lush green. A rooftop window in the vaulted ceiling opened up views to the white, billowy, fair weather clouds overhead. I relaxed in comfort in a grand king size bed made of rich mahogany. A bowl of scented potpourri sat on the nightstand.

When we headed down the steps toward the car Ralph remarked, "We owe you big time for this one, Duke!"

He smirked, "No, you owe me twenty bucks apiece."

We could never be sure if Dominick was telling the whole truth about all of his stories but we never questioned him again about his far-fetched escapades. After the Pennsylvania incident, in our eyes, he was validated.

* * * * *

Ralph and I loved going to all of the sports events in our area. We usually didn't have the money for admission, so we devised four or five ways to sneak into McCoy Stadium. We enjoyed the challenge of it all, but some of our methods were dangerous.

"Zeke, do you remember the winding cement walkway leading into McCoy Stadium?"

"Sure I do. I've been up and down that walkway many times."

I continued, "One way in was to have one guy sit on the lower walkway railing, while another stood on his shoulders. A third guy, who was already in the stands, could then lean over and pull the second guy up into the stadium. That last stretch was about six or seven feet!"

"Yeah, I remember seeing kids do that. I was always afraid someone would get hurt."

"I guess *we* were just lucky, but one time Jackie Barron slipped off Fuzzy Fusco's shoulders. Jackie landed on the side of his foot and broke his ankle."

There was one other circular walkway entrance where the gate was always locked. A pipe wrapped in barbed wire extended out from the fence, discouraging illegal entry. If you were careful, you could step out on the pipe and go around the barbed wire. There was always the danger that the barbs would tear into you. If you slipped off the pipe, there was a twenty foot drop to the pavement below. The one time we gained entrance at this location, Ralph left a piece of his khaki pants on the barbed wire.

Another time, we waited behind the scoreboard until the National Anthem ended. The policemen were still standing at attention. We ran across the field to the baseball screen and scooted behind it so we could climb up into the stadium. Everyone was able to get to the top of the screen, step across to a railing, and duck into the first row–except Biffa McFearson. He bolted up the *front* side of the screen and climbed up to the foul ball netting. With no place to go, he climbed back down. The policemen were waiting for him and promptly escorted him off the field, as the spectators gave him a big cheer.

The next time Ralph spied Biffa, he commented to me, "Look, there goes McFearson, Pawtucket's wrong way Corrigan."

One night, we wanted to see the Rhode Island Reds, a semi-pro hockey team, play at the Providence Arena. We met up with some savvy kids that lived in the neighborhood. They had an aluminum ladder that they used to scale the ledges on the side of the building.

"You guys came prepared," Ralph observed.

I chimed in, "Yeah; mind if we join you?"

One of the burley guys nodded, and we all climbed to the roof, then pulled the ladder up behind us. There were glass panels on the slanted roof. Ralph scratched the green paint off one of the panels. We could see the teams warming up on the ice below.

I looked at Ralph and said, "Looks like the only way we can get in from here is to *parachute*."

Ralph answered while puffing on his cigarette, "There's gotta be an easier way than this. The only way we're gonna get down from here is to retrace our steps."

As we backed down the ladder, I noticed a partially open window on the first tier and said, "I'm gonna check *this* out."

I carefully raised the window and whispered, "Hey, guys! This is the Reds locker room! There's no one in there."

Ralph peered in and gave the command, "Let's take it and make it!"

I climbed in, clung to the sill for a moment then dropped to the floor. When Ralph was ready to lower himself, two security guards burst into the room. They didn't see me because I was behind the door when they stormed in. I slipped into the stadium, but Ralph was still outside. I eventually went outside, found Ralph, and told him, "I guess it's time for our old standby!"

This involved moving ahead of an older fan who was waiting in line. We made sure four or five people were between us. At the gate we'd nonchalantly say, "Our uncle has the tickets," as we pointed our thumbs back toward the unsuspecting guy. By the time the man got to the gate, we were inside the stadium, bolting into the crowd. This ploy always worked because the ticket collector couldn't leave the gate unattended. At the time, getting into the events without paying was a sport in itself. We were always ready to take it and make it.

* * * * *

After football season was over, I had a short stint on the basketball team. As a sophomore, I started every game on the Junior Varsity, alternating with Ray Oney. Ray always ended up playing more than me. I was on the Varsity Team in my junior year, playing very little, but I expected to play a little more in my senior year. Our football coach, Mr. Farley, also coached the basketball team.

During a scrimmage with North Attleboro, I went after a loose ball that was going out of bounds. Leaping for the ball on the dead run, I turned in the air, and threw the ball back on the court, as I hit two big doors at the end of the gym. The doors flew open with a bang and I cruised through them, sliding down the long corridor. I landed in a sprawled position on the slippery floor. When I got up, I casually strolled over to a bubbler, took a long gulp then ran back onto the court as the Saints cheering section gave me a standing ovation. Coach Farley just stood there shaking his head and looking perplexed.

In another pre-season game against Pawtucket West, we were loosing by a good margin. Their star player, Norm Dorsey, was dribbling and weaving through our team, making us look foolish. He could out-dribble the best of them with his superb skills. Coach Farley put me in the game and said, "Stop Dorsey."

I thought it would be easy, but when Dorsey came down the court, he reversed directions as he dribbled behind his back. He blew right by me. The second time, he dribbled down the court near the sideline. I ran at him low and threw a cross body block that caught him just below the knees. It sent him flying up into the stands. He jolted back to the court, swinging his arms wildly in the air, almost inciting a riot. The refs threw me out of the game. The next week, I started looking for a job. I realized that working was a better option for me.

Saints had great talent on the basketball team. Bill Allwood was an All-State basketball player. He could have been All-State in baseball and football, too. He was the best athlete at the school. In his junior year, he was late coming out for the football team. The good helmets were taken and Bill was issued a soft old leather helmet that gave little protection. Early on, he suffered a concussion that kept him out for the rest of the year.

In his senior year, Bill elected to only play basketball. He averaged twenty-five points a game. A national sports magazine rated him one of the five best high school basketball players in the country. Bill was left handed and could shoot jump shots from outside the perimeter. He was extremely fast and versatile on driving lay-ups. He led the fast break and could pass the ball, as if he had eyes behind his head, just like the renowned Bob Cousy of the Boston Celtics. Bill went to Cousy's Basketball Camp during the summers of 1955 and 1956.

One day, Bill was asked to be the equipment manager for five Celtics team members. On a warm summer night, they traveled to Hyannis, Massachusetts, where they played against five New York Knicks players, in an 'under the lights' exhibition game. Al Bartels, a Knicks player, hit his head on the hoop rim during warm up drills. He was taken to Cape Cod Hospital for stitches. Bob Cousy asked Bill Allwood to be the fifth player for the Knicks, replacing Bartels. Bill played in the backcourt with the renowned New York McGuire brothers and scored seventeen points. When the game went into overtime, Cousy jokingly told Bill, "If the Knicks win, you won't be going back to *my* camp."

The Celtics finally prevailed. Bill was thrilled to have had the opportunity to play with nine professionals. The next year he was a point guard playing with Lenny Wilkins on an undefeated freshmen team at Providence College. Lenny became an All-American and starred in the NBA as a player and coach.

* * * * *

My sister dated Joe Moret, a freshman on the Providence College basketball team. Nancy had a part time job in a dental office and earned a little money. Joe asked to borrow a hundred dollars and promised to pay her back within a month. As the weeks went by, Nancy realized Joe didn't intend to *ever* pay her.

I came home from school one day and found her crying, "Joe won't pay the money he owes me...and besides...we just broke up!"

I was appalled and became angry. "Why, that no good... where is he? Where does he live?"

She sniffled, "In the dorm on Smith Street."

Later that evening, when I rang the bell at 156 Smith Street, a student answered. "I want to see Joe Moret," I demanded.

Joe appeared at the door. In a calmer voice, I said, "Come out on the porch so we can talk.

"Who are you?" he asked with a quizzical look on his face.

"I'm Nancy's brother, Mike," I continued, as I moved right up under his chin. "You borrowed a hundred bucks from my sister. Pay her back."

He looked down at me and said "I'm not going to give her anything," as he pushed me backwards.

"Oh, NO?" I retorted.

I had to jump up to hit this six-foot-six basketball player. My right fist only grazed his head as he turned. He ran inside the house and locked the heavy, wooden door with a glass insert. Furious, I slammed into the door with my whole body. I knew I could bust right through that door if I kept pounding it with all my might. Looking scared, he picked up an empty beer bottle from a trash barrel near the door. I thought Joe could have knocked me into next week, but we *both* knew I was on a mission!

I glared at him and demanded, "You better have that money at my house by noon tomorrow—or I'll be back!"

The next day, Nancy noticed an envelope sticking out from under our front door mat. It was addressed to her and contained ten crisp ten dollar bills

Chapter 13
The Salesman Always Rings Twice

Singer hired me! I answered an ad in the *Pawtucket Times* for a part-time sales job at Singer Sewing Machine Company, in downtown Pawtucket. It was too cold to caddy and I wasn't playing any sports. I could work after school and on weekends to fill the gap.

During the interview, the manager asked, "Do you know how to sell, son?"

In a positive manner, I answered, "Yes, sir. I've had experience selling Bibles–beautiful, leather-bound Bibles."

He took a shiny, Parker ball point pen out of his striped shirt pocket and handed it to me, saying, "Here, kid, sell this to me."

I thought for a moment then asked, "Do you have another pen?"

He opened his desk drawer and handed me another one,

then tilted back in his chair and pulled his tie taut under the gold clip. I could feel a little perspiration under my arms, but my mind was sharp.

I lifted the pen in my right hand and spoke. "This pen is guaranteed for a lifetime, to never run dry. The other pen is nice; however, it will run out of ink by the end of this year. Both pens cost fifty cents but the pen in my left hand will cost you more because you will have to replace it every year. You'll lose the Parker pen before it runs dry." Appreciating the smile that came over his face, I asked, "Should I put in an order for one pen, sir, or would you also like a second pen for your wife?"

With a wide grin, the manager replied, "You're hired!"

While we were shaking hands at the door, I still had one more thought in mind. "My best friend, Ralph McGreavey, sold Bibles with me. Do you think we could work as a team? I know Pawtucket like the back of my hand and Ralph used to live in Central Falls. We could cover the whole area for you."

The manager's eyebrows lifted. "You can split the territory with your friend any way you want, Mike."

"Great idea! And, sir; just wait 'till you meet Ralph!"

Ralph was excited when I told him that I had secured a job for both of us, selling sewing machines at a high commission rate. After a day of orientation, we felt confident that we were ready for the next phase of our training…learning the ins and outs of a sewing machine. The training room located in back of the retail store was filled with sewing machines and attachments. The doorway leading to the back room was covered with a long, gray curtain. The room was well lit, with florescent light bulbs that buzzed overhead. The strong smell of the beige paint on the newly manufactured machines was evident throughout the room. A small storage room was filled with old-fashioned, used machines taken in as trade-ins. There was only one small section for the repair of the older black machines. The ladies of Pawtucket and the surrounding communities were anxious to own the latest wave of new, modern sewing machines that were introduced in 1955.

We studied the literature and learned how to screw on the pressure foot, the buttonhole maker and zig-zag attachment. We learned threading. We learned to straight stitch, top stitch, bottom stitch and double stitch. Then we learned how to reinforce stitches. After two days, Ralph had had it!

"For Christ sake, Mike, my Aunt Florence should be doing this kind of work! When are we going to do some selling?"

I looked at our schedule. "Hang in there, Ralph. Tomorrow we're going to the New England headquarters in Middletown, Connecticut."

Ralph snickered, "Well, at least things are looking up… anything's better than this!" Ralph lit his cigarette, puckered his lips and slowly pushed out smoke rings. "My car didn't start today so we're gonna hafta' thumb."

Dressed in sport jackets, white shirts and ties, we headed out to Armistice Boulevard to hitch a ride to Middletown. We were picked up right away and got there in record time. Sales trainees from all over New England arrived to learn how to operate the new sewing machines that were lined up row after row throughout the entire first floor of the building. Instructors were positioned at the end of each aisle, ready to assist anyone who needed help. After they explained the functions of the machines, and showed us again how to sew a straight stitch, how to lift the pressure foot and all the other basics of sewing, they demonstrated how to use each attachment. Then they provided a large piece of material to practice sewing on. Ralph was pissed.

"Mike! Come here! Not another lesson on the machine! I know all about this stuff!"

I shrugged my shoulders and said, "Augh, Ralph; pay attention! We *have* to know what we're selling."

"I'll be right back. I need another cigarette."

A short time later, I smiled as I glanced over at Ralph and saw him making a perfect straight stitch. He even seemed to be enjoying himself. The instructor looked pleased with Ralph's progress. I carefully guided the fabric, progressing to the wavy stitch with ease. The contrast between the white thread on the navy blue fabric made it easy to see if we made any mistakes. Soon we were both working the machines like pros, threading the needle, adjusting the sole plate and sewing fabrics together. The various stitches became automatic, but we still had trouble with the attachments once in a while. When it was time to work with the zig-zag attachment, Ralph showed a little apprehension.

I was still screwing the attachment onto my machine, when I heard Ralph scream, "YEOOOH! Son of a bitch!"

The room became silent. Every machine stopped and everyone stood up and glared at Ralph. His finger was pinned under the pressure foot! He hollered out, "The needle went right through my finger! God damn finger, right through! This darned thing zigged when I thought it would zag! For Christ sakes, it zigged when it should have zagged! Son of a bitch."

Just then, the door swung open and the Pawtucket manager came in to check on his two new salesmen. The instructor was manually reversing the round wheel to draw the needle back up and out of Ralph's fingertip.

I looked up, "Oh, sir. I'd like you to meet Ralph McGreavey."

With beads of sweat rolling off his nose, Ralph said, "Hi–just a scratch."

Blood was spurting out all over the machine and the fabric he was practicing on. Ralph clamped his finger to shut off the spray. He quickly stuck his finger in his mouth, trying to draw the blood, while biting hard on his fingertip. Finally, it was bandaged with a big wad of gauze and tape. "Mike, look at this! Will you just look at this? My finger's the size of a baseball. How am I gonna thread a needle?"

When we got home, Joe and Jim were in the living room waiting for us. Low and behold, little did we know they held the key to Ralph's predicament. Joe beamed, "Have we got a deal for you guys! We're gonna sell stainless steel cookware!"

Jim piped in, "A twenty-five piece set sells for just $299 and we make fifty dollars a sale!"

Ralph said in a serious tone, "First sewing, now cooking."

I laughed at the thought of him trying to cook after his experience with sewing. Jim said, "You won't be cooking, you just need to show it to prospective customers."

Ralph was looking for just about anything to get him out of selling sewing machines and this sounded good to him! "Count me in!" he bellowed. "I don't think I can get hurt showing cookware!"

Proudly Joe and Jim dragged over a heavy suitcase, opened it up, and gave us a professional demonstration. The shiny stainless steel cookware set was comprised of various sized polished pans. There were one quart, two quart, and three quart pots, with bakelite handles. There was a large frying pan, a small frying pan, an eight quart Dutch oven, and an egg poacher that was equipped with an eight cup insert disc. Also contained in the package were a colander and a double boiler. Matching covers, with bakelite knobs completed the set.

Jim stated, "It's the top grade of triple-ply stainless steel cookware on the market and it comes with a lifetime guarantee."

Joe's eyes gleamed as he said, "If the customer buys our cookware the first time we show it to them, they have a choice of a five piece bake ware set, or a three bowl mixing set, as a bonus. We call it our '*first call special*.'"

When they finished, I said, "Well, Ralph. We might as well stick together, pal."

A few days later, Ralph was rapping on my aluminum porch door. **BANG–BANG Bang–Bang–Bang**. I opened up the door. Ralph was holding a large frying pan in his hand. "Look, Mike. It's here." We jumped in his car and sped off to practice our demonstrations on his Aunt Florence.

After cutting out the engagements listed in the *Pawtucket Times*, we made appointments by phone, or just went to houses '*cold turkey*.' We split up the leads. Ralph covered Central Falls and some of the surrounding towns. I concentrated on the city of Pawtucket. My brother, Jim, and I eventually got our own franchise to sell stainless steel cookware when we were in college. We earned our way through school, selling cookware on weekends and on occasional weekdays when we could break away from our studies.

We hired many of our friends and trained them to sell all throughout Rhode Island and Massachusetts. Bill Allwood sold the cookware before starting his own well drilling company in Vermont. Ron Kornfeld and Jim Buckley also joined the cookware sales team. Joe met Johnny Zee at URI and recruited him to sell in the Armenian section of Providence where his family lived.

John was a terrific athlete at Central High and was an outstanding defensive back on the University of Rhode Island football team. He came to a meeting wearing a bright yellow sport jacket that was tailored to fit him like a glove. He was enthusiastic and explained, as Ralph ran his fingers through the cloth, "I picked up a fifty dollar deposit. It's great that we get to keep it. I used my first deposit to buy this new sport jacket." John looked great in that jacket and he did a wonderful job selling cookware.

I still run into people who are using and enjoying the cookware we sold them more than fifty years ago. Apparently, the lifetime guarantee is still in effect.

* * * * *

The Zambrowski sisters were planning a double wedding. They sounded excited when I made an appointment over the phone, so I had high expectations of two nice sales.

They liked the cookware, but I was dumbfounded when they giggled every time I moved to get another pan. Then as I bent my knee to kneel down, I noticed my fly was open. *Yikes!* Then the corner of my starched white shirt popped out like an inch worm…and then it went back into my pants when I stood up again.

"Oh, my God!" My face flushed with embarrassment! I whirled around, zipped up my fly, and finished the demonstration… and…the Zambrowski girls each bought a set.

Meanwhile, Ralph was in Central Falls, at a third floor tenement apartment. He rapped on the door and the knocker fell off in his hand. He tried to reattach it, but couldn't fix it. The door swung open–and he was greeted by a very hefty, overly excited lady in a dark blue dress and pink apron. In a high-pitched voice she screamed, "Yvonne, Yvonne! He's here! The guy's here with the cookware." Then she acknowledged Ralph. "Come in…come in."

Ralph handed the doorknocker to her and made his way to the TV room to prepare for his demonstration. The room smelled of toll house cookies, freshly baked for Ralph. Mr. and Mrs. Robitaille sat on a sofa and out came shy, petite Yvonne. Then there was a loud boisterous little boy, Emile, with his arms stretched out like an airplane, buzzing around his parents, Yvonne, and the pots and pans. BUZZ–EYOIE!

His mother said, "Emile! Emile, sit down!"

His father yelled, "Emile! Emile, sit down and stop acting crazy!"

Ralph proceeded with his demonstration. As he spoke about each piece, Mrs. Robitaille was beaming. Yvonne's engagement ring was glistening as she sat and listened to Ralph.

BBBBURRPFF! Everyone turned to look at Emile as the smell of the toll house cookies vanished. Ralph began to stutter as he struggled with this distraction. He noticed that Mr. Robitaille looked embarrassed and had to think fast before he lost the sale. After all, this was expensive cookware and a large investment for this family.

BBBBURRPFF! It was Emile again. Ralph mumbled to himself, "My God, this is bad." Ralph tried to regain his composure and walked over to Mr. Robitaille and said, "I can offer an easy payment plan."

The details were being discussed. Mr. Robitaille pulled Ralph aside, "My Emile has a medical problem. I'm sure you understand."

Ralph put his arm around Emile and said, "Someday you'll outgrow it. I know you will because I outgrew it, too."

Mr. Robitaille smiled as he got the deposit money from a cookie jar and gave it to Ralph, along with a cookie. With a skip in his gait, Ralph got in his car. **BBBBURRPFF**–"Well, I almost outgrew it–must be the cookies."

* * * * *

It was seven o'clock. It was raining and I was late. The windshield wipers could hardly keep up with the driving downpour. I hurried into the driveway. My heart was pounding as I gathered up the heavy case of three-ply stainless steel pots and pans for my biggest demonstration. I knocked on the door; it flung open and I could hear the excited voices of six women sitting in the room. I was going to be center stage for the evening, with my dazzling culinary presentation.

"Come on, Mikey. We were wondering if you were even going to make it in this weather, but of course, a little rain couldn't stop our guys from going bowling as usual tonight."

"Sit down," said the excited hostess, "and have some hors d'oeuvres."

"No thanks," I said holding my hand on my stomach. "My mother fixed pork chops and sauerkraut tonight and I ate more than my share, especially the sauerkraut."

I was all set, ready to go. The moment I started my presentation, all the girls gathered closer around me. I knew this was going to be a good sale by the smiles on their faces. They were ready for a good time and they were already asking leading questions. All of a sudden I could feel my mother's sauerkraut moving its way through my intestines, and crawling like a German soldier behind enemy lines.

"Ladies, before I really get into this, could you direct me to the bathroom?"

The hostess said, "The lavatory is right behind you."

As I stood up, the cramps attacked. It was a bayonet to the solar plexus, direct and excruciating cramps.

Once inside the tiny bathroom, I pushed the door to seal it. My forehead was dotted with sweat. Now my stomach was rolling like a Sherman tank out of control. What followed could only be compared to the Battle of the Bulge.

BING, BANG, BOOM! I EXPLODED!!

The voices beyond quieted. The battle echoed through the walls and a purple cloud began to engulf the small area. Surely, my malady would be discovered when the barrier was unsealed and I re-entered the room. I had to do something. I had to think fast. I threw open the window; it wasn't enough. Air freshener–air freshener–air freshener. I frantically searched for something to dilute the air–something, anything to dilute the air. Medicine cabinet–nothing. Under the sink–nothing. I threw open the shower curtain. Damn. I had to do something. I went back to the medicine cabinet and found myself staring at the door, with a bottle of Old Spice After-Shave Lotion in my hand. I pulled the pop top...SPLAT! SPLAT! As I thrust it against the walls–SPLAT on the mirror. SPLAT in the air and on the ceiling. The panic increased inside me. It had to be enough. Frantically, I splattered up, down and around the room. The last splat misfired and was a direct hit in my right eye.

"Jesus, I'm hit. I'm hit! I'm going down. I'm going down." I yelled out loud, "YIKES!"

The burn engulfed my eye socket and numbed the side of my face. I found the sink and began to flush my eye. The sting and burn began to ease and my vision returned. I shut off the running water. It was deathly quiet.

There was a knock on the door, "You okay in there? You okay, Mikey?"

I could hardly speak, but managed to say, "Ah–yeah, I'll be out in a minute."

After several more taps on the door, I got myself presentable. I had been in there an entire hour. I meekly emerged with my bloodshot, watery, red eye protruding from my face. I couldn't keep it open and as I started to become more focused I noticed the room was empty. "I'm ready to show the cookware. Would everyone please come back in and take a seat."

The disappointed hostess replied, "It's too late now. They had to go."

I apologized, saying, "Sorry. I wasn't feeling well. Can we set up another appointment?"

"We'll let you know," she said in a soft voice.

I thought, "*Six hot leads down the drain. Literally down the drain!*"

I never got another opportunity to show the cookware to this particular group of girls. After that incident, I never ate sauerkraut again before going on a sales call–but I do use Old Spice After-Shave!

* * * * *

Two weeks later on our way to Foster, Rhode Island near the Connecticut border, Ralph pulled the car over to use a pay phone and get directions.

"Are we almost there, Ralph?" I sighed.

"Yeah, sounds like these folks are in the boonies, Mike. They said they've got some sort of a surprise for us."

We turned into a long driveway with a two car garage and an old barn. Between the barn and the house was a large doghouse with the name 'LUSH' inscribed in dripping black paint. A thick, rusted chain was wrapped around the doghouse. The length of the chain lay among several large holes in the bare, grassless dirt. Before Ralph could knock on the door, I tripped over an old mixing bowl half full of filthy water, **Ka-Bang**! The door opened. An old, white-haired, unshaven man in baggy overalls motioned for us to come in. The kitchen smelled like wet dog.

An elderly woman came into the kitchen smiling and said, "Our granddaughter, Suzie, will love the cookware. She's gittin' married next month. Show us whatcha got."

The cookware was arranged on the large, empty kitchen table. From the other room, the unmistakable sound of a scratching dog came across the wooden floor. From around the corner, a scruffy, long-legged dog with a jutting jaw and a bushy black tail sauntered around the kitchen table. He licked the back of my hand and then he went around to Ralph and licked his hand. Ralph squatted down and petted him, and the dog licked his cheek.

"And who's this guy?" Ralph said.

I looked at Ralph and said, "Looks like you've made yourself a real good buddy."

"Name's Lush…got him at the pound," slurred the old lady over gums that had no teeth.

Ralph asked, "What breed of dog is he? I've never seen such long legs."

206

"Breed? No breed–Lush is pure wolf–but we didn't know it when we got 'em. He looked like a shaggy dog as a pup."

"Now for the surprise I told you about," the man said as he opened up the refrigerator and took out two tall Narragansett beers. "Ever see a wolf drink beer?"

Ralph looked at me with raised eyebrows and said, "Not really."

The old guy poured the beer into a bowl at the corner of the kitchen. Lush shot to it like a missile, almost knocking the old man down. He lapped up the beer as quick as he could, grabbed the bowl in his jaw and tipped it straight up in the air to get every last drop. He slammed the bowl down and stared at his master with fire in his eyes.

"Okay, boy. I'll get ya two more."

You could have heard a pin drop. We were amazed at how fast that animal could drink. The next round, like the first, was gone in seconds. Four empty cans were next to the bowl and Lush began to growl at them. Ralph sensed that the situation had become unstable and that this animal had just undergone a change in personality. Ralph nervously reached for a large frying pan at the end of the table while keeping a wary eye on Lush. Lush didn't take his eyes off Ralph. Suddenly, in the middle of the presentation, Lush bolted under the table toward Ralph and locked his huge jaw right into Ralph's crotch like a bear trap ready to be sprung. Ralph was paralyzed. He could not move. The breath of the wolf was like a locomotive engine, fueled by four beers and blasting hot fumes over Ralph's family jewels.

Ralph's knees were locked and beads of sweat poured down his forehead as the old lady gummed, "Paw, you know Lush gets a little too feisty when he has more than two beers."

The old guy hollered, "Go lay down, Lush!"

Ralph stuttered in a faint, quiet voice, "D–d–does he ma-mind?"

Lush opened his mouth and released his grip on Ralph, slowly pulling away. Then Lush nestled up to the old kitchen stove. Ralph let out a loud sigh of relief. He fumbled his unlit cigarette in his shaking hands then continued his presentation. The old couple loved the cookware and bake ware set.

After collecting his deposit, Ralph said to me, "I didn't know if Lush was going to back off. I thought any minute I'd be singing soprano."

The couple put a leash around Lush's neck. We had to get out the door. We had to get out fast. We had to beat Lush to that door. The door appeared three miles away. Lush was starting to go berserk. We didn't know if the old folks, with their arthritic hands, could hold that wolf back. The hair on the wolf's back was standing straight up and his sights were intensely fixed on Ralph. Ralph's whole body began to tremble and he turned pasty white. The alcohol appeared to have reached its peak in Lush's bloodstream. His eyes were bleary and his mouth was foaming.

I said, "At the count of three, make a run for it." I yelled "THREE" and dashed out the door.

Lush went wild and dragged both of the old folks across the kitchen floor. Ralph was still paralyzed. He couldn't blink. He couldn't flinch. He couldn't move–in fact he completely stopped breathing! The old man threw a beer into the den as a diversion.

"Go get the beer, boy–the beer."

Lush dashed into the den. Ralph grabbed the case of cookware and ran to the door. Lush reacted to the sounds of Ralph fumbling with the doorknob. He came flying across the kitchen floor and slid into the door as Ralph slammed it behind him. **SLAM! BLAM!**

Ralph was finally safe outside and flung open the trunk and threw the cookware inside. Then he slipped in a pile of wolf dung.

"Holy shit, Mike."

He got in the car. I looked at him clutching the steering wheel as he stared off into space with a broken cigarette dangling from his lips. "Holy shit," he mumbled.

We drove off and as the car turned onto the paved road, Ralph shifted into third gear, took off his messy, stinking shoe and winged it out the window.

"A wolf, Mike! Who the hell has a damned beer drinking wolf? Shit. I don't know who's gonna come back here to deliver the cookware, but it sure ain't gonna be me!"

I laughed, "Poor Mr. Jenkins will get a surprise when he delivers *this* set."

Zeke said, "I hope *Suzie* liked her cookware. That's gotta be the toughest sale you guys ever made! That wolf story reminds me of my poem about a coyote."

Eager to hear more of Zeke's words of wisdom, I nodded as I leaned back against the big oak tree. Zeke began to recite:

COYOTE

"Coyote, I no longer hear you howling in the depths of the
forest, like I used to.

The wind now is silent and the ground is as frozen as it used to be.

Where are you coyote?

Are you watching now?

Do you notice the same glitter on the open fields, where
butterflies used to fly?

They're all gone away.

Hiding, waiting for the summertime.

Show not coyote, your golden fur in the moonlight.

The hours are passing by.

Coyote you once stood so strong, now pretend I am gone.

Pretend I am gone."

Chapter 14
We're Awfully Glad We Met You

The wind gently rustled the leaves above Zeke. He pulled a cigar out of his shirt pocket, using two fingers like a pair of tweezers. As soon as he took the first puff, the scent placed me in my father's 1950 Nash.

Dad was smoking a Haddon Hall cigar while driving Ralph and me to Archie's Tavern. My father said over the rush of wind through the windows, "You boys have never had swordfish until you've tried Archie's swordfish."

I looked over my shoulder and saw Ralph pull out a cigarette and hesitate. He slowly slid it back into the pack. Even though my father was smoking, Ralph had more respect for him than to light up. Instead he asked, "How long have you been smoking those Haddon Halls, Mr. Ryan?"

"Well, Ralph," he answered flattening his hair with the palm of his hand, "Ever since I became the wholesale manager for Hudson Terraplane. I was twenty-one; they shook my hand, gave me a new car, a raise and a cigar. That was my first break into management." He went on to say, "As a youngster I worked in a cotton mill in New Bedford."

Ralph perked up, "Oh, Mike told me about that. I heard you had a little trouble with the bobbins, Mr. Ryan."

"Yes Ralph. I was all thumbs. I could never stand those looms clacking and crashing, clacking and crashing. How could anyone concentrate on those bobbins?"

"Actually, Mr. Ryan, I tried my hand at sewing but my finger got in the way."

"Well, boys," my father said with the cigar in the corner of his mouth, "Most of the things that seem to be a disaster at the time turn out to be a blessing in disguise. Like when I delivered meals at the Hathaway Mills. Because I was all thumbs, they decided to have me take meals to the managers at the mill instead of setting up the bobbins. One time I tripped on the sidewalk when I was carrying a pail of pea soup for the owner. It wasn't my fault, really. I was wearing a pair of hand-me-down shoes that didn't fit right. I didn't know what I was going to do. I had to think fast, so I scooped the soup back into the pail as fast as I could. I thought no one would ever know.

"An hour later I was summoned to the owner's private office. 'James,' he said, 'Do you like pea soup?' I couldn't look him straight in the eye, 'Yes, sir.'

"Well, so do I,' he growled. 'I love pea soup. I love pea soup with salt. I love pea soup with pepper. I love pea soup with crackers, and sometimes I love pea soup with a nice tall glass of milk. But the pea soup that you brought me, James, had no salt, had no pepper and had no crackers. But it did have plenty of stones from the sidewalk and plenty of dirt from the gutter. The next time you drop the soup, just bring a new pail, James; that's all you have to do.'

"I looked up at him and into his eyes and said, 'Yes, sir.' And as I walked away, I knew that was the last pail of soup I would carry up those stairs. The very next day I was off to a job interview at the New Bedford Hotel."

"Hey, Dad, tell him what happened with Buster McLacklin."

"Oh, yeah, good old Buster. Well see, I heard they needed a bellhop at the hotel. On my way to the interview, I ran into my neighbor, Buster, and he walked along with me. When we arrived at the hotel, the manager eyed the two of us and stated, 'We're only looking for one bellhop.'

"I told him, 'He's not looking for work.'

"Buster piped up, 'I'll take the job!'

"The manager took a quarter out of his pocket and said, 'I'll flip a coin and whoever wins, gets the job.'

"Buster quickly yelled, 'Heads' as the coin landed on the desk.

"He looked at Buster and said, 'Son, you start at eight o'clock tomorrow morning.'"

My dad bit deep into his cigar, "He scooped the job and I walked home alone."

Ralph grabbed the back of my shoulder and whispered under his breath in my ear, "*That bastard.*"

"So, Dad, what did become of Buster?"

"Well, Mike, you see, it's like this. Buster had a short life–in and out of jail for petty offenses. He never really got squared away. Even when he was in prison, he was bucking the system.

He thought it would be a slick idea to filter rubbing alcohol through bread to get drunk. One inmate died, another went blind and Buster was never the same."

He took a long puff on his Haddon Hall. "Well, I'll tell you, I got a new car every three months. If it wasn't for Robinson Snow and the Wamsutta Club, my future would have been a lot different. Professionally, instead of being on the trail of a wooden duck, I was right around the corner from 'Easy Street.' I was a bellhop at the club when I met Mr. Snow, a well respected and successful cotton broker. I liked being a bellhop. I liked the clean uniform, I liked the free meals, and I liked working in the card room. They liked me enough to give me a raise.

"Mr. Snow took me aside and asked me what I wanted to do with my life. I said, 'Business school.'

"He lifted his eyebrows and said, 'Then, business school it is.'

"He was a member of the elite club and liked my work ethic. I worked the card room three nights a week getting sandwiches for the members along with my day job as bellhop. I took night classes a couple of times a week at Herrick Business School and Mr. Snow footed the bill. I was so fast on the typewriter that my friends Slip and Skip called me 'Speed.' I can still type the words, 'Thank you, Mr. Snow' in half a second. Shorthand was a natural for me. In fact, I was approached by the Headmaster and invited to stay and teach shorthand after graduation, but I had different plans. Gil Foley, another member of the Wamsutta Club, brought me in as an accountant for his used car dealership in New Bedford. I filled in for the salesmen during their breaks. Then I joined the sales department full time and quickly became one of their top salesmen. A Hudson Terraplane distributor in Providence offered me a job as Wholesale Manager at the age of twenty-one. I was only twenty-one...and the world was my oyster. So you see, boys, everything always works out for the best."

Ralph looked up to the sky and said, "My Dad went to Brown Medical School. I was too young to hear any of his stories, but I know he was a brilliant man."

The Nash shifted into third gear.

Dad went on, "Ralph, like you, I lost a parent. My mother died when I was very young. My older sister raised my two younger brothers and me. The four of us were very close. Paul, the youngest, went to Holy Cross, where he was a soloist in the Glee Club. He was constantly asked to sing his favorite song, 'Ave Maria.' Eddie was playing semi-pro baseball while he was a senior in high school."

As we approached the stoplight I said, "Ralph loves hearing your stories, Dad. Tell him about the "Honeydales."

Dad eased on the brake. "Okay. I was the pitcher for the Honeydale Hitters. We were a step-and-a-half above sandlot." Now Dad's cigar was out and he was chewing on the juicy end. Talking out of the corner of his mouth with a tilt to his head, he said, "We were playing the 'Bloomer Girls.'"

Ralph brightened, "Girls?"

"They had us 22 to nothing in the third inning, but they were lucky; it started to rain and the game was called off." The three of us burst out laughing. "Seriously, guys, one day when I showed up on the field, the rest of the team was going to quit if I pitched. My brother, Eddie, barked, 'Let him start, and if he doesn't strike them out, take him out.' Well, Eddie was all over the outfield making spectacular plays. He also hit two homers. Miraculously, I lasted the whole game."

"Ralph," I said, "My mother was the athlete in our family. At eighteen, she won the Greater New Bedford Women's Tennis Championship. She beat the perennial champion, Frannie Ford, of the famous automotive family, in three sets. My mother's name was Mildred, but all of New Bedford knew of her affectionately as 'Little Mo'."

A Harley Davidson came alongside as we slowed to take a right onto Mendon Avenue. Ralph rolled down his window and yelled, "Hey, Magic!" The cool-looking guy was wearing a Tolman jacket. He gave us a big wave. Ralph had a broad smile on his face, "Magic was elected to be the Tiger's football captain for next year."

"So, Mr. Ryan, Mike told me you taught him how to play the ukulele. I gave him my mandolin, but he had trouble tuning it."

I said, "Yeah, I wonder if it's still in the pawn shop."

Ralph mused, "I'm sure someone snapped that gem up right away."

Dad reflected, "I used to play the ukulele a lot, but my brothers and I always sang barbershop. When any of the six of us got together and sang, everyone would say that we had a nice blend of voices. My two oldest brothers, Johnny and Tim, were tenors. Eddie sang air, Paul was a barri, and I sang bass."

Ralph perked up, "I sang bass myself, in a school minstrel show."

My father continued, "Did Mike ever tell you about my brother Eddie's orchestra?"

"No."

"Well, believe it or not, I managed and funded a fifteen piece orchestra. Eddie was the Bandleader. It was during the mid-thirties. They all had white tuxedos, and that's not all...they were better than Guy Lombardo. In 1936, during competition in Boston, they were voted the top band in New England. They were ready for the big time and I had them booked at the

DeWitt Hilton Hotel in Albany, New York. We rode through a snowstorm to get there, only to find another band playing."

I interjected, "Dad, Uncle Ed told me the rest of *that* story. Let *me* tell Ralph." I continued, "You went to the agent's house and told Uncle Ed to wait outside because *he* was so angry. He waited a while then peered through a window. There you were, chasing the agent around a table, yelling, 'I'll drag you through the Goddamn gutter.' Uncle Ed said you were so mad, Dad, that he had to get you out of there right away."

"Yes, the guy wanted a pay-off, but nothing good ever comes of a pay-off, son. The band shut down shortly thereafter."

The car pulled into Archie's parking lot. Ralph said in an alerted tone, "You know, they've been stealing cars around here, Mr. Ryan. I heard it on the news. I think you should park in a spot where you can see your car from inside the restaurant."

"Good idea, Ralph."

When we walked into the restaurant people were watching *The Honeymooners.* Jackie Gleason and Art Carney were going through their zany antics on the television in the lounge area. The restaurant was buzzing with the early bird crowd and you could smell the fish and chips special.

The waitress approached, "Three?"

My father said, "Yes. Can we sit by that window?"

"Sure; window seats seem to be very popular these days."

Ralph quickly grabbed the menu and cried out, "I'll have one egg-trilbie-on-a-double decker."

The waitress looked perplexed and said, "What?"

"Okay, I'll have an olive and anchovy sandwich."

217

I said, "Ralph, don't start that again."

"Well, Mike," my father said, "Sounds like Ralph always has his own way of expressing himself."

I said, "Ralph, did I ever tell you that when my Uncle Johnny was in the Navy, he was asked to sing with the Elsie Jannis Troupe?"

"No."

"They put on shows to entertain the soldiers in Europe during World War I. Uncle Johnny was only eighteen years old and a little wild. He went with his buddies to celebrate the night before the troupe left on tour. He didn't make it back to join them the next morning. He was a signalman. On November 11th, 1918, he used the signal flags on his ship to inform the British Fleet in the harbor that the First World War was over. When his mother died, he couldn't get a furlough. He stowed away on the Leviathan Troop Ship leaving Brest, France for the United States. He stayed in New Bedford for six months. When he heard that his own ship was docked near Boston he attempted to rejoin his mates, but they threw him in the Deer Island brig."

Dad cleared his throat and changed the subject. "Uum, people seem to enjoy listening to my brothers and me sing whenever we're together. We love to harmonize. We actually had a few opportunities to make it big. But something always got in the way. My brother Tim was our second tenor. He refused the offer we got to be on the Horace Heights Talent Show in New York because he didn't want to leave New Bedford. He was a 'home body' and only wanted us to sing for family and friends. He was determined to keep it that way."

Dad continued reminiscing as Ralph and I wolfed down our desert. "We all have a favorite song."

I winked at Ralph and said, "Every song has a special meaning to them."

218

Dad said, "You're absolutely right, Mike. Eddie likes *In a Gay Old Garden Concert.* Paul's favorite is *If I had My Life to Live Over.* Tim sings *Chicago Town.* My special song is *Down the River of Golden Dreams.*"

I interrupted and said, "You know, Ralph, when my Uncle Leo Patrick can make it back to New Bedford from Washington, D .C. he sings *Smile Awhile.* I remember how people loved to hear their beautiful blend of voices as it rang through Buttonwood Park when we were kids."

Dad said, "Since the forties, Leo has been the Master of Ceremonies for the Saint Patrick's Day shows in Washington that are sponsored by the Friendly Sons of St. Patrick. He has entertained three Presidents...Roosevelt, Truman, and Eisenhower. President Truman told him he loved his singing."

Dad continued, "During the summers, the family meets in New Bedford. We swim in the ocean near Fort Rodman then go up to Hazelwood Park for a clambake. When we start singing we seem to draw a crowd. The evening always ends with everyone coaxing Tim to tell his Arsene and Philias story. He uses a French-Canadian accent that has everyone in stitches.

"This story is about two guys named Arsene and Philias who were hunting bears in the Yukon. As the story goes, Arsene went into a cave to look for a bear, but the bear was outside. When the bear blocked the entrance to the cave, Philias grabbed him by the tail and held on for dear life. The cave became very dark and Arsene yelled out, 'Philias, Philias, who blocked 'de light?' Philias, struggling, called back, 'If this tail comes loose from this bear's 'R A S S,' you'll find out who blocked 'de light.'"

Ralph put down his fork and burst out laughing.

I said, "When we were kids, we were treated to cherry cider every fall on our ride to New Bedford on Route 6. Those were great family times. When we got to Swansea, we looked for a homemade sign made by a farmer that was placed at the edge of the road. It read, 'Horseshit- fifty cents a bucket.' The cider stand was in the next driveway. The cold drink was delicious. The cider smelled like sweet cherries—not horseshit."

We walked out of the restaurant laughing.

Ralph looked around and said, "Hey, Mr. Ryan; where's your car?"

Dad walked over to a gray car. "It's right over here. I haven't taken my eyes off it. C'mon boys, get in."

"DAD! This is not your car!"

"Whoa…wait a minute! Whoa, whoa, whoa! This isn't my car." He looked around frantically and with a lost gaze, almost as if he didn't believe it himself. "I've been watching the wrong car—the wrong gosh dang car—and mine's been stolen."

It was the beginning of a nightmare for him. He didn't have time for hassles, and this incident proved to be one big hassle after another in dealing with the insurance company. Another car was provided as a loaner…a 1946 Ford Coupe. It was a real clunker. The Nash was finally replaced, but the replacement was a lemon. My father hated that car because it had a lot of mechanical problems and it was hard to drive. He had to bring it to Manny's Arco Service Station for repairs almost every week.

* * * * *

On a Friday evening, when my father arrived home from a business trip to Lake George, New York, I knew he would be tired. I thought that this would be the perfect opportunity for me to gain possession of the keys to the Nash. I also knew that to get the keys, I could volunteer to unload the jewelry in the car. His small store was merely a mile away, near Pineault's Corner, and he would surely appreciate my gesture of good will. I just wanted the car. Drizzle gathered on the windshield, the last remnants of torrential downpours that had created a swamp behind his jewelry store. I splashed into the area behind the building and unloaded the jewelry boxes through the back door of the store.

Smoke was steaming from the pipes on the underside of the Nash. I sat motionless for a moment then turned the radio down. I knew that the smoke rising around me was somehow the result of the car being stuck deep in the mud. I slowly eased the shift into reverse and gave it a little gas. It seemed for a moment like the car was going to back straight out, but then it stopped. The back tires began to cry out a worried-sounding song as they lost traction and spun. I felt the rear sink. I slowly stepped on the brake and shifted it into first gear. Surely moving forward a bit would help...forward and reverse, forward and reverse, forward and reverse. I thought I was gonna rock that car right outta the mud, but it was buried right up to the axles. Persevering, I gave it more gas and tried to rock the socked-in vehicle harder and faster. Forward, then slam, reverse, until the smell of a burning and beaten clutch filled the car. The hissing of the muffler in the mud made my Adam's apple rise higher in my throat. The next sound was the idle of the motor, a motor that had been defeated by the elements. I was stuck and I had to call my dad. He would know what to do. Dad would understand. It could happen to anyone, I convinced myself.

The Nash looked like a docked submarine in the newly-created mud pond behind my father's jewelry store. A tow truck picked my dad up at the house and brought him to the store. As it lifted the disabled car and pulled it out of the mud, my father said calmly, "It's okay, Mike; it could happen to anyone."

We both got into the car. I started the ignition and shifted into first. I was ready to go home. The car didn't move. When I shifted into reverse, the car still didn't move.

He bellowed, "You burned out the God damn clutch. Now it'll cost a fortune!"

I bolted from the car and didn't look again. I ran all the way home. Dad called the tow truck and the car was taken to Manny's Service Station. The truck brought him home, just before midnight. He was exhausted, completely shot, and his three piece suit needed to go to Wong's Dry Cleansers.

* * * * *

I said, "Zeke, do you see that gray tombstone at the top of the hill over there?"

"Yes. That's Mrs. Wiser's tombstone. Did you know her?"

"Well you might say I knew her by blood, specifically, my father's blood."

It was a Friday night and my father came home exhausted. He came through the door with his briefcase in hand. His shoulders were slumped over from a long drive home from Lake Winnipesaukee in New Hampshire. He draped his coat jacket over a kitchen chair and shuffled toward the refrigerator.

As he gripped the handle with the last of his strength, my mother shot into the kitchen. "James! James, you can't eat anything tonight! You have to give blood tomorrow morning and you can't have any food!"

He slowly released the latch on the door. "What are you talking about, Mildred?"

"I'm talking about Mrs. Wiser. You have been volunteered to give blood."

My father was too exhausted to argue the point. All he said was, "And who volunteered me?"

My mother gave him a peck on the cheek as she pulled the bow to release her apron. She said in a soft sweet voice, "Well I did, dear."

In the morning the hospital was humming with harried nurses. My father sat down under the sign that said '*Blood Donors.*' He waited patiently for two hours. A nurse finally appeared in front of him. She said, "I know you have been waiting for some time, sir, but it will be another hour before we are ready for you."

He wanted to leave. He was tired and famished, but Mrs. Wiser was promised his blood. There was a painting of a bowl of fruit in the hallway. The longer he stared at it, the more he convinced himself that he could reach right into the frame to pluck a grape, but he even resisted that for Mrs. Wiser. Two hours later, he was summoned to give blood. The nurse walked down the hallway with him to the donor area.

Looking like a basset hound he said, "Do I get a sip of brandy?"

"Oh, Mr. Ryan," she giggled. "That's funny."

"What? I thought I would get brandy after I gave blood."

She said, "That custom went out during Prohibition."

My mother knew everything about donating blood. That was expressed by the delicious meal she made that afternoon. When she heard the Nash pull into the driveway, she hurried to get a plate fixed up and on the table for my dad to enjoy. That was her way of saying 'thank you' to him for donating his blood for Mrs. Wiser.

The side door opened. Dad was white as a sheet and by the

223

way he lolled to the table in slow motion, I knew he was light headed. Before him were sixteen ounces of sirloin steak, cooked to perfection. Nancy pulled the chair out for him. To the left of the steak was a mound of whipped mashed potatoes, fluffed up like a cloud in heaven and to the left of the mashed potatoes was my little brother, Gary. On the side, away from everything else on the plate, was his favorite–boiled onions. He gazed at the feast and savored the aroma. He blinked once and on the second slow blink his eyelids lifted, and he became as cross-eyed as Mrs. Wiser's callico cat. Then **blam**! He collapsed head first, right into the mashed potatoes. He was out cold.

We carried him upstairs and put him to bed. He slept like a log all day. When he finally woke up, he said, "When my blood went into Mrs. Wiser's system, she ran around the house twice before she kicked the bucket."

* * * * *

Dad traded in the Nash for a used '51 Chevy Station Wagon. Nancy was the only girl in our family. With three brothers, she was my father's princess. She took his new car out for a drive one night and when she returned, the gas gauge was on empty. The next morning she came rushing down the stairs only to see the taillights of the school bus pulling away from the stop. My father was also running late, and now he realized that he would have to zip Nancy over to Sacred Heart Academy, so she wouldn't be late for class. He didn't have time to shave or even put in his false teeth. Still wearing his cotton pajamas with matching slippers, he threw on his bright red bathrobe, grabbed his watch, and put on his prized soft hat to try to hide his rumpled hair. He ran out of the house, holding his hat to his head with his left hand, while clutching his bathrobe shut with his right hand.

When he jumped into the car, Nancy said, "Gee, Dad. I hope no one sees you."

"Naugh, it'll only take a minute, Honey."

When she got out of the car, Nancy poked her head back inside and gave him a peck on the cheek and said, "Thanks, Daddy."

As he drove through downtown Pawtucket, the car started to sputter and cough. Then the engine completely conked out. Fuming and embarrassed, he got out and slammed the door shut. He was horrified to discover that his keys were locked inside. There he was at eight in the morning, standing in his bathrobe, slippers and top hat, toothless and unshaven in the middle of Main Street, with wind and rain swirling around his head.

Luckily, a few minutes later, our postman recognized my father and pulled up to help. "Mr. Ryan, is that you? Are you okay?"

Dad quickly explained, "I'm in a real pickle. I'm locked out."

"Your rear window is open a little. We can try using a clothes hanger."

He took his postal uniform off of its hanger and bent the wire. He pushed the hanger in and lifted the tail gate latch. My father crawled over the rear seats, wriggling on his stomach and weaving his body over boxes of jewelry, until he was able to maneuver into the driver's seat. "Thanks, pal. Can you give me a push so I can get gas?"

Reluctant, but agreeing, he replied, "I'm not supposed to do this, but how can I say no to a man still in his bathrobe and slippers."

When Dad applied the brake to turn into the gas station, the rear headlight on the station wagon and the front headlight of the mail truck collided and glass was strewn on the driveway. The mailman threw up his hands and took off, leaving my father to figure out his next move–how to pay for the gas while his wallet was sitting on the bureau in his bedroom. The attendant suggested that if he wanted to get five dollars worth of gas, he could leave his watch as collateral.

When he returned home, my mother reeled, "What took you so long, James. Is everything okay?"

"You don't want to know! Get my teeth, my wallet, and my comb. I have to go back to the Texaco station to get my watch."

* * * * *

Skowhegan, Maine was not too far from Pawtucket for my father to deal with a family crisis. As mater of fact, no place on earth was too far for my dad to be there for his family. Skowhegan just happened to be where he was when he got a phone call from the North Attleboro, Massachusetts police. "Mr. Ryan," he said. "Young Michael and one Ralph McGreavey are now in our custody."

The morning business appointments were cancelled in his mind, before he even put down the phone. That evening, he was hurrying the officer to release us. Ralph was as happy to see my father as I was. He had a tear forming in the laughing cracks at the corner of his eye.

The police chief began to read the report. "Mr. Ryan, it seems the boys, here, purchased a vehicle at an auction, a 1941 Chevrolet, and had obtained no registration permit for the use of the roadways in this state. Instead, they decided to remove the rear license plate of your wife's 1950 Ford and affix it to the

226

rear of Mr. McGreavey's untitled vehicle. They were intercepted on Route One, opposite Jolly Cholly's Drive-In by our patrol car. When interviewed by the patrolling officer, Mr. McGreavy stated that the two vehicles should be excused from detainment. Further, he stated that the rope that was connecting the vehicles joined them together to make one long vehicle. He insisted that a plate on the front of the forward vehicle and a plate on the back of the towed vehicle qualified as proper registration for both vehicles, under the 'limousine act.' Presently the vehicles have been separated and impounded."

The next morning, after hiring Randall Parmenter, a local attorney, we all appeared at the hearing. When the lawyer informed my father that we would be charged with a minor offense, my father asked, "Will it show on their record?"

Mr. Parmenter nudged in close to my father, "Look, it's *already* been dropped to a minor offense, but there *will* be a finding here on record."

My father leaned in closer, "I do not want these boys to have a police record."

Mr. Parmenter said, "I could try, but I'd be indebted to the clerk of courts."

"Well, Mr. Parmenter, be indebted. For these boys, be indebted."

After a lecture from the judge, we left with no record. We always had a lot of love and appreciation for my dad, especially that day. A good and kind man, his deeds were always interspersed with humor. He was handsome and dignified. A meticulous dresser, he carefully coordinated shirts, ties, and suits; he matched right down to his socks! When complimented on his classy attire, he'd smile and say, "I just threw it on and it happened to match."

Everyone liked my dad. He articulated a story or joke of some kind to everyone he met. He was a proud man. He was proud of his Irish heritage. When he was in his cups, he would recite a poem he learned from relatives in Cloonainra and Tumgesh, two townships in Ireland.

"Hooray for the men of the west
Hooray for the bravest and best
When Ireland lay broken and bleeding
They looked to the men of Tumgesh"

He also liked to remind us of his recipe for a happy family:

Combine happy hearts.
Melt hearts into one.
Add a lot of love.
Mix well with respect.
Add gentleness, laughter, joy, faith, hope and self-control
Pour in much understanding
Don't forget the patience and the prayers
Blend in listening ears
Allow to grow and share
Sprinkle with smiles, hugs and kisses
Bake for a lifetime.

He taught us a family song called *We're Awfully Glad We Met You* that he said was written by one of our ancestors. With a smile on my face, I quipped, "That could be blarney, Zeke, but we're the only family I know of that sings this song."

When my father passed away, my sister started to sing *We're Awfully Glad We Met You* at his funeral. Everyone joined in as we said our last good-bye standing by his gravesite. It was a tribute to a wonderful man. I'm sure it pleased him.

Chapter 15
Are You Ready, Adele?

It was December and the snow was piling up in Pawtucket. A group of us decided to take a ski trip to Vermont. Jim Buckley was a good skier and Ron Kornfeld had skied many times at the Suicide Six Ski Area in Woodstock, with his family. Shawn O'Neill had never been on skis and I was a ham 'n egger—a real beginner. Ralph was still working at the bowling alley when it came time for us to leave Pawtucket. He said, "I'll drive to Vermont tonight. I'm not going to ski, but I'll be the best apre' skier that mountain's ever seen!"

On the first run down the mountain, O'Neill wiped out. He landed on his wrist and cracked a small bone. I had to drive him to the hospital. He was put in a cast up to his elbow. When I got back to the ski area, Buckley was waiting for me to take him for x-rays. He did a 'daffy' trying to imitate a guy practicing ski ballet. He flew off a mogul, spread his legs while airborne and crash-landed. The result was a chipped bone in his knee.

Kornfeld wrenched his knee in a spectacular wipeout on the last run.

The sun set over the mountain at the end of the day, with two guys in splints, complete with crutches and one guy with his arm in a cast. I was fine, in great shape, except that I was completely exhausted. I had a day pass hanging from my jacket that never saw even one chairlift ride. I didn't volunteer, but I became the non-stop express vehicle between the mountain and the hospital. The receptionist began to recognize me and said, "Von Ryan's Express is back," as she assisted the next casualty.

That night we went to the turkey supper at the Methodist Church in White River Junction. Someone on the mountain told Kornfield about the 'all you can eat' dinner. One of the servers greeted us at the door and noticed our Rhode Island license plate. As my injured buddies hobbled down the stairs, the man announced over the loudspeaker,

"Here come the FLATLANDERS!
The score is: MOUNTAIN: Three,
RHODE ISLAND: Zero!"

It felt like all eyes were on us. Then I heard a big round of applause.

After a hearty meal, Buckley wiped the gravy from his chin and said, "Boy, this is just like Thanksgiving–and will you just look at those home-baked pies!"

We stayed at a little country inn near the gorge, in the small village of Quechee. Ralph appeared late that evening, whistling and carrying large pizzas and two bags, full of Narragansett six-packs. He was in a hell-raising mood and drank late into the night. At three in the morning, he woke me up, shaking the bed and bouncing my mattress up and down.

"What-za-matter with you, Ralph?" I groaned.

Moaning, Ralph said with a slur, "I'm deathly sick. I need to go to the hospital. And I mean it!"

"Ah, for cryin' out loud, Ralph. Get some rest. I'm exhausted. I had a rough day."

He crouched down, agonizing in a low tone, "Mike, I'm gonna die! My stomach is gonna burst!"

Rubbing my tired eyes, I blurted out, "I've been back and forth to the hospital like a God damn yo-yo! I am not going again at this hour of the night."

"I'm too sick to drive and besides, you know the way. C'mon, Mike; I've never been more serious. You've got to take me."

"Oh, for cryin' out loud, get your boots and your jacket on; help me find the keys. Let's go. For Christ's sake, let's just go."

We drove back over the Connecticut River, to the Mary Hitchcock Hospital in Hanover, New Hampshire. A sweet little nurse, dressed in a white starched uniform and nurse's cap, white nylons and soft white shoes looked at me and said, "You again?"

Ralph rushed past her and crawled up on a gurney. "I feel like I'm gonna die," he grumbled.

I pointed, "Ralph here figured it was his turn, and I had nothing better to do than to drive this sick water buffalo to the Emergency Room."

They quickly wheeled him into a small area with an examination table in the center. Moments later, nurses were running in and out carrying bags, bottles, hoses and water. "We need more water. Get more hot water!"

Meanwhile, the waiting room started to fill up. The roads

were icy and cars were slipping and sliding all over the place. Then the doors swung open and a young father rushed in carrying his three-year-old son in his arms. The boys' siblings trailed behind their mother. The grandmother sauntered in huffing and puffing behind them.

The man bellowed, "Thomas has kept me up all night. He's wound up like a clock. He's been jumping and diving on the bed for hours, acting like a helicopter out of control. He took a flying leap right into the headboard and now he needs stitches! Where's the Doctor?"

I thought, "*Oh, boy. I thought I had problems.*"

I tried to pretend I didn't know the guy behind the thin wall that separated the exam room from the waiting area. When I heard a loud, "**W H O O A!**" coming from the cordoned off area Ralph was in, I raised the *Valley News* a little higher, to obscure my face. The pretty nurse stood in front of me, looking down at a clipboard she held and said in a soft tone, "He's going to be okay. All he needed was an enema."

"An enema?" I said too loud. Then I lowered my voice. "We drove two hundred miles to go skiing and Ralph winds up with an enema!" I shook my head and thought, "*Just wait 'till I tell 'The Duke' this story.*" Ralph whistled as he walked back into the waiting room and interrupted my thought.

"Mike, don't you *ever* breathe a word of this to 'The Duke.'"

"Mmm. I would *never* give that a thought, Ralph."

Three breaks and an enema had taken its toll on me, but the next morning, Ralph woke up fresh as a daisy. "Hey Mike, just smell that coffee 'a-brewin.' I'm getting a whiff of the bacon and sausages sizzling downstairs. Let's go!"

I wanted to sleep, but couldn't resist the thought of a hearty breakfast. It smelled so enticing. We finished a big breakfast of fruit, cereal, bacon, sausage, ham, eggs, toast, and pancakes with real Vermont maple syrup.

Carefully placing his cigarette on the edge of his saucer, Ralph suggested, "Ya know, Mike, I haven't felt *this* good in a long time. The enema was just what I needed. I think I'd like to try skiing. I'm in the mood for it."

I replied, "We're here, we might as well take advantage of it."

Ralph hooted, "We're gonna have a blast!!

Our injured friends Buckley, Kornfeld and O'Neill found a nice spot by the crackling fire in the base Lodge. They amused themselves by talking to a lot of skiers who came in to warm up after a few runs on the slopes. Ralph and I rented skis for five dollars. Ralph thought we got a pretty good deal when he found out the poles and lace-up boots were included. We studied how the other skiers mastered the chair lift, lowering themselves to sit down.

Ralph became impatient, "C'mon Mike. I've got the hang of it. We're ready. Get in line."

We got on the chair with no problems. Looking back, we were stunned at the beauty of the majestic mountains, covered with snow and towering over the valley below. The scent of balsam and pine lingered in the cold air. My nose was stinging from the breeze and my eyes were watering. When we tried to open the gate at the top of the lift, it wouldn't open. Ralph's feet were firmly planted on the foot bar. He had neglected to raise his skis to allow the gate to open. Before we knew it, around the bull wheel we went, careening back down the mountain like a couple of flatlanders out for a joy ride. Skiers riding the chairlift up laughed as they passed us riding it down.

"Well, Ralph, now what?"

The attendant stopped the lift and showed us how the gate operates.

Ralph said, "We're not going to let a little thing like *that* stop us!"

We rode up on the chairlift once again. This time, we both lifted our skis off the bar. When the gate flung open Ralph wailed, "We did it, Mike. We did it."

We managed to balance ourselves and lifted our bodies out of the chair with ease. We skied smoothly off the chair with our skis in the snow plow position and our ski tips pointed firmly inward. The wind was howling. We could hear the voices of a young girl and her father echoing across the mountaintop. They spoke to each other in a foreign accent as they were about to ski down the mountain.

"Are you ready, Adele?"

"Yes, Pa-Pa."

"Completely?"

"Yes, Pa-Pa."

And off they skied.

Ralph looked at me, "Are you ready, Adele?"

I laughed and answered, "Yes, Pa-Pa."

Mimicking the foreign accent he asked, "Completely?"

"Yes, Pa-Pa."

We started flying down the hill *completely* out of control with our skis chattering like Mrs. Manning's teacup. A guy stopped skiing and put his hands on his hips and hollered as we whizzed past him, "Slow down! You guys are nuts! Slow down!"

234

After a few runs, we were really enjoying ourselves and had gained some confidence. We advanced from the snow plow and attempted shaky stem-christies making turns all the way down to the bottom of the run. We then headed right back to the long lift line. Ralph skied over the top of a guy's brand new, shiny double shellacked skis. Creech–creech!

The irate skier was quick to survey his deep gouges and bellowed, "Jesus Christ! I just got these." He shook his head in disbelief.

Ralph turned back to look at the guy and meekly said, "'Scuse me." He then pointed down and said, "Your tips are crossed."

Ralph spotted a pretty girl at the beginning of the lift line, gave me a 'thumbs up' and said, "I'll ride up with her, Mike." Shoving himself through the crowd toward the snow bunny, he called out, "Singles–singles–any singles?" As the chair scooped them up together and carried them off, Ralph looked over and said, "Well, H E L L–OOOO."

Before they prepared to lift the gate, Ralph had her convinced that he was an expert skier. When the chair neared the top, Ralph instructed, "Watch your feet, time to lift the gate," and he opened it with finesse. When he raised his rump off the chair, Ralph wildly flung both arms wide open and knocked the girl back into the seat. She was startled and screamed at the top of her lungs, "HELP, HELP! SOMEBODY–PLEASE HELP ME!"

She couldn't get off and the chair whipped around the loop at the top. She was headed back down the mountain with the safety bar still open. The lift operator threw the switch to stop the lift and two ski patrollers caught her as she jumped out of the chair. Ralph snow-plowed his way toward her, but he gained speed as he headed downhill. He couldn't stop and he headed directly for her, with a lit cigarette dangling from his lips. He plowed right into her, causing the cigarette to singe her nylon jacket, as his face nuzzled into her right breast. He tried to brush away the ashes, but she pushed him away and gave him a glaring stare that stopped him in his tracks. She quickly turned and skied down the trail in parallel fashion.

I met up with Ralph, nudged him and asked, as if I didn't know, "Where's the girl, Ralph?"

He was quick to answer, "She didn't know how to get off the chairlift. She could use a few lessons and a fire extinguisher!"

Ralph and I raced to the bottom of the mountain with the cold, clear wind whipping across our rosy faces. We were on Bunny's Boulevard ski trail. It was covered with moguls and small, bushy evergreen trees with icy branches that glistened in the sun. Riding the chairlift together on our next run, Ralph dropped his pole when he tried to lift the leather loop on the handle over his oversized ski glove. It landed in the snow below the chair and a ski patroller retrieved it.

Ralph said, "Don't worry about it, Mike. He'll send my pole right up. I'll just wait at the top. Ski down and I'll catch up to you."

When I got to the bottom of the run a half hour later, Ralph was shivering and still waiting for his pole at the top of the mountain. He finally made his way down with only one pole. When the ski patrolman noticed Ralph, he pointed to a guy in a red jacket riding the chairlift and said, "I just sent your pole up with him."

"No way! I just killed myself trying to get down here with one pole!"

After a whole day of vigorous skiing, Ralph was completely exhausted. By our last run, he could only ski a couple of yards without falling. "**Eyeough!** Oops!" **PLOP**! He must have fallen ten times. The harder Ralph tried not to fall, the more he fell!

The whole ski patrol team surrounded him on their final sweep of the mountain. By the time he made it to the bottom of the trail and joined our friends in the lodge, we were all anxious to head home.

I grinned at Ralph and asked, "Are you ready, Adele?"

Sipping a hot chocolate, Ralph surmised, "I just finished a suicide run! Whoever named this mountain 'Suicide Six' sure knew what they were talking about."

I rode with Ralph to make sure he didn't fall asleep at the wheel. We were enjoying snow capped mountain views and the picturesque streams and rivers of Contoocook, New Hampshire. Suddenly I spotted a deer running out of the woods. **"Look out for the deer Ralph! He'll hit us!"** I shouted at the top of my lungs.

Ralph retorted. "Holy cow!" He's running right at us!" Ralph jerked the steering wheel to the right and hit the brakes with full force. **S-C-R-E-E-C-H! S-M-A-C-K!** The deer flew through the window on the driver's side as Ralph dove under the dashboard on my side. The dazed animal sailed across the backseat, and crashed through the window behind me. The stunned deer got up off the ground, shook his body, and wobbled off into the woods.

I yelled, "My God! It flew right through the car! I can't believe he's still alive!"

Flabbergasted, Ralph said, "HIM? What about US?"

When the police arrived, the officer told us, "If the deer got hung up in the car, he could have thrashed the both of you."

Ralph turned to me and quipped, "NO SHIT!"

As he stood on the pavement, his whole body shook. He

cupped his hands over his cigarette just before lighting it. Fur clung to the seats of Ralph's car and slivers of glass covered the tight nap of the gray upholstery. Once we gained our composure, we found a general store and bought some plastic sheeting and masking tape to cover the shattered windows so we could drive back to Rhode Island. The next day we sprayed the upholstery with a mouthwash solution to try to get rid of the strong, musty animal odor. Remnants of deer fur lingered in Ralph's car for months. Ralph reported the accident to his insurance company. They insisted on a copy of the police report to verify his claim before they would proceed.

"Wow, it's been a long time since I've told that story, Zeke. I guess because I felt people didn't really believe it."

"I've heard of a lot of tall tales but this takes the prize! Did he ever get the money for the damage?"

"Yeah, there was enough proof for the insurance company, but not enough proof for our friends in Rhode Island. They never believed this story."

* * * * *

In 1955, everybody in our neighborhood had a heavy black rotary telephone in their den next to an overstuffed lounge chair. Our phone was ringing. My brother, Gary was watching *Howdy Doody*.

"Oh, hello, Uncle Leo. This is Mike." I cupped my hand over the phone, "Gary, turn that thing down. It's Uncle Leo."

"Yes, I've been following your favorite team. Maryland's doing great. Gee, I never thought I'd be eligible to go there. Yes, our team had a fantastic season. Sure, I could get my coach to give me a recommendation. I've got a good write up, too, from when I made 'All Blackstone Valley.'"

"Gary," I said, "Turn that down." I continued on the phone, "Yes, I can take the nine o'clock train out of Providence and meet you in Washington. Okay. I'll tell Mom and Dad. Say hello to Aunt Amelia and cousin Lee Ann."

"Hey, Gary, I'm gonna spend some time with Uncle Leo in Arlington. Maybe I've got a chance to go to college out there."

"I wish I could go to Washington." He then turned back to watch Princess Summer Fall Winter Spring dance across the screen.

I mused, "Maybe you will someday, pal. Maybe you will."

A couple of days later, I was on a bus from D.C. to College Park, Maryland. My heart pounded as I looked around the huge campus. Cutting across the grassy common I stopped a wiry student and asked him where the Athletic Department was. He pointed to a tall brick building. The front desk was littered with schedules and programs. The secretary looked at me, and trying not to feel like a stranger, I calmly said, "How are you today. I was wondering if Coach Most is available."

The pleasant woman smiled and said in a welcoming voice, "Who should I say is here?"

"I'm Mike Ryan."

She led me into the coach's office and introduced me to him. He read the letter and news clipping I handed him as I sat looking around at the array of plaques and trophies throughout the room. The door opened after a gentle knock and a Maryland Terrapin football player ducked under the door casing. He musta' been six feet seven. Even the number '89' on his red and white jersey looked huge.

Coach Most said, "Come in. Mike, I'd like you to meet Bill Johnson."

I was dwarfed by his size and once again, I felt like I was standing in a cleat hole. I think it was at this point that I realized I was never going to be a lineman at this Division One school. Coach Most was cordial but said the scholarships had all been given out.

When I got back to Saints, Coach Farley called me into his office. He said, "Ryan, shut the door. You left quite an impression at UMD!" I sat down. He pulled a letter out of his drawer and handed it to me. "I thought you'd like to see this from Coach Most. He said the scholarships have been filled for this year, but don't give up."

I said, "It was already 'Katie, bar the door,' coach, but I gave it my best shot."

The next week I received a letter from the football coach at Northeastern University. I called and made an appointment for first thing Monday morning. I thumbed to Boston, clutching a briefcase containing my letter of recommendation, news clipping and Northeastern brochure. The weather was raw. My gray wool jacket felt damp and heavy. The oversized hood hung like a mop with Mickey Mouse ears. In my pocket was a soggy, wet handkerchief, my only comfort. I was freezing, I had a fever and my nose, as red as a Popsicle in the cold rain, was running like the Ten Mile River. Standing by the side of the road, I looked like a Mouseketeer who needed a ride real bad.

Huntington Avenue was bustling. The trolley heading to Northeastern was as packed as sixteen ounces of Boston Baked Beans in a twelve ounce can. The wheels squealed, dampening the background hum. The seats were all taken, so I reached up for a ceiling strap. I was ready for the ride and was glad to be out of the rain. Every time the lurching trolley stopped, more people packed in like stewed tomatoes. In the corner of the car, next to some flattened cigarette butts, I could see a sardine tin.

I guess I was starting to get hungry. When I looked up, there was a girl standing face to face directly in front of me grasping a vertical pole for stability. I looked at the sardine tin, then at her. She was beautiful, perfectly beautiful. I didn't want her to see me stare, especially since we were inches apart. I looked up to the strap. I looked over to the pole, then back to the sardine tin, then back to her. She stared right through me. Suddenly I felt my nose begin to run. I was in a complete state of helplessness—one hand on the strap, the other clutched the briefcase handle. There was no possible way that I could figure out, to ask this girl that I didn't even know, to reach into my pocket for the soggy handkerchief and wipe my nose with her free hand. So my nose just continuously dripped like an I.V. The heat in the trolley must have been on full blast. I could have sworn I smelled fish oil from that sardine tin.

The trolley stopped and so did the rain. Northeastern was riddled with puddles. My head was splitting. I made my way to the university gym and blew my nose. I took two aspirin and washed my face with water cupped in my hand. I pulled a bottle of Old Spice After-Shave lotion out of the briefcase and splashed it all over my face. Somehow I felt it would give me confidence at the interview.

Coach Tuchapski's office reminded me of an insurance company office. It had bare walls and gray metal furniture. I sat there cold, like the weather outside, in damp clothes. The nameplate on the door was etched with the name 'Joseph Tuchapski.' The phone rang just as I was sitting down and he picked it up as he bit his lip. "Yes, Holly, he's here now. No–In my office–Great, you have his application–Great. Thank you, Holly." Then he looked to me, "So, Mike Ryan, Holly's got your application."

Then I leaned forward. "Did you have a chance to look at my college boards?"

He snatched the phone and dialed, "Hi, Holly. This is Coach 'Two Chops' again–On Mike Ryan–Do you have his college boards up there?–You do. Oh, you don't." He held the phone away from his ear gripping his hand to muzzle his voice and whispered to me, "We don't have your college boards."

"My guidance counselor at St. Rays has the scores."

He put the phone back to his ear. "Holly, would you do me a favor and call the guidance department at St. Raphael's in Pawtucket, Rhode Island and get his scores and get right back to me? I'd like to a have a decision on Mike Ryan today." He stood up "C'mon Mike; I'd like to show you around the school and take you over to our football field on Kent Street in Brookline."

When we returned to his office, he picked up the phone. "Hello, Holly, 'Two Chops' again–What's the scoop on Ryan?–That's great–And he got a good recommendation too–That's wonderful." Hanging up the phone he extended his hand and said, "Congratulations, Mike. Welcome to Northeastern."

I thumbed home. The chilly winter weather made my cold worse. I trudged down Greenfield Street, dragging my feet through the puddles of water. Jeff Scott, a neighbor, walked briskly past me. When Jeff reached the corner, he suddenly turned back to me and yelled, "Mike Ryan!" I stopped abruptly. He was laughing and roared, "I thought you were an old lady, with a face that just looked like yours! Heh, heh, heh. I can't believe it's really you! Where did you get that hood?"

I flashed him an annoyed look and answered, "Yeah, it's me, all right. I just got back from Boston and I'm sick as a dog!"

Northeastern University had the best Co-op work-study program in the country. I knew it would be the right choice for me. I could earn a college degree, play football in a good league, get scholarship money toward my tuition, and continue selling cookware to help pay for my room and board.

In October 1959, Hofstra University came to Boston for a game against Northeastern. Hofstra was undefeated and going for the Lambert Cup. Two Pawtucket natives, Chet O'Dell of Hofstra and Mike Ryan of Northeastern faced each other at right guard for their respective teams. Northeastern upset Hofstra 24–14. In 1960, Chet O'Dell was elected captain of the Hofstra football team. He later became an outstanding coach at Hofstra, Colgate, and Harvard and was voted into the Rhode Island High School Football Hall of Fame.

On September 25, 1960, I started at right guard at Northeastern against the University of New Hampshire in Durham, New Hampshire. Years later I found out that on that same day, Jim Hennessy scored two touchdowns for Boston College—one on a 60 yard punt return, and the other on a 40 yard pass—against Army at Miche Stadium at West Point, New York. Army coach, Earl 'Red' Blaik named Jim to the 'All Army Opponent Team' that year.

Other members of our championship team were also playing that day for various colleges across the country. Jackie Shannon played quarterback for Cal-Poly, tackles Rod Kornfeld played for Northwestern, and Doug O'Toole played at the University of Kentucky. Ends Charlie Mont played for Rhode Island and Charlie Palumbo captained the Brown University team. Half-back Bobby Perry played for Boston College.

Chapter 16
Memories to Last a Lifetime

"Our Father…Who art in Heaven…Hallowed be thy name…" I looked around to make sure no one was there. "Thy kingdom come…Thy will be done…" I thought, "*This is a new piece, a totally new piece.*"

I was standing in the cellar among the many boxes of my father's jewelry samples. In my hand was a necklace, uniquely different from anything I had ever seen. Inspired by the Northern Lights, this necklace was named Aurora Borealis. My father had an exclusive contract with a manufacturer in Providence. He was the only representative who could sell this item. The woven metal chain had a gold-plated cross hanging from it. Colorful, inlaid stones were neatly arranged on the cross. In the center was the Lord's Prayer, engraved on metal encased in a magnifying glass bubble. The entire pendant was a magnificent work of art. Not only that, I liked the fact that I could read the prayer through the round top when I put it up to my eye.

That evening, my mother made one of my dad's favorite dishes–liver and onions, so at supper, he was in exceptionally good spirits. Liver and onions, just the way he liked it. I put the necklace on the table and ran my fingers along the chain to the cross.

"Dad, I think the guys at school would love to give one of these to their mother or girlfriend for Christmas. I could probably sell them at lunchtime in the cafeteria."

My father took a long gulp of coffee and raised his eyebrows. With a shine in his smile he said, "You're a chip off the old block, son."

The cafeteria was humming with activity. The smell of hamburgers and grilled cheese sandwiches was everywhere. Hennessy flipped the patties as they sizzled on the grill. Wally Ossinchowski was entertaining his friends by imitating the sounds of cars racing down the highway. The room was buzzing with friendly chatter.

I looked up just in time to see Billy Cavanaugh squirt ketchup on his hamburger and splatter his tie. Of course he noticed the splatter, but never cared. The tie was already cluttered with many various condiments, some of which would never be identified. What started out as a light blue tie when he enrolled in Saints, now was an Aurora Borealis of its own. The tie was a living menu of the last four years of school lunches. It was merely a prop that fulfilled the mandatory tie requirement for the dress code. It lived in Bill's desk, waiting for him to don it each morning. When class was dismissed, so was the tie–back into the desk it went. The tie never knew where Cavanaugh lived, nor did it ever see the light of day outside the classroom.

I never understood why Saints didn't have standard height tables and chairs in the cafeteria. We had to stand at tables that were chest high to eat lunch. There were no chairs. We sometimes swapped sandwiches. I always loved it when I could get the sliced chicken sandwich loaded with Miracle Whip that Freddie Fernold brought every day. Paul Patnaude frequently brought a bean and onion sandwich. Anyone who ate his sandwich was not popular when they returned to class for the afternoon session! No one would want to sit in front of or behind *that* guy!

I set up shop on one of the tall tables, and before long, I was surrounded by potential customers. When the guys saw my merchandise, they loved it and it practically sold itself. Long lines formed around me. Brother Thomas, the Assistant Principal, also came over. "What's going on, Mike?"

Handing him a cross, I said, "Here, Brother; hold this up to your eye."

He looked inside the magnified bubble, nodded his head and said, "Very nice. Very nice, indeed, Mike. God Bless."

I was glad to have his approval, and got a blessing to boot! In the first few days, I sold over two hundred pendants at three dollars each and I made a dollar profit on each sale.

Christmas was near. The plan was set. On Saturday morning, Packy, Ralph, 'The Duke,' and Rocky left at four o'clock in the morning to go up to northern Maine in a borrowed truck to pick up Christmas trees. They spent the whole day traipsing in the deep snow, packing up the heavy trees. They headed home in darkness as night was falling. Ralph jumped on the truck bed and flung a rope across the trees to tie down the branches. He employed his favorite ship shank and square knot to secure the rope to the sides of the truck. "I'll ride back here. I've got lots of experience riding on top of trees. I'll be a gladiator, gloriously riding his chariot once again."

'The Duke' cupped his hands over his freezing jaw and shot

back, "Suit yourself, Ralph." When they hit the Maine Turnpike, the gears grinded to a stop at the tollbooth.

Ralph hollered, "What're we stopping for?"

"Toll."

"You're God damn right it's cold!"

He shifted his body and crawled a little deeper into the arms of the Christmas tree branches. The loaded truck finally chugged into the empty parking lot across the street from the Spa. Out jumped Rocky sporting a set of tree branch antlers that Ralph had fashioned for him.

Blowing into my hands to try to keep warm, I greeted them. "Holy Cow, Duke, look at how much weight this truck is carrying."

'The Duke' stretched his legs and back and said, "I didn't think a hundred trees would weigh so much. We're lucky we didn't get pulled over for being overloaded."

"Well they certainly look like super trees, Duke."

"Maine's got the best, nothing but the best, Mike."

A few days later, all the trees were sold, except for three. We gave them away and headed home after a long, exhausting, but profitable experience. The next morning I ran into Ralph. He was relaxing on a stone wall just puffing away on his ever present Lucky Strike. Contemplating, he said, "We can make money singing Christmas Carols in Countryside."

"Great idea, Ralph. I'm game. Let's make a little more moola for the holidays."

The plan was set. At nightfall on Christmas Eve, John Manning, Lenny Driscoll, Ralph and I paraded through the glistening snow surrounding the lavishly decorated homes in Countryside. We rang each and every doorbell. We sang with voices blending as if we were the boys from a church choir and our audience loved it. Lenny stood out front, holding a small coffee can. People threw in coins that made a tinkling sound as they hit against the sides of the cold metal. Sometimes we were invited into their magnificent homes for cookies and hot chocolate, or warm apple cider. We'd sing in front of blazing fires, roaring in crackling fireplaces. The warmth of the homes was a welcome relief to our chilled bodies.

After visiting a few homes, Ralph leaned against a lamp post, quickly lit a cigarette and thoughtfully said, "We're here to make money. I've got an idea. We should be able to 'double our take.'" He draped several dollar bills around the outside of the can and secured them with an elastic band. "Okay. All set."

We rang the next doorbell…and the next…and the next… and…now everyone put dollar bills into the can. We more than tripled our take.

I said, "That worked like a charm, Ralph."

When we finished caroling, we stopped at my house and I gave my fifteen dollar share of the money to my mother. Coyly I said, "Merry Christmas, Ma. Now you can buy the sleeve of a mink coat. Maybe someday I'll make enough so you can have the whole coat."

Ralph was restless and said, "Come on, Mike, the night is still young. We have plenty of time to catch the dance at Warner's." When we got to Warner's in Central Falls, Ralph looked around and said, "How'd I know that everyone would be paired up by the time we got here? Looks like there's nothing here for us. Let's head back to Pawtucket."

* * * * *

I started singing *Memories are Made of This.* "Mike, knock off the Dean Martin act and pass me my drink."

"You don't like my singing?"

"Setttle down, Mike. We have to make it to Midnight Mass."

We ended up at the *Happy Day Club* on Newport Avenue in Pawtucket, where Billy Faye was 'taking on all comers' at the pool table. He had a stack of beer checks from his previous wins lined up on the window ledge, but that didn't matter to Ralph. Ralph was interested in the challenge. He blew smoke rings up to the ceiling, then proposed, "If you win, Billy, we'll buy you a beer. If you lose, you'll buy me a screw driver." He threw me a fast wink, "...and Mike, here...a Bloody Mary."

A city slicker was about to meet two more suckers. We were no match for Billy. Alternating games, Ralph and I didn't win one challenge and now there were a lot more beer checks stacked on the ledge.

A dim light hung on Billy's brow as he looked over the eight ball. He pointed his cue stick to the corner pocket with authority that had been gained by playing pool at the Pawtucket Boys Club for fifteen years. He was slight of build, a little round shouldered. He wore high-water pants with white socks and loafers every day. His crew cut made his ears appear bigger than normal. His eyes were always squinted and his face had a serious look as he contemplated his next shot. To Faye, losing was never an option. The loser's debt was Faye's beer. Winning meant drinking and, in time, winning became a problem for Billy. Like Freddy 'Luck Box,' he had found an angle. He didn't have to work. His forte` was the pool table and he mastered his occupation.

The barroom smelled like sour mash and cigarettes. Every

other time I took the stick, I miscued on the ivory ball. One more Bloody Mary... another miscue.

Ralph mumbled out of the side of his mouth as he chalked up his stick. "Midnight Mass in half an hour."

I said, "Billy, the last time I felt this loose was two years ago when I had my first beer."

Ralph butted in, "Oh Jesus Christmas, not this story again."

I said, "Pipe down, Ralph."

I faced Billy and said, "One day Buckley and I met Georgie Nipp at the red light on the corner opposite Ziggy's Grille. He was thumbing up Newport Avenue to the racetrack."

Georgie was from Alabama and was a 'bug boy' at the track. We had just finished two Coney Island hot dogs with coffee milk and I started a conversation with Georgie. He was nineteen, but seemed closer to our age because he had a young looking face and a slight stature. He had the perfect build for a jockey. His blonde hair had loose bangs that flopped on his forehead. Each morning as he exercised the horses, he longed for the day he would be an apprentice. He wanted to eventually become a professional jockey.

Freckle-faced, young-looking Buckley said, "Georgie's old enough to buy beer!"

I said, "Yeah, he's well over eighteen."

Georgie was parched from the cold, dry day and said, "You guys chip in and I'll get the beer!" He dashed into Laverty's and bought each of us a quart bottle of Budweiser. We sat on the ground behind the Darlton Theatre. It didn't take long for the three of us to get that mellow glow.

Georgie got his wish a few years later. He was an outstanding apprentice and became a top jockey in the racing circuit. During Narragansett meets, I often saw Georgie riding around Pawtucket in a brand new powder blue Cadillac. He always had a different tall, striking girl in the passenger seat. I'd say to myself, "*There goes a famous jockey.*"

Ralph mimicked me and mouthed, "*And he bought me my first beer!*"

"Well, Ralph, what about your first drink?" He took another sip of his screwdriver, "Do you remember when we were sophomores at Saints and I worked as an electrician's helper?"

"Yeah, so…?"

"Well, Mr. Gastineau hired me after I'd had two dates with his daughter, Collette. His French-Canadian relatives were visiting for the weekend and I was invited to their Saturday afternoon cookout. They drank Canadian Whiskey all afternoon. Mr. Gastineau was a man who was proud of his heritage *and* his Canadian Whiskey.

"He hoisted his drink, 'To the Canadian Mounties, bottoms up!'

"During the afternoon, he slipped me a few shots of that smooth and mellow blended whiskey. Well, that strong booze got a grip on me and soon I was overcome with a Canadian glow. I went up to the second floor bathroom. So the next thing that happened, Mike, is that I suddenly realized that the people in the backyard were no longer talking in a friendly way. Something was going on. I could hear their voices getting louder. I peeked through the Venetian blind and pushed the window open wider, so I could hear what the commotion was all about.

"I saw Mr. Gastineau's sister pointing her finger at his wife yelling, 'She said that you said that I said something about her. She said that you said that I said something about her.'

"I heard it being said over and over again. I repeated it to myself and it started to click in my mind. I actually made sense of who said what to whom. I repeated it louder and louder.

"I pushed the window open wider and shouted at the top of my lungs, until everyone knew that I knew that, 'She said that you said that I said something about her.'

"The whiskey was making me yell loud enough to be heard in Canada. Finally, I realized that the yard was empty. Then bang!! The bathroom door flew open. Mr. Gastineu charged in and before I could say, 'She said that you said......' I was wrestled into a headlock and wrangled into the spare room. I conked out, never to see the Canadians again. My relationship with Mr. Gastineau was solidified. Yes, we formed a bond that only Canadian Whiskey could bring about. Unfortunately, Collette was not part of the bond."

* * * * *

The next half hour at the Happy Day Club was sort of a blur. All I can tell you is the drinks kept coming. We were singing along with the Ames Brothers. *My Bonnie Lassie* was playing at the bar. We slammed down the last three drinks; then Ralph and I headed out to the cold parking lot. The crisp air snapped our senses awake. I turned the key in my mother's Ford. The radio was on too loud so I turned it off, only to find the tone of drunken silence.

"Hey, Ralph, we'd better roll down the windows. I need all the fresh air I can get right now."

"You okay, Mike?"

"I'm good; just roll 'em down."

The Ford knew the way home; it knew we were late, and

probably knew that Ralph and I had way too much to drink to make the trip on our own. As we rolled softly into the driveway, Nancy came rushing out of the house in a full blown panic. "Where have you guys been?" she said through the open window. Her left hand held down her red beret as the wind tried to tug it away. "And you've both been drinking!"

Ralph said, "Who, us?"

She gasped, "Really drinking and it's time for mass and we're late, we're late for Midnight Mass! I'll get Mom and Dad and don't say too much when they come out. Now roll up the windows."

The five of us rode in silence, with Ralph and me sitting straight as soldiers in the front seat and my family in back. The Ford reeked of smoke and vodka. A car sped out of a side street unexpectedly and almost side-swiped us. It wasn't my fault, but I heard my mother nervously say, "James, I think you should drive."

Reassuring her while patting her hand, he said, "Relax, Mildred. We're almost there."

We arrived safely at St. Joseph's Church. I dropped my family off at the front door. The silent parking lot was filled with empty cars.

I said, "They know we've been drinking, Ralph."

Nodding, he said, "Yeah, but if we get through this Mass, things will smooth over."

As I looked around, I spotted my parents seated about half way down the right side of the church. Our next door neighbors, the Murphy's, were seated directly behind them. I recognized just about everyone in the church. There was 'Lieutenant Jack,' 'The Duke,' and even Willie the card shark, shuffling through his church prayer book as if it was a deck of cards. It seemed like a good idea to stand in the back of the church because Mass had already started.

Ralph whispered, "Let's work our way down the aisle. We can get a seat at the end of a pew, in the front of the church. Your folks will see that we made it in here, and they won't think we're sitting in the car."

I was reluctant but nodded in agreement. Sporting his open collared shirt and Navy sport jacket, Ralph briskly walked down the aisle in a big, exaggerated gait. He dipped into a pew that was about five rows in front of my parents. Following him and trying to act nonchalant, I genuflected and entered another pew on the left side of the aisle. When I looked up, all I could see was a maze of white lights. Flickering candles all over the altar made my head dance and I began to sweat from the heat I was feeling. The Bloody Mary's in my system started taking over my whole body. When everyone stood up I realized I was the only one in my row sitting. I clenched the rail in front of me as tight as I could. I felt like I was on a roller coaster, holding on for dear life.

Then I saw Ralph get up and stagger across the aisle. He held himself up by grabbing onto the end of my railing. His face was as white as a sheet. He stretched his neck, straightened up, and then wobbled up the aisle, right out of the church. I could hear the congregation gasp.

I thought to myself, "*Oh, my God! Now I've really got to last through the whole Mass. I'm on my own.*' I prayed, '*Listen, God. You get me through this one and I'll get all A's and never have another Bloody Mary as long as I live…Ohhhh boy…*"

Everyone seemed to be looking at *me*. I could *feel* the glaring stares. People in my row moved away from me when they smelled the stale odors emitting from my body. A woman sitting in front of me was wearing a shiny, brown mink stole. The whole damn mink! *The heads and tails of the whole damn mink!* She had a

255

hair-do styled in a high beehive. She was following the Mass in her prayer book. The sophisticated lady looked affluent and pious as she concentrated on the priest's solemn words during the Liturgy. The priest motioned for everyone to sit. I was still clutching the back of the pew in front of me.

The best way that I could describe what I felt like is to compare it to something I experienced at Rocky Point Park. Oh yes, it was just like being at good 'ole Rocky Point, sitting in the roller coaster car as it was going up, up, up, and click, click, click to the highest part of all of Rhode Island. I looked out at the candles flickering on the altar and it seemed as though I was at the very top of that roller coaster ride, looking down at all the twinkling lights in the harbor. That place where time stands still and there's a complete calm before the wild ride down. Everything was a blur. I felt the pew dive, turn, and dive again. I couldn't stop the ride.

I felt my stomach heave. "Oh, no!" I said out loud.

I got a mouth full of vomit. I swallowed, but that only primed the pump. My jaw locked wide open. I felt the pew tilt and bank. Now my whole body was completely locked up. I could swear the mink winked at me. The Bloody Mary blast exploded over the pew in front of me, blowing the beehive a foot in the air, drenching the mink and her left ear with vodka and tomato juice, compliments of the Happy Day Club.

At this point, it was no secret to anyone what I had been doing before Midnight Mass. The lady's furious husband turned toward me with a closed fist as she let out a loud scream. Then she ran up the aisle with her irate husband close behind. He was steaming, she was soaked and I was sick. I could see my father dashing toward me, but my sister tackled him in the center aisle before he could reach me. The whole congregation was in a state of confusion. The priest stopped speaking. His jaw fell open as he peered through his thick glasses. I managed to get up the aisle and out the door without getting killed by *anyone*! I found Ralph on the front lawn, throwing up.

I said, "Do you know what I just did?"

He looked at me with bloodshot eyes, "No, but I can just imagine!"

Filled with remorse I said, "That poor lady with the mink stole is now wearing ten Bloody Mary's and now I'm an orphan."

My disgusted family walked the two miles back to the house. Not daring to go home, Ralph and I circled around the block for an hour or more, before I got enough courage to go in. My sister had calmed my father down, until he *saw* me! He had never hit me in my life, but this time, he went into a rage and started to pound at me as I climbed the stairs to my bedroom. He turned around to Ralph and bellowed, "...AND YOU!" Ralph didn't wait to hear any more. He ran out the front door, jumped off the porch and bolted down the street!

On Christmas morning, I was the black sheep of the family. My brother Gary is ten years younger than me; therefore, Christmas in 1955 was just about the biggest event in his life. Of course he had no idea of what his older brother had done that Christmas Eve. Gary bounded into my room and rustled me out of bed at six o'clock in the morning, by jumping up and down on the mattress. "Get up Mike! It's time to open presents."

A turkey was roasting in the oven. Everyone was gathered around the tree. Gary was finally quiet, playing with his new Play-Doh and building Lincoln Log cabins. My head was splitting. Gary suddenly sprung up to his feet and jumped onto my lap, hollering, "Merry Christmas!"

I held my head in my hands and quietly moaned, "Oh, please! Don't do that!"

Dejected, Gary slowly backed off and ran to Mom, asking, "What's *his* problem?"

Joe had been on a date with Lori on Christmas Eve and didn't know what had happened at Mass. No one else was talking to me. My head was pounding and I felt like I had been run over by a cement mixer. I went back to bed and snored for hours. I woke up with a feeling of dread and loneliness. "What a Christmas," I mumbled to myself.

I thought my father was going to kill me. 1955 surely was going to be the last Christmas for Mike Ryan. There was a slow knock on my bedroom door. "Yes," I said nervously.

The door slowly opened. I was hoping it would be Gary again, but it was my father this time. He walked in with a somber expression. His vest was buttoned up tight and his hands were in his pockets. "Listen, Mike. It's Christmas. I'm sorry for getting so mad and upset, but I hope you never have a son act that way in front of you!" Feeling lower than whale shit, I knew those poignant words would sting for a long time. My father broke the silence by saying, "It's Christmas, go give your mother a hug. I know Ralph is your friend, but he's having a misspent youth and you're going along for the ride! Now go give your mother a hug."

I called Ralph the next day and told him what my dad said. He chuckled, "Misspent youth! Just don't be surprised if you see that on my gravestone!"

I said, "Just make sure it's in your will."

Zeke strolled over to Ralph's headstone, with his hands in his pockets and a somber look on his face. He reminded me of my father, as he brushed his fingers across the lettering and said, "Gee, Mike. By golly, now I know why '***Misspent Youth***' is engraved on this headstone."

258

Chapter 17
Life is for the Living

The day was getting on. Shadows from the evening trees were long, and sent pin-striped patterns across the cemetery. Zeke and I began to walk slowly through the monuments.

Then I said, "I often thought about how Ralph's father's death influenced his life. Ralph was only three years old. How could he have fathomed it; how could he have known it would have such a huge impact on his life?"

After we went over the falls on the Ten Mile River I asked him why he insists on doing so many wacky things, and, how I always wind up being with him.

He answered, "Life is so short; it can be taken in an instant. I want to live it to the hilt. My motto has always been: 'Life is for the Living.' As for you, I don't know. As for why you always wind up with me, I don't know. It's just friendship, pal—just friendship. Friends are thicker than water."

Ralph revered his father's memory, but almost never spoke of that tragic day in St. Louis. Dr. McGreavey had just started his medical practice when he was killed. His widow and the two small boys returned to Rhode Island. Ralph's life was changed forever. They lived on the third floor with Ralph's Aunt Florence in Central Falls. His aunt had an aura of sincerity that surrounded her, and a sweet, innocent outlook on life. She loved her nephews and they loved her. Ralph was her pride and joy. She thought he could do no wrong. As Ralph grew older, it became harder and harder for his aunt to guide her unpredictable nephew. Ralph's mother had to work in the mills to support her sons. She married Sal when Ralph was fifteen years old. Ralph loved Sal and never gave him a hard time. Sal was a good family man and moved them to a small house on York Avenue in Pawtucket.

Ralph's older brother Leo joined the Navy when he turned eighteen. When his stint was up, he came home, got a college degree at Bryant College and became a well respected teacher at Hope High School. He then taught at Cumberland High School, but was killed in an auto accident at a young age, leaving a wife and five children.

After graduating from Tolman High School, Ralph joined the Navy, touring the world. Then he returned to his home in Rhode Island, got his degree at Bryant College, and married a sweet girl he met there. They moved to California and then to the Midwest where Ralph started a successful sales promotion business. He raised his family in Shaker Heights, Ohio, near Cleveland.

After graduating from St. Raphael Academy, I enrolled at Northeastern University. I thumbed back and forth between Boston and Pawtucket on weekends so I could continue selling cookware. One of the reasons I chose to enroll at Northeastern was because they had a great co-op program. I was placed in a training program at Texas Instruments in Attleboro, Massachusetts and learned about clad metals and their applications. I've made selling in the metals field my lifelong career.

Joe and I took a ride on an Easter Sunday and stopped at Frates Dairy, on Route 1 in Plainville, Massachusetts. When I ordered ice cream cones at the take-out window, a blonde girl slid open the screen to take my order. I thought, "*Gee, she looks familiar. This is the girl I met at Indian Mound Beach.*" I asked, "Are you Patty Stalinka?"

She smiled brightly and said, "Are you Mike Ryan?"

I was overwhelmed as I answered "Ya…wow! Are you able to date yet?"

With a blush she said, "Oh, sure. I've been going out for some time now."

Her sweet smile melted the ice cream all over my hands, but I didn't mind. I took the ice cream cones to the car and then went inside to the restroom to wash my hands.

When I came out, I leaned over the counter and said, "Have you been getting my greeting cards? I didn't know your street number so I addressed them to Patty Stalinka, halfway up Maxwell Street, Taunton, Mass?"

She nodded, "Yes, I got one for every holiday. I still live in Taunton."

I said, "I'll give you a call." She gave me a nice smile.

Five years later I graduated from Northeastern University and Patty became my bride. We moved to the Midwest, then back to Massachusetts where we raised three sons and then moved to "God's Country," the beautiful resort town of Quechee, Vermont. Patty and I celebrated our forty-seventh wedding anniversary in April.

Zeke slowed to a stop back at Ralph's grave and extended his hand. As we shook hands he said, "Mike, that's wonderful. I'm really glad I met you. Now I feel like I know the person buried here and understand the close friendship you and Ralph had. You guys had one heck of a year!"

I nodded, "Yes, Ralph was certainly one of a kind, just like this mandolin. He could never be tuned, he could never be tamed, and he certainly danced to the beat of a different drummer." Feeling a little melancholy, I continued, "Just like our mandolin, he was the neck, and I was the body…forever glued together in friendship. Good memories never die. Ralph certainly had what my father called a misspent youth…and I'm glad I was along for the ride! Yes, it was a good time to be young.

"I remember this poem he had memorized. It depicted how he lived his life.

> "The clock of life is wound but once
> And no one has the power
> To tell just when the hands will stop
> At a late or early hour.
> Now is the only time you own…
> Live, love and toil with a will
> Place no faith in tomorrow
> For the clock may then be still."

A cool, refreshing breeze ruffled the leaves on the tree above.

As we both looked up, Zeke said, "This is the most beautiful tree in the cemetery. It inspired me to write *Trickery of Trees* a few years ago." He spoke in a melodious poet's voice, gazing at the clapping leaves.

TRICKERY OF TREES

"I'm no fool
I know these trees laugh and sing; they even dance.
Yes, they hear, and see, and know when you are near.
They smell you.
We all see them in their paralyzed act.
In autumn we enjoy painted leaves silently gliding on a gentle breeze.
Although, I know they scream.
And they die of fright before they land.
I have been watching these trees for a moment of twenty-one years.
I know they have dreams and fears.
Walk in the woods and find a tree, stand straight and tall; then freeze.
Wait a moment of twenty-one years and you won't be fooled,
you'll see."

Zeke silently strolled off and got into his rebuilt, 1948 two-ton, Chevy truck. I turned toward Ralph's gravestone and spoke, "Well, Ralph. Your gut feeling was right. Someone did pay two hundred dollars for this old mandolin."

With a tear rolling down my cheek, I gently leaned the mandolin against Ralph's headstone. The strings softly hummed with the breeze as I walked away.

Patrick J. Payton

Patrick attended Unity College in Maine and Hampshire College in Amherst, Massachusetts and is a graduate of King Philip Regional High School in Wrentham, Massachusetts. As a senior he was the recipient of the prestigious Creative Writing Award and also earned a Kodak Medallion of Excellence Award for photography in the state of Massachusetts. He and his wife Sheryn have a son, Thomas, and reside in Vermont.